Geordie shrugged, then lifted her up until she could grab a branch. She appeared completely unconcerned by the fact that she was showing her legs and giving him the opportunity to have a look up her skirts. He crossed his arms over his chest and watched her scramble up the tree with true skill. Even he could not climb a tree with such ease and grace. Then she studied a number of apples, putting several in her pocket, and he was pretty sure that muttering she was doing held a lot of swearing.

She started to climb back down, and when she got within his reach he grabbed her by the waist and pulled her the rest of the way down. Then she put her hands on his shoulders to steady herself, so he tugged her close against him and held her there. She tensed slightly and narrowed her eyes. He just grinned.

"You can let me go now."

He smiled. She sounded so prim and proper, a bit like his brother's wife, Emily, when she got cross with one of them, but actually a bit primmer. Belle sounded much like a queen ordering her subject despite the fact that she had just been climbing a tree with her skirts hiked up to her knees. He was just going to have to show her he was neither a subject nor very obedient.

"Why? I think I deserve a reward."

She felt good in his arms, and fit perfectly. Leaning his face a little closer to hers, he brushed a kiss over her mouth. She did not jerk away and she tasted sweet. Her kiss also stirred his manly appetites in a way none had before. Then she sagged a little in his arms and he went down with her as he deepened the kiss . . .

Books by Hannah Howell

The Murrays

HIGHLAND DESTINY
HIGHLAND HONOR
HIGHLAND PROMISE
HIGHLAND VOW
HIGHLAND KNIGHT
HIGHLAND BRIDE
HIGHLAND ANGEL
HIGHLAND GROOM
HIGHLAND WARRIOR
HIGHLAND CONQUEROR
HIGHLAND CHAMPION
HIGHLAND LOVER
HIGHLAND BARBARIAN
HIGHLAND SAVAGE
HIGHLAND WOLF
HIGHLAND SINNER
HIGHLAND PROTECTOR
HIGHLAND AVENGER
HIGHLAND MASTER
HIGHLAND GUARD
HIGHLAND CHIEFTAIN
HIGHLAND DEVIL

The Wherlockes

IF HE'S WICKED
IF HE'S SINFUL
IF HE'S WILD
IF HE'S DANGEROUS
IF HE'S TEMPTED
IF HE'S DARING
IF HE'S NOBLE

Stand-Alone Novels

ONLY FOR YOU
MY VALIANT KNIGHT
UNCONQUERED
WILD ROSES
A TASTE OF FIRE
A STOCKINGFUL OF JOY
HIGHLAND HEARTS
RECKLESS
CONQUEROR'S KISS
BEAUTY AND THE BEAST
HIGHLAND WEDDING
SILVER FLAME
HIGHLAND FIRE
HIGHLAND CAPTIVE
MY LADY CAPTOR
WILD CONQUEST
KENTUCKY BRIDE
COMPROMISED HEARTS
STOLEN ECSTASY
HIGHLAND HERO
HIS BONNIE BRIDE

Vampire Romance

HIGHLAND VAMPIRE
THE ETERNAL HIGHLANDER
MY IMMORTAL HIGHLANDER
HIGHLAND THIRST
NATURE OF THE BEAST
YOURS FOR ETERNITY
HIGHLAND HUNGER
BORN TO BITE

Seven Brides for Seven Scotsmen

THE SCOTSMAN WHO SAVED ME
WHEN YOU LOVE A SCOTSMAN
THE SCOTSMAN WHO SWEPT ME AWAY

Published by Kensington Publishing Corporation

The Scotsman
Who Swept Me Away

HANNAH HOWELL

ZEBRA BOOKS
KENSINGTON PUBLISHING CORP.

www.kensingtonbooks.com

Chapter One

Geordie MacEnroy picked up a small stone and tossed it into the creek. It should have been a fast-flowing river at this time of year, but rain had been scarce so far this spring. The snowmelt was late as well. There was even a lot of ice still on the water, although much of it was breaking up, but the slow current allowed the ice to gather in untidy lumps close to the banks.

Picking up a flat stone, he again tried to skip it across the river, but it ended up caught in the ice dams. He had come here to try to ease a yearning he was suffering more often, and it grew stronger as time passed. Now that the weather was warming, that yearning was growing keener. He wanted to see the ocean.

As he scrambled up the hillside to make his way back home, he struggled to understand why he even had such a yearning. Usually he just tried to shake it off, but this time he fought to find out what he was actually wanting. There was a chance his yearning for the ocean meant something else, the ocean simply a symbol.

When he and his family had arrived on the East Coast of this country from Scotland, they had not found the best of lives. For a while they had lingered in New York, but the only places they could find to live were rat-infested tenements. Worse, crime had been pervasive and one never felt safe. His mother had yearned for a small place, a quieter place with a small patch of land for gardening, so his father had painted again and sold his paintings until he had earned enough to buy them a wagon like the ones people used to move west. They packed up and wandered up the coast until they reached a place called Boston, only to find the living there was little better than it had been in New York. Disappointed, they had continued wandering up the coast, thinking it might be better to go west like so many others.

That was definitely not what he was yearning for, he told himself firmly when he reached the road, mounted his horse, and started on his way home. The journey west had been interesting, but they had found little to make a good life for them all. Their hopes had not completely died with their parents, but they had taken a long time to be fulfilled. Geordie did not even want to think about where they would all be now if Iain had not been ready, willing, and eminently able to step up in their place.

What they had now was good, and he could not really see how he could do much better. The land provided a decent living for all of them and room to grow. Two of his brothers were now married and growing their own families. Their land had provided for the Powell brothers, the shepherds hired by the MacEnroys, and their new families, as well as a living for Mrs. O'Neal and her children. They had gained more land from Iain's and Matthew's wives to add to their living opportunities. It was just what most people would want, yet Geordie still battled this yearning to see the ocean.

It was as if the ocean called to him, a thought which, he decided, was a ridiculous fancy. He rode by his brother Matthew's house and waved at Abbie, Matthew's wife, who was weeding her garden with little Caitlin's help. As he rode through the big open gates of the stockade, enjoying that sign that things had calmed in the hills since the end of the War Between the States, Geordie returned his brothers' greetings as he went to put his horse in its stall. He removed the saddle and the rest before he began to brush down his mount. By the time he had finished that as well as fed and watered the animal, his brother Robbie walked up to him.

"Hey, ye coming in for the evening meal?" Robbie asked.

"Aye. Didnae ken so much time had slipped by. Got lost in my thoughts."

"Ye have been doing that a lot, Geordie. Troubles?" Robbie asked as they walked out of the stables and headed toward the back of the house.

"Nay. Just trying to make up my mind about something."

"What?"

Geordie shrugged. "Whether to stay or to go."

"Go? Go where? Have ye found some land ye want, or a lass ye fancy?"

"Nay, sad to say, I haven't found either of those things here. I just have an urge to see the ocean again."

"So, ye want to go west?"

"East. What tales of traveling west I have heard make me think it might be far more dangerous than I want to deal with. The way east is more settled and has regular train service."

"Isnae that safe. Still has some lingering troubles from the war."

"Nay so much. Talked with Emily's grandfather, the Duke, when he came last, and got a lot of information. He did say a man needs to harden his heart when he rides through the country now. There is still some ugly destruction and a lot more signs that people are in dire need than he had seen before. Too many people crippled and limbless. Too many children without a father or with a mother either broken or dead."

"So have ye decided yet?"

"Nay, I was trying to figure out why I had such a fool longing."

"Oh, nay so foolish, I wouldnae mind seeing the ocean again. It's a wondrous thing to watch. Strangely calming."

"Aye, it is."

They stopped at the porch to wash up. When they entered the kitchen it was to find everyone already seated around the table. Geordie and Robbie quickly took their seats and hurried to fill their plates before anyone began reaching out to take second servings.

"So where have ye been for most of the afternoon?" Iain asked Geordie as he passed him the rolls, which Geordie quickly passed on to Emily after taking what he wanted.

"Why? Was there something I needed to do?"

"Nay, ye did all your chores. I was just curious. Ye dinnae often go off on your own like that."

Geordie finished the bit of lamb he was eating and then sighed. "I just had something to think over and needed to be alone to do it."

"Hard to find solitude here, no doubt about that. Care to share? Lot of people here who could help."

"Dinnae ken how. 'Tis just a foolish craving I cannae shake."

"Are ye sure we cannae help ye get what ye want?"

Geordie laughed briefly. "Nay, Iain. It is a craving to see the ocean. It is nay something that ye can just drag up to the door for me." He smiled at his family when many of them laughed. "I dinnae ken why, but it has become a yearning that keeps on growing."

"Cannae fully understand that." Iain shook his head.

"Once we all got off the boat from Scotland, I had no urge to ever see that huge body of water again."

"Surprises me, too. Maybe I was just too young to be scared by it all. I remember Mum always complaining about how she couldnae see any land at all. Ye could see that sore troubled her when we journeyed up the coast later. Looking out and seeing nothing but water for miles bothered her."

"My sister was always troubled by that, too," said Emily. "She would rarely stand on deck with me."

"It is because you can see nothing to swim to if the boat flounders and you end up in the water." Mrs. O'Neal shook her head. "The realization is quick to rise up whenever you see that huge stretch of water and no land."

As Mrs. O'Neal began to clear away the meal with Emily's help, Iain pulled a letter out of his pocket. "Heard from James today. Bit of a surprise as I wasnae his brother-in-arms, Matthew was."

"And he is well?" asked Geordie.

"Aye, he just wanted me to ken that he would be stopping by as he headed toward home. Was asking if he could stop here for a bit."

"Ah, you're the head of the family. Best one to ask. But, why here? It is a fair long trip from his home in Maine."

"He wasnae in Maine. He came south to see our major and Maude, one of the women who cared for the orphans, then decided to come by here on his way back home. It seems they collected the orphaned boys from Mrs. Beaton's home, so he took something for them too."

"That is good news. Abbie will be pleased, as will Emily. Abbie was troubled by the orphans left behind and it hurt Emily's soft heart"—Geordie smiled and winked at her—"to think of the boys stuck with a woman who didnae sound verra motherly. Matthew kept waiting for Abbie to come up with a plan to get them here."

Iain frowned. "Ye would have objected?"

"Nay, of course not. We have plenty of room and can make more. Just understood his concern. She already has three children and this land hasnae completely shaken off the harshness and hate the hostilities stirred up. Dangerous. Especially if the trip ye plan would be encumbered with a wife and children." Geordie grimaced. "And I suspect that the boys there might have picked up a few irritating ideas and habits after staying with Mrs. Beaton for a few years. They willnae be like Noah, I am thinking. After all, we also have Ned."

"I am nay sure this family has a need of another Noah," Iain said with a grin.

Geordie laughed. "Nay. I shall have to ask James how the major and Maude are doing with their new family. Lads couldnae find a better man, judging from how Matthew speaks of him. If Mrs. Beaton gave the children some odd ideas, he will sort them out."

"It will be good to see James. Thank ye, Mrs. O'Neal," Iain said when the woman handed him a large slice of pie and nudged the pitcher of fresh cream closer to him.

Emily and Mrs. O'Neal served everyone some pie, then sat down to enjoy their own. Geordie looked at everyone around the table as well as the young ones seated at their own table. This ever-expanding family was why he had difficulty making any decision. He did not want to leave them, did not want to miss these gatherings at the end of each day. The table filled with family, laden with Mrs. O'Neal's cooking, and all the talk they shared were as much a part of him as a limb. When the wish to see the ocean pulled at him, this was what pulled him back.

A sharp elbow was jabbed into his side so he turned to look at Iain. "What?"

"Ye were staring. Rather blankly as weel. Something else troubling ye?"

"As I told ye, I cannae shake the craving to see the ocean again. Couldnae think why I waver so much. Then I realized it was all this." Geordie swept his hand around to include the whole kitchen and everyone in it.

"Are ye planning to go to the ocean to live?"

"Nay, I just want to go, to visit for a wee while." Geordie could tell by the look of relief that spread over Iain's face that his brother had worried about that.

"Then why do ye worry o'er this? We arenae going anywhere."

Geordie shook his head. It was just like Iain to see things so clearly. He had allowed himself to get too tangled up in his emotions. There was no need to fret over it all; he was just going on a brief journey.

"I got too focused on the leaving," he muttered.

"Aye. It isnae like ye plan to go away for good, but even if ye find a reason to stay there, like a woman or some good land, we arenae going anywhere. So, ye would ken where to find us when the mood strikes."

"Although why I would, I cannae say." He laughed and rubbed his face after Iain gave him a light rap on the back of his head.

"Just wait until James comes by. He is only stopping here for a night or two and then traveling home."

"Why? I dinnae need a nursemaid."

"Nay, but he is an experienced soldier who is headed in the same direction and that would be handy."

"Ah, aye, it would. He maynae be willing though."

"And I suspicion he will be. Always better to ride with someone than ride alone."

For a while they spoke of the many ways he could make the journey. Geordie was not that interested in taking the train. He had heard it was dirty and crowded. Iain had no real knowledge on that to share, but he did think Geordie ought to at least look into using it if only for part of the way. It would make the journey shorter and Geordie liked the idea of that.

By the time he retired for the night, Geordie felt much calmer. The yearning was still there but it was quieter. He suspected it was because he had decided: He was going. Now the excitement was building. He was trying to find a way to tamp that down before it kept him from sleeping, when a knock sounded at the door. A moment later, Iain and Robbie came in, walked over to the bed and sat down on the edge.

"What? I dinnae need company to go to sleep. Outgrew that years ago," Geordie grumbled as he sat up.

"Ha! Funny guy," Iain said. "We've come to talk about this trip you are going to take."

"Thought we did. I'm going to go along with James."

"Aye. And Robbie."

Geordie looked at his grinning younger brother. "Ye want to come?"

"Aye," Robbie answered. "I can manage."

"Are ye sure? It is a long trip."

"I am much stronger than I was. So long as we arenae galloping across the country for days at a time, I will manage just fine. And ye will have James with ye, so it will nay be just the two of us who dinnae usually travel much. I have been riding regularly, Geordie. I can hold up."

Geordie looked at Iain. His eldest brother did not look worried about it or even inclined to argue with Robbie's decision. Geordie could not decide if that was because Iain and Robbie had already argued over it or if Iain was truly not concerned. Iain was very skilled at saying what sounded right, just what you wanted to hear, but if you sat and looked very carefully at what he said, you would find it was a rather empty package of words, and that he was placating you.

"Weel, all right then. Now let me sleep." He lay down

with his back to them and tugged the covers up. "I need rest for the journey."

"Rude," Iain muttered as he stood up.

Geordie kept his eyes closed as he listened to them leave, then flopped onto his back and stared up at the ceiling. He had no real objection to Robbie coming along, but he did have a worry or two. Robbie's leg injuries still left him with a serious limp and his hand could occasionally go so weak it was useless. It also remained too stiff for him to do some things, like the weaving he used to love doing. A long trip could possibly set him back in the healing he had done.

Then he shook his head and closed his eyes. Robbie still managed to work at the cider business he and Emily's brother Reid had begun, and suffered little from it. He just had to trust that Robbie knew what he could or could not accomplish. It would also be a good adventure for him, and Geordie suspected his brother needed one, needed something to make him a little more sure of himself.

He hoped James would agree to travel with them. It would make Geordie feel even more at ease about taking Robbie. There was a lot of good the ocean could do for his brother. Many people felt the water had a healing effect on people. Geordie was not sure he believed that, but he did feel it could soothe a person and he strongly felt there was something in Robbie that needed some soothing.

Just sitting and watching the waves come in might do Robbie a lot of good. Geordie could easily recall how that worked. The years had soothed away the memories that could cause his brother to wake up screaming, but maybe a trip to the ocean would help even more. It was odd that the ocean could be so powerful, so destructive at times, yet, when it was calm, it could also soothe.

Sleep began to creep over him and he welcomed it. There was a lot that needed thinking on, but it could wait until morning. He would make better decisions with a well-rested mind.

Robbie rubbed the cream, which Abbie and Mrs. O'Neal swore would help him fight the aches he suffered at the end of the day, into his wounded leg. He had not told them that there were times during the day when it was painful. It did soothe it at night and he was grateful for how that helped him to fall asleep. It did nothing to quiet his mind, however. His mind was crowded with thoughts of all that could go wrong and doubts about his taking part in the journey, but he fought to banish them. He could not decide if that fear and worry was born of reason, or of unreasoning fear.

Shaking his head as he put the cream away, he settled down in his bed. He faced his fear and wrestled it down. His leg was ruined but it was also healed. Crooked and ugly, but healed. Travel could not ruin it more than it was already ruined. Robbie told himself yet again that he was fortunate he still had it despite the pain that too often troubled him. During the war, the solution for such an injury was usually amputation, a solution not everyone survived. At least he had escaped that fate.

He would have to have a talk with Reid. The East did seem to be the place with the innovations and ideas. He might find one that would help them take a big stride forward. Their business was doing well enough, but it needed to be built up a bit before it got them a really nice return for their efforts. It was probably a bad time to just go off for a while. He hoped he could explain why he felt he needed to.

As he closed his eyes he wondered if this trip would inspire him, if he would return with new ideas and new strength to work on the business. He promised himself he would go visit any cider mills in the area they were in while he was in the East. Sleep slipped over him as he wondered if that would be enough to calm any anger Reid might feel.

Chapter Two

Studying the clothes he had laid out on the bed, Geordie decided he had all the clothes he needed. It was probably more than many men would take for a short journey with no plans for a long stay, but he needed to be sure he would not have to wear dirty clothes. The journey they had taken to find their new home, with all the dirt and mud that had constantly assaulted them, had left him with an abhorrence of unwashed clothes. He was so particular he had even learned how to wash his clothes himself. His brothers questioned him about it often, wondering why he did not just wait for washing day when the women did it, but he knew several of them had picked up a few of their own odd habits. Mrs. O'Neal referred to them as "twists."

Despite the fact that James had not yet arrived or agreed to travel with him and Robbie, Geordie had begun to pack the rucksack Iain had given him. When he was done he saw that he had a lot of room left in the bag. He was about to choose a few more clothes when he caught the scent of breakfast cooking and decided packing could wait. Tossing what he had chosen to add to the rucksack onto his bed, he followed the scent of food.

Geordie took a seat at the table after saying good morning to Mrs. O'Neal. Iain walked in a moment later and stared at him in surprise before sitting down next to him.

"Ye are up and about early," Iain said as Mrs. O'Neal set a platter of ham down on the table. "I have a loud bairn. What is your excuse?"

Geordie shrugged. "Despite how far and wide your bairn shares that loudness, it wasnae that loudness that roused me. Figured I might as well pack so I am ready when it is decided whether I go along with James or nay."

"I was wondering why we havenae seen the mon yet. Thank ye, Mrs. O'Neal," Iain said as the woman put a mound of scrambled eggs on his plate. "I pray that cough your Marie was struggling with yesterday hasnae developed into anything worse."

"No. It never does. Beginning to think it is from all that dust or whatever it is, floating around in the air at this time of year, that is the troublemaker. You can see it on the fences or anything else left outside."

"Ever wonder what it is?"

"Comes off the plants and trees this time of year."

"Huh. How do ye ken that?"

"Ever look at a bee when it is in a flower?"

"Nay, seems like a good way to get your face stung." Iain grinned when Geordie laughed.

"Well, when I was young, bees fascinated me. Didn't see that many of them in the city. I used to watch them closely when I could. They would land in a flower, wriggle about, and get loaded up with all this yellow dust, then fly off to another flower. So, if it is there for bees to collect up, it is obviously all round us and the wind can move it. I wager there are some fellows who have studied it and can tell one why and when and all that. Probably even have a name for it."

"Undoubtedly. And some fast-talking man sells a cure

off his wagon. Do you think those who may study it can make a living from that?"

"Who cares?" asked Geordie "If anyone does something about it ye will ken all about it then, for they will have some concoction they will be wanting to sell ye. Or, while ye wait, ye can just try out some things on her, all on your own."

Iain muttered something about Geordie being heartless, then looked at his wife and brothers as they shuffled into the kitchen and took their seats. "Ye all look like ye had to dig your way out of a cave to get down here."

"And ye look all cheery and weel rested," snarled Nigel, one of Geordie's brothers. "Dinnae ye e'en stir when the bairn screams?"

"No, he does not," said Emily and glared at her husband before turning her attention to filling her plate.

"I wake when I am needed."

"What nonsense are you spouting? Are you trying to tell us you can tell why she is wailing?"

"Aye." Iain ignored his wife's scornful disbelief. "When she is crying for a cuddle or food I just go back to the sleep she rudely pulled me out of. I willnae spoil her with a cuddle in the middle of the night or whenever she demands one, and I cannae feed her, so I just go back to sleep. Seems the only reasonable thing to do." Iain quickly took a sip of his coffee to hide his grin when his wife actually growled at him.

Geordie shook his head as he gathered up his empty plate and took it over to the sink. He had to wonder why he thought he would miss this crowd. When Emily's nephew, Ned, came up and held up his empty plate for him to put in the sink too, Geordie ruffled the boy's hair. Well, he mused, there were some he'd miss, he decided, and grinned down at the boy. Then he sighed and wandered back to the table to have some more coffee.

He was about to refill his mug when a knock came at the door. Iain hurried out to the front door to see who it was. The greetings were loud enough that Geordie suspected James had finally arrived. When the two friends walked into the kitchen it was clear Iain was very pleased to see the man. Geordie was surprised Matthew was not with him.

"Matthew didnae come?" he suddenly asked and almost grimaced in embarrassment.

"No," James said as he sat down at the table. "He said he'd come round later. Seems he promised Abbie he'd watch the bairns while she went shopping."

"How are the major and Maude doing?"

"Just fine. Seems marriage suits them both and they arenae suffering much for fighting on the wrong side. I got the feeling the whole town, where they get their supplies, had split and guess people have decided the only way they can stay in town is to just ignore the reasons for the war. The major and Maude are not in the midst of a town or village, but out in a farming community. Though I got the impression Maude is very skilled at redirecting talk so that it is as if they have landed in a place that doesn't know the war ever happened. She is also very kind to the people in the area who lost someone."

"One has to believe that happens more than we know," said Mrs. O'Neal as she poured James some coffee. "Folk are always fighting somewhere, and yet things settle afterward. The ones that seem to hold hard to what caused the fight are the men who planned to fatten their wallets if they won or the ones who lost what fortune they had because they picked the wrong side."

"Always comes down to money and power, and they are not the ones who get out and do the fighting."

"The way of the world," muttered Iain. "So ye are headed back to Maine."

"I am. Stayed away for the worst of the cold season, but my mother just sent word that I am to trot my backside home because my fool dad hurt his foot and cannot work."

"Ah, aye, a request that must get a swift response," said Iain.

"Definitely, though I told her it was unkind of her to make me come home during fly season and she should not say such insulting things about Da." He grinned when the MacEnroys all laughed.

"Fly season?" asked Iain.

"Black flies. Biting flies," James replied. "They swarm all over the place at this time of year. Tormenting little beasts."

"And this is the place you have been wanting to go back to since you joined the army?"

"Oh, yes, I should get home in time to offer the mosquitoes a meal."

Geordie laughed. "I remember those creatures. Hated them. Don't get that many up here, although there are days when they can be thick in the air."

For a while they talked idly about what Iain was still doing, what Reid and Robbie were still working hard on, and what James had plans to do. Then, when James idly asked Geordie what his plans were, Geordie thought for only a minute before telling him.

"I am planning a journey east. Want to see the ocean again," he said.

"Why not go west? There's an ocean that direction too, and a lot is happening that way."

"Too much, I am thinking. I dinnae want an exciting or dangerous journey just to see any ocean. I want to see the one we traveled on, the one I have always looked on the times I got close enough to do so."

"It is just water."

"So speaks the mon who has lived near it his whole

life. Probably can step out on your front stoop and stare at it."

"Nope, not that close. Only a fool builds that close to it. It can be as destructive as it is beautiful."

"Really? I suppose we did hit some rough waters on the way here."

"Well, picture those rough waters hitting the shore. They have washed away many a man's home."

"Sad, but I dinnae have a wish to be living there, just a craving to see it, sit on shore and soak in the sight and sound of it when it is calm."

"Before the two of ye get caught up in whether the ocean is calm or nay, dangerous or good, let us discuss what we were wondering about before ye came here, James," said Iain.

"Oh? Am I going to like this?"

"Dinnae ken. Ye are headed back to Maine, aye?"

"I am. Hoping to spend a night in a bed here, then riding out."

"Mind if Geordie and Robbie ride out with you?"

James looked at the two young men, then back at Iain. "Company is always good, but"—he looked at Geordie—"are ye hoping to stay with me? Because I am nay certain there will be much room. Had a bad storm come through and had some damage there. That damage is what caused Da to hurt himself. My sister and her family had to move in with us until they get their home fixed. Tree came down and took out their roof."

"I wasnae expecting to be housed," said Geordie. "I rather assumed there would be rooms to let or something, since I suspect ye get a lot of folk coming in for a summer visit."

"Yes, we do, and that number appears to be growing. Also, a bit of trouble with men using underhanded legal tricks to take homes or land the owners don't want to sell.

I made sure I can get the money I saved quickly and easily in case it is needed by my folks. Mother often had a room to let so she could get some extra money, but my sister and her family are in it now. I have neighbors who even built a couple small cabins to let on their land, and do quite nicely when the summer folk wander up. It may be a slowly growing business, but it is a *growing* business. Trains going up that way have really added to the numbers. Haven't decided whether I like it or not, but doubt I will get much say in the matter."

"I am nay sure I could abide dealing with strangers wandering in every year," said Iain.

"Seems a relatively good way to get some money and there arenae that many ways to do so in some places now," said Robbie.

"Too many businesses destroyed and fields burned and towns pummeled into dust. From what I have seen it is being cleaned up fair swiftly though."

James nodded. "Not that much ruined up my way. So, are ye ready to set off as soon as tomorrow? Hate to rush you, but when one's mother sends out an order . . ."

"Aye, I have already started packing and can finish that tonight," answered Geordie, and then he turned to look at Robbie. "Are ye ready?"

"I can be by morning."

"Good," said James. "I promise I willnae be up at dawn snapping out orders."

"Verra kind of ye," muttered Geordie, as Robbie got up to put his dishes in the sink and walked away.

A moment later, James looked at Iain and asked quietly, "Are ye sure Robbie can deal with a trip like this?"

Iain sat back and crossed his arms. "I suspect he will need a lot of resting when he gets there, but, aye, he has healed enough to do it. True, he might make ye have to go a bit slower but nay by much. He has not healed as much as we hoped, yet probably as much as he can. There is a slight weakness that comes and goes, but it is there and I fear it always will be."

"He wants this," said Geordie. "I am nay sure why, as he didnae show any great interest in the ocean when we were near it, but I can feel that he really wants this."

Iain nodded. "I could see that. He needs to go, yet I dinnae think he is trying to prove anything."

"Nay. I didnae get that feeling, either."

"He just needs to move, to go for a wee wander." Iain shook his head. "He really hasnae gone anywhere since we arrived here and nowhere since those men beat him and left him on our doorstep. We arenae the wandering kind." He frowned at Geordie. "Usually. Mayhap Robbie just believes that, if he can do this, then he can do anything he chooses to. I do feel he will come back feeling less uncertain of himself."

"Maybe more confident that he can lead a normal life?" asked James.

"That may be some of it. A lot of men didnae come back whole, and ye see too many of them in the big towns and cities, many of them broken, poor, drunk, or dazed on something to kill pain, and homeless, rootless and alone. I can easily imagine him seeing that and fretting about his own fate."

"Well, I hope a long, boring trip to Maine will help him." James looked around at the people sitting at the table. "Although, I can't believe the boy has any concern about finding himself alone with this lot around."

"I dinnae ken why he frets, either, but maybe he will stop after traveling a bit."

"Needs to test himself," James said and Iain nodded. "He knows he can manage around here but doesn't know for certain if some things have been arranged to cater to his injuries."

"Told him we havenae."

"And I suspect he quietly accepted what you said but still doubted. He will know for certain on this trip that nothing has been arranged to make things easier for him. So, yes, now that I think on that, it could well give him some confidence." James turned to look out the door to the kitchen when he heard the front door open and shut. "Expecting company?"

"Just Matthew. You did say he was planning to come round. And here he is." Iain smiled at the small girl Matthew held as he walked in. "Hello, sweet lady."

"What? No greeting for your brother?" said Matthew as he sat down across from Iain.

"Ye arenae as bonnie. So, Abbie has gone shopping?"

"Gone and returned. Then she got started on some curtains she wanted to make and Caitlin was helping too much, so I said I would bring her here with me." He frowned. "She agreed rather quickly." He kissed his daughter's cheek, making her giggle. "Guess ye were making her feel inept with all your help, dearling."

"Isnae it a wee bit warm to be wearing a scarf?" Iain asked, frowning at what appeared to be a long knitted scarf draped around Matthew's neck.

"It isnae a scarf."

On the chair next to Matthew, Mrs. O'Neal set down the square of wood they used in the chairs for small children. Matthew set Caitlin on it, then used the scarf to tie her in the chair as Mrs. O'Neal set some strips of buttered toast smeared with jelly in front of her. Mrs. O'Neal was just securing a small piece of toweling around the child's neck when Caitlin picked up one of the strips of toast.

"So, are ye going to give this vagabond a bed for the night?" Matthew asked.

"Aye," said Iain. "And he is going to take Geordie and Robbie with him when he goes."

Matthew made no attempt to hide his shock. "Why?"

Geordie excused himself and left to start packing.

"Geordie has a sudden hankering to see the ocean and Robbie decided he wished to go as well," said Iain.

"Why would he have a strong wish to see the ocean? Would have thought he'd seen enough of it when we traveled here from Scotland, especially when we were hanging our heads over the railing, emptying our bellies."

"I dinnae think even he could answer that question clearly. He just wants it."

"Ye think Robbie can make that kind of trip?"

Iain explained what had been said and was pleased to see Matthew slowly nod in understanding. Robbie was a grown man and no one could tell him not to go, but it was still good to see that Matthew agreed and understood. It would make it easier. A big family argument would only upset Robbie.

"It seems an odd thing for Geordie to crave, but it might help Robbie in some way, and possibly make him stay home. Just nay sure how Reid will take the news."

"I think he has gone to talk with him. I dinnae think the mon will have a big problem with it. Nigel MacEnroy can step in. He has before and has recently worked with Robbie and Reid."

"Weel, that is good. That business shows promise and it would be a shame to lose that because he has an itch to wander."

Iain nodded and turned to James to talk about the major, the man James had just spent time with. He was just laughing about an incident with the kids the couple had taken in when Geordie returned and a moment later Robbie returned. They lingered for coffee and Robbie gave a report on how things had gone with Reid.

"Is he going to want Nigel to work with him then?" asked Matthew.

"Aye," answered Robbie, "so I mean to have a chat with Nigel before I go. Reid can sometimes get caught up in an idea and want to just go ahead with it, so I thought it might be a good idea to give him my opinion on that plan, and gave him some advice on what to go forward with and what to hold back, then tried to turn him away from anything too crazy. Now I will go do some packing."

Chapter Three

Looking around as James got them tickets for the train, Geordie wrinkled his nose. Missouri had grown despite the war. He had forgotten how much he disliked the smells and constant noise of such places. What Geordie noticed now was the shocking lack of men, the streets full of mostly women. That was going to cause some trouble soon with the losses in the war and the movement of men into the West now that the war was over.

A glance at Robbie made it clear that riding the train was the best choice for them. The younger man was quite pale and, as Geordie watched, a man left his seat on a bench set out for waiting passengers and Robbie hurried over to take it. His gait clearly revealed the pain he was in.

"Got our tickets and passage for our horses," said James as he looked at Robbie. "Is he all right?"

"He hasnae complained, hasnae said he wishes to turn back." Geordie frowned. "I do think it will be better for him if we travel by train for a bit. Coming down from the hills wore him out, I think, as it required a lot of strength in the legs, which he lacks."

James nodded. "We can gather up his things when we get the horses settled, so he doesn't have to carry them around."

Geordie went over to tell Robbie what they were doing,

then joined James in leading the horses to the stock car. After a quick look at how the other horses were settled, he helped James to settle theirs. They secured the saddles as well and took their saddlebags and blankets with them. Collecting a sleepy Robbie from his bench, they then hunted down their seats on the train. To Geordie's relief their compartment had two seats facing forward and two facing back, so one seat was left open after they took their seats. Hoping it would stay unoccupied, he encouraged Robbie to take the inside seat and put his weak leg on the seat opposite it, where he and James had piled their blankets to make a pillow he could rest his leg on. It was not long before his brother fell asleep.

"It never healed right, did it?" said James softly, his voice weighted with pity.

"Nay. In truth, I think what little the men who captured him did ensured that it wouldnae. Same problem with his hand. If he wasnae going to take up arms for them, they apparently wanted to make sure he wouldnae take them up at all. It was all senseless. Just plain mean."

"There was a lot of that during the war. And the scars of it will linger a long time. Of course, it was never terribly quiet and peaceful once you got west of the Mississippi."

"Well, my family found a quiet place, I think. We have had trouble but nothing we couldnae handle ourselves."

"Appears so. Of course, there are seven of you, so not hard for you to handle trouble. Quiet, far enough away from the cities to stay that way, too, so long as you keep a close eye out for encroachment."

"Oh, Iain did, and always has. Every time he can afford to, he buys up more land, putting a wider buffer around us. As he says, he can always sell a piece or two if he needs some money. I think he is hoping we will all settle on it like Matthew has."

"Then name that section of the hills after your family?" James asked and grinned when Geordie laughed and shrugged.

"How long will this train ride be?" Geordie asked as he frowned and glanced out the window.

"Too long, and there will be stops we have to suffer through. We will even have to switch trains in places. Never took one for so long a distance before. Did short journeys and they were mostly out of curiosity."

"Cannae see the point of paying for just a short journey."

"Some of them are worth it because of the route taken."

"True enough." Geordie picked up a book he had packed in his rucksack and opened it.

"Reading?"

"Ye have something better to do to pass the time on a train?"

"Not really. Did bring some cards, which may be of interest later." James looked at the cover of Geordie's book. "Shakespeare?"

"Aye. *King Lear*. I promised myself I would go through all his plays by Christmas."

"Why? I saw a performance of one of them, *Macbeth*, I think it was, and it wasn't too bad but cannot imagine what it would be like to read it."

"Ye saw it acted out? In Maine?"

"No. In Boston. Went to university there. I was trying to impress a girl. Was pleased it didn't make me fall asleep. That would have been embarrassing."

"Especially considering all the killing that goes on in it."

"True. If I remember right, there is a fair bit of slaughter in the one you are reading."

Geordie laughed. "Aye. Still have some trouble with the words, but getting better. Emily was a good teacher.

Still not sure I understand all of it because the language is so different."

"Maybe next time you should read something written in this century."

"There's a thought." James had stretched out and closed his eyes, so Geordie struggled a while longer with his book until he had to follow the man's example and sleep.

Geordie stepped off the train and headed to the stable car. Robbie and James followed him, Robbie prodding James for information about Maine. Geordie hoped Robbie was just curious and not looking to find a new place to live. Trying to explain to his brothers how he had come home without Robbie was definitely not something he wanted to have to do. It would upset a lot of people, family and friends. Unfortunately, he was not sure he had the heart to deny Robbie much of anything, nor did he have the gifted tongue to talk Robbie out of a plan to move east.

They fetched their horses and took them to the stables. Collecting up their baggage and saddle packs, they went to the boarding house. They got two rooms side by side and went up the stairs to get to them. Geordie could still smell the newness of the wood. This had been built simply because the train came through the area. He wondered how much of the rest of the town was so new.

He could see why people fought to get a train coming through their town as he looked out the window, having settled into his room. Trains brought noise and dirt but they also brought business. He promised himself he would try to remember that about trains when next he was grumbling about the smell and noise of the machines.

James rapped on the door and then walked in. "Shall we hunt down some food? I saw a place just round the corner."

"I could do with some food," Robbie said as he slowly

sat up on the bed he had chosen for himself. "We have eaten everything Mrs. O'Neal packed for us. Only have some sweets and a few bottles of cider left."

"We'll see if we can pick up a few things to add to that."

Taking just a little time to tidy up, they all walked to the place James had seen. It was large and looked a lot like a saloon except the tables had cloths on them. They sat at one near the doors, a wall at their backs, and a pleasantly attired young woman came over to hand them a small listing of what they offered.

"I think this is pretty new as well," said Geordie when the woman left to fill their order.

James sat back and looked around, then nodded. "Think it used to be a saloon. They obviously decided to keep the bar and use it for more proper things. I suspect they are still in the planning stage and deciding exactly what they want to be."

"As long as the train keeps passing through and stopping, they will have business."

"Aye," Robbie agreed, then stared at the table across from them. "We arenae wearing uniforms, but I think some people have a good idea of which side we fought for."

Glancing at the men Robbie had been watching, Geordie sighed. "Weel, dinnae stare at them or they will think it is a challenge."

"If they have such a difficult time dealing with people who may have supported the Union, wonder why they are coming this way? They are headed right for the heart of the Yankees."

"To work and make a living."

"Suspect that galls them."

"Oh, aye. Ah, here comes our food."

The plates set before them were clean and the food plentiful if ordinary. It was the kind of thing Mrs. O'Neal would make them. Geordie hoped they did not decide to imitate fancy city restaurants. Once he had gone to one with Emily's grandfather, a duke, and had found it stifling, even unsettling because he was so unsure of how to act.

"So, just how long a train ride do we have left, James?"

"A few days. We switch trains here for a more direct route. We will end up in New York at the end of this trip. Then we ride or take a short train trip to Boston. Then we ride again. Should get to my home in about a week if the weather is kind."

Geordie laughed. "If I recall right, that isnae something one can count on in that area."

"Not at all. But, if we are lucky, the weather will at least remember it is spring now. It will be close to planting time when we get there."

"Weel, we can probably give ye a hand if it is needed."

"If it is, I will be sure to call on you."

"What does your da plant?" asked Robbie.

"He had not decided by the time I left, so I am not sure."

"He doesnae have a regular crop?"

"No. Used to, but he has lately taken to deciding closer to planting time. Depends on what markets he can sell to. War made for a lot of changes, and the markets he used to plant for are not there any longer. He makes more than enough to keep his house and land, pay what he must in fees and taxes, and feed his family.

"He was talking about planting some herbs when I left, as there is always a market for them and it appears to be growing. Mother said she would deal with them. With the lot of us grown and setting out on our own, he seems to be farming for himself."

"And why not? Sensible. Keeps him busy and feeling useful and his pockets full."

James smiled at Robbie. "True enough."

"I ken that none of us, including Iain, have any great

wish to herd sheep, though we all can if needed," Robbie said. "And we help with the shearing. Ye really have to love something to do it right up until ye die."

"That is how Iain got the Powells. He doesnae have to worry much about it," said Geordie. "The brothers were born into the trade and love it."

"I think they love the dogs they say they need to do the work," muttered Robbie, and then smiled at the woman who came to collect their empty dishes.

"That is quite possible," agreed Geordie before turning to the woman to sort out the bill.

As they left the eatery, Geordie looked around and shook his head. It was a town in Missouri that was rapidly growing, and by the look of it, already had all the problems that could bring. When Robbie and James stepped up beside him, he headed straight for the train station. He appreciated traveling by train but he really did not like the towns they stopped in. At first look they were thriving, but a closer look revealed not everyone was sharing in that bounty and some of the big losers were the original citizens, the ones who had settled there before the trains had arrived.

When they stopped at the place that sold the tickets, he slipped some money to James so he could get passage for them and their horses. He told his friend he was going to the stables to see the animals, then strode away. The moment he was in the stall with his horse Romeo, he felt his growing tension begin to ease. His horse's name may have been a foolish whim of his, but the animal was a good choice. This journey had showed him one thing—he was not a man who should try to settle in a city or even a large town.

* * *

"Is your brother all right?" James asked as Geordie marched ahead of them while he and Robbie started to walk to the stables.

"Aye. He just hates the crowds, the noise, the smells, and all that. He kenned that years ago when we had to leave our cottage and had to spend some time in the city, but I think this journey has really set the knowledge in hard." Robbie looked around. "Cannae say I disagree with his opinion of such places. I dinnae think I am made for such a living."

"Not everyone is. I am not that fond of it but get the feeling Geordie would not even want to be a regular visitor."

"Probably not."

"Well, someone has to live in the little towns and on the farms."

James shrugged and Robbie laughed. "And I suspicion there are many who feel as he and I do. The war drained the country of men better than people like me or Geordie, and it could soon leave cities begging for residents."

"True," James murmured as he watched a group of four women slow their march past the storefronts to stare at him and Robbie. "I have begun to wonder if three unwed men traveling through the country are actually safe from all the dangers."

Robbie laughed again. "There is that. Dinnae fear, we are nearing the ports where boats crammed with people are landing and searching for a place all the time so we won't be the only targets."

"True. Let us hope they do not all tote their families along."

"Weel, I warn ye, the one running the stables is female and I got the feeling she is looking hard, so ye arenae safe yet."

James stepped into the stables right behind Robbie to find a tall, strapping woman cornering Geordie while he struggled to get his mount out of his stall. The softest feature on her was her long, red-streaked gold hair tied in a loose tail that ran down her back. Then she spoke and James softly cursed. Her soft Irish accent could easily stir the interest of one of the men still alive and, probably more important to her, single.

They moved to the stalls where their horses stood and got their things so they could board the next train. James took the time to thoroughly check his mount for any signs that the train travel was troubling him physically, relieved to find none. He would prefer riding to Maine but could see that even the train travel was hard on Robbie, as he had taken his cane out of his pack. The filth that had tried to beat him into fighting for them had not just caused him untold pain but had done what they could to cripple him for life. That had just been vicious and unnecessary, but he feared the war had bred a lot of men who were so inclined.

"I got my cousin's boys to help me and we took them out for a little ride. Thought they might need it. I think they appreciated it."

James looked at the woman who stood by the door of the stall, resting her arms on the top of the door, and idly wondered if she was on the hunt, too. "I suspect they did. Not used to being shut up in a train for days."

"So, I hear you are heading east."

"We are. Only left because of the war. Going back home to Maine now."

She shook her head. "The call to war. Men can't seem to ignore it. Long way to come to let some fools shoot at you. Should have stayed home. Suspect you could've found someone to shoot at you there."

He laughed. "I could have, except the need to keep the country whole stirred me to go. The worst is trying to accept that you are killing people. Even though they are trying to kill you, it is a hard thing to adjust to. Then there is the fact that it is nasty, dirty, and, certainly, damned uncomfortable. I am a man who greatly appreciates his comforts." He grinned when the woman laughed.

"I bet. Saw some soldiers, some going and some coming back from a battle." She shook her head. "Some of the boys returning, too few of them in my opinion, looked like they had aged ten years." She stepped back and held open the door as he led his horse out of the stall. "Come on. No need to worry. Already did my hunting and caught me a good one: he is only missing a piece."

"Which piece?"

"Bottom half of his leg. He's pondering a peg leg, like a pirate," she said and smiled slightly.

James nodded. "There will be a lot of broken men for a while."

She nodded. "My man has accepted it, but he is constantly searching for something he can strap on to make up for it. To give him balance, he says. I am glad my cousin stood in her door with her rifle in hand and stopped her boys from marching off. And not just because that would leave her with no one to help her keep the house by working the fields and dealing with the animals. They had only just entered their teen years. Handsome, good-hearted boys. Too damn young."

"Drummer boys," he muttered as he started to walk his horse around the building and recalled one horrific memory of finding pieces of a body left on a battlefield, just enough to let him know it had been a very young boy. He had stood there and wept that day, and it still haunted him. He suspected it always would, then frowned as he felt someone rub his back and looked back to see the woman had come up and was trying to comfort him.

"I am fine. It is just a quickly passing memory and I get it often, though it begins to fade."

"Good," she said as she stepped back. "This damn fool war left too many of you young men scarred by bad memories. Filled your heads with ugly memories to haunt your thoughts and dreams. Well, you fellows have a safe trip."

After settling his horse in the stock car, Geordie stood outside and watched the milling crowds as he waited for Robbie and James to do the same. He could understand Robbie's dislike of such crowds because he shared it. They were pleasant to mix with on a celebratory occasion, but he would find them a chore when the crowds were a constant part of your life, always waiting just outside your door. He had no plans to live in a place like Boston or New York, but now he wondered if he would find even these small cities cropping up along the train tracks difficult to settle in.

They finally got on the train and found their seats, making sure Robbie would be able to put up his foot. He needed that or he could end up with a bad ache in his leg. This train would take them into Boston with only one switch to a smaller, local train, and Geordie thought it might be a good idea to let Robbie rest for a bit when they got to the city, to get a room with beds and stay a night or two. He considered their finances and figured they could do it. It would be a resting stop, he decided, and one he felt Robbie needed. He was not sure how much rest Robbie would need after the hours, the days, they had spent traveling, but felt sure it would help him as they made their way up the coast.

He watched as a woman they had seen earlier on the streets came in and took the seats across the aisle from them. She settled her little girl next to her, set a cloth bag down by her feet, and pulled out some knitting. He slouched in his seat and wished he could do something like that, as he found riding the trains somewhat boring. The scenery was pleasant, but there were only so many trees you could gaze at and fields you could watch before boredom swept over you. Sleep passed the time, he decided, as he closed his eyes.

Chapter Four

The whimpers of a small child pulled Geordie from sleep. He rubbed the sleep from his eyes as he sat up and looked around. He was not home; he was on a train. Once he had that clear revelation, everything came back to him and he sat up straight. The woman and the small child still sat across the aisle from him. Now six men had surrounded her. One knelt on the seat behind her and played with her black hair, undoing her careful styling and sneaking caresses of her long, slender neck. The others crowded the seats around her, forcing the young girl into her arms so that she could not even attempt to fight off the men. It was an effective trap and he had to wonder if the men had used it often.

"Aw, hell," muttered James, and he reached for his gun but Geordie reached out to stay his hand.

"Tempting as it is, I dinnae think we can have a shooting match in the train car," Geordie said softly. "The child or the woman could end up hurt or dead."

"Can't just ignore that."

"Wasnae suggesting that we do. Just that we shouldnae start shooting." Geordie looked at his brother, who was staring at the scene next to them and looking furious. "Robbie, remember the awkward stumble?"

"Of course I do. Nay that fond of it. It hurts a bit, ye ken."

"I thought maybe it did, but it is for a good cause this time, nay just a bit of foolery."

"Ye saying that doesnae really help."

Robbie stood up while Geordie made a big show of helping him. Together they staggered into the aisle as they drew abreast of the seat where the men were harassing the woman; they feigned a small tugging argument with Geordie saying they needed to go left and Robbie adamant that they should go right. Then Robbie stumbled, conveniently whacking a couple of the men with his cane as he fell heavily on the man sitting next to the woman. Geordie saw the punch Robbie gave the man and knew they could count that one out. He actually had to bite back a laugh when the little girl hit that man in the head with her wooden doll.

Geordie stumbled back when Robbie made an attempt to sit up. He felt a man move behind him and swung as he turned toward him, knocking him out by slamming his elbow into the man's jaw. Robbie got to his feet, flailing his cane around again until he caught the man standing behind the woman, square in the face. It was clear to see that Robbie had practiced flailing his cane around.

James slid over the back of his seat and across the aisle, then, a moment later, Geordie saw the man facing the woman being grabbed around the throat by James and being held tightly until his thrashing body stilled and he slumped down. It was something James had done when he and other soldiers were creeping around doing a little spying on the enemy and he apparently had decided to keep and hone the skill.

James moved to stand beside Geordie as a couple of the

porters rushed in. While James talked to them, Geordie dragged the unconscious men more fully into the aisle, then sat down facing the woman. Out of the corner of his eye he noticed Robbie sitting down in his seat and watching him, all the while using his cane to whack any man who showed signs of regaining consciousness.

"Are ye hurt, ma'am?" Geordie asked the woman, deciding she was pretty, nicely rounded yet slender, and probably several years older than him. She was also weighted with sorrow and pain, but was that pain emotional or physical? "Do ye need a healer?"

"No," she replied, brushing her long black hair back off her face and smiling faintly. "Thank you for your help."

"It was no trouble." He watched as more men arrived to drag off the ones they had left in the aisles. "Looks like they willnae be able to trouble ye again."

"Where you from? You talk funny," said the little girl, who was ignoring her mother's whispered scold.

Geordie looked at the child and smiled faintly, suspecting it was a scold she heard often. She was a small copy of her mother, although her black hair was very curly, and her big eyes were a deeper blue. "I came here from Scotland with my family. We all talk this way."

"Is that far away?"

"Pretty far, aye. Ye have to sail over the ocean. What is your name?"

"Morgan. I was named after my daddy, but he got sick from something he got in the war." She held up her doll. "He made this for me."

"Verra nice and a good weapon." He shared a grin with the child and then watched as the woman blinked back tears before he looked back at the child. "Did your da decide to stay home, or do ye live just up the track a ways?"

"No. My daddy went to live with God. We miss him a

lot but it is a good place. He will be with a lot of his family and friends. We are going to stay with my grandmother in Boston."

"I am truly sorry about your da, Morgan." He looked at the woman. "And my condolences to ye as weel, ma'am."

"Thank you kindly. And you, too, sir," she added with a smile and a nod to Robbie, who was struggling to settle back in his seat. "And my name is Jane Benson Haggert."

He nodded. "I am Geordie MacEnroy." He pointed at Robbie. "My brother, Robbie." He then pointed at James, who sat beside him and grinned. "And this disreputable fellow is James Deacon." He winced dramatically when James jabbed an elbow into his side.

"Very nice to meet you. And fortunate." She frowned. "Are you only now headed home after the war?"

"Nay. I suddenly wanted to see the ocean. Robbie decided he wouldnae mind visiting it, too."

"I am headed home after visiting my commanding officer, once he settled down somewhere and got married," said James.

"Why east? Most men seem to be rushing west and there is an ocean there."

"Weel, I suspect they are flocking there because they think they will find gold and get rich," said Geordie. "Nice dream, but it doesnae leave a place to have a quiet sit to watch the ocean. The East doesnae have that scourge, and once ye leave the cities there are a lot of quiet places, if I remember right." He glanced at Robbie, who nodded. "The time to go hunting gold in that place was when it was first found, nay years later. Now ye just get the ruffians who will shoot ye for a nugget or two. Ye only have the desperate and the deceitful, now." A look passed over her face, which made him sigh. "Your husband went there."

"He did. Took us with him. He knew he was sick,

suspected it was something that could kill him. He wanted to leave a legacy for us. Whatever had burrowed into him did not want to wait for him to accomplish that. It robbed him of his strength, so the doctor said we could bring him home. He got fretful near the end. Kept telling me to watch for it in Morgan."

"He thought it was something one could catch?" asked James.

"No, but he said his father had died of something similar, so there might be a weakness."

Geordie just nodded. "Just keep recalling those words, that he said there *might* be a weakness."

"Oh, I will," she said and smiled, holding Morgan closer when the child leaned against her. "To tell the truth, I do not really think it was what he feared it was. In the war he was shot several times, then was caught close to explosions so fierce he and some other men were tossed into the air. Something inside may have been weakened, maybe even bled, because he did start getting some horrible bruises, and it took a while to break him down completely. Some organs may have been badly damaged, so they could no longer sustain him. But he spent his last days with us, so I can thank God the doctor who tended him sent him home with us. Seeing as he could stand and shoot, since he was still in the army, he should have been returned to the battle as that was what they usually did."

"And he made me my doll, Lily. I gave her a girl's name."

Geordie almost laughed, for she sounded terribly condescending. He had to smile when the child frowned at her mother, obviously blaming the woman for her own name, which did not sound sufficiently girlish. "Morgan is a very nice name."

"I named you that in honor of your father. You should be proud, young lady."

Morgan sighed heavily. "I know and I am. Just wish his name had been Julia or something," she added in a soft mutter.

Geordie had to bite the inside of his cheek to keep from laughing aloud. "That might have been difficult for him."

"Maybe," she muttered, then suddenly smiled. "But it would have been great for me."

Geordie saw Jane grin then quickly don a serious face and close her eyes. Geordie noticed those eyes looked bruised, but without a closer look he could not be sure if it was because of actual bruising from a blow to the face or because she was tired to the bone and probably still grieving a bit. From all she had said, he imagined watching her husband slowly die had been no blessing and probably still robbed her of sleep.

He had seen too many deaths like her husband's. It was a true curse, but he seemed to be around whenever a man got that sort of injury, the kind that damaged the insides in ways many doctors could not fix, sometimes did not even see, at least not the ones who came to small towns or were in a medic's tent on a battlefield. He knew what the bruises she mentioned had been. Kicked by a mule or caught in even the edge of an explosion could leave a man with injuries one did not see, at least not until one recognized what those growing bruises meant. They meant a slow death and quite possibly a painful one.

But he saw no reason to bring up the subject of internal injuries. Stirring up the woman's bad memories and pain gained nothing. At least she was right about the doctor sending the man home. The doctor had probably known what was going to happen, had seen the signs of what was coming, and was kind enough to allow the man to be cared for by family until the end came. He suspected the woman knew it too.

And there were undoubtedly hundreds of widows

who had suffered so, he thought. Widows, mothers who lost their sons, fatherless children. War was a vicious waster of lives, destroying not only the men who so proudly marched off to join the fight but so many people around them.

It destroyed places as well, he thought, recalling too many savaged towns he had seen. He could only pray that his people had learned something from the bloody mess. Then he thought about the place he had come from in Scotland and all the blood repeatedly spilled there and sighed, shaking his head.

He glanced at Robbie and noticed his brother was already sound asleep. James was asleep as well. He wished he felt sleepy, but unfortunately he did not. Even the woman had gone to sleep, but her daughter was wide-awake. The little girl looked at her mother, then looked at him and grinned as she advanced in her seat until she sat on the edge near the aisle.

"You all done reading your book?" she asked as she hugged her doll.

"Nay. Just tired of it for now. Thinking I might try to sleep like my companions."

"And my mum."

Her mother opened her eyes and looked at the child. "Not sleeping," she said in a voice that strongly hinted that she had been. "You shouldn't bother the man, Morgan."

"I wasn't. Was just talking."

"It is all right, ma'am. I was only wondering if I could sleep like my companions are. But, afraid I did that coming here."

"It is the motion of the train."

"Aye, a wee bit like a rocking cradle."

"Where are you going? Boston, like us?"

"I think we will stop there for a change of trains. We are then going up the coast, might stop somewhere along there or go on to Maine with James at least for a while. Robbie and I are going to see the ocean, and once we get to the coast we can choose where we stay."

"Oh. So you have no plans to be at a set address?"

"Only his for a bit. But if ye ever need a hand"—he dug a small scrap of paper out of his pocket—"this is James's address, his parents' house, where he will be staying. Before the war, I would have said he was going to go back to Maine and settle down. Now I am not sure he kens where he wants to be."

"I think there will be many men who are roaming about looking for a place to settle."

"I fear so. Anyway, notify him, as he will ken how to notify us. We might even be there already."

"Thank you," she said and pulled a piece of paper from her bag. "This will be our address. I always find it a comfort to simply know someone is near or reachable."

They only talked for a few moments more before she clearly needed to go to sleep. Geordie thought hard on where he and Robbie would stay. He did not want to impose on James's parents and he did not want to stay in Boston. That city had certainly grown bigger than it was when they had first arrived in America. He hoped there would be something in-between that was reasonable.

Someplace near enough to the ocean so that he could walk the shore whenever he wanted to. That was the whole point of this journey. He was determined to find someplace to stay near the ocean. A small part of him was a little worried that he might decide to stay, but he ignored that worry. He suspected he would fight that battle right up until he had to get on his horse and head home. Would he turn to a new life or would he ride back to his ever-growing family?

Not a question he would easily find an answer to. He would have to keep it to the fore of his mind as he searched for that answer. He would also have to be brutally honest with himself, he thought, and grimaced, as he knew he had no history of that and would have to find it within himself. Once a person settled somewhere, it could be difficult and costly to turn back, so he needed to be absolutely sure he wished to settle.

"Ye arenae looking cheerful or expectant as one would expect when ye are making a trip ye so wanted," said Robbie as he woke up and tried to stretch out the aches caused by sleeping in his seat. "Having second thoughts?"

"Nay. Just wondering exactly what I plan to do."

"What do ye mean? Ye are going to see the ocean because we dinnae have it in the Ozarks."

Geordie nodded. "And I think it might be best to cease wondering if there was anything else to it."

"What else were ye wondering about?"

"Whether I wanted to live there, if I was thinking of, or searching for, a place to settle."

"Ah. That would displease Iain."

Geordie laughed and nodded. "It would, and not just because he has always worked to keep us all together. He hasnae said it, but I really do think his plan is to make his own clan." He grinned when Robbie laughed.

"Possibly. We will ken for certain if he ever starts trying to contact clansmen from back home and bring them over."

"God help us. Some of those people arenae missed by me."

"Nor me." He pulled out a deck of cards. "Want a game?"

"Why not," Geordie answered and sat up straight. "Cannae sleep right now and it will pass the time."

"Ye could watch the country go by out the window."

"Trees, fields, messy towns swollen by people from the trains or people searching for a new place to live. Nay. Seen enough of them. Thought getting the train stopping in one's town was a great thing. After having seen some, dinnae think it is."

"Nay," agreed Robbie as he dealt the cards. "Train service takes over a town and changes it."

"And no' really for the better. What game are we playing?"

"Poker. Need to practice for all those wild nights in the saloons I plan to indulge in."

Geordie laughed and then concentrated on his cards. It would at least pass the time and might help him get in the mood for another nap.

Chapter Five

As Geordie stepped down from the train he tried not to breathe too deeply, a little afraid he would fall into a coughing fit. The smell of the train was starting to cause a deep-set itch in his throat. He also missed the lady and little Morgan. Their talk had made the time pass faster. Morgan's mother, Jane, a quiet, troubled woman had, at times, seemed eager to share conversation with an adult. He was still amazed that her husband, sick and dying as he had been, had managed to hold off the forces chasing him for as long as he had.

She had told him a wild story about how her husband had given her a chest to hold and keep secret. The man had only told her what was in it when he was close to death. The chest was filled with gold coins from a Confederate supply payment, and he told her some long tale of catching the thieves and finding the small chest where one of them had stashed some for himself. Her husband kept it, thinking he might find a chance to return it to the men who were with him, or put it back in the hands of the men who had been with him when they found the gold. He warned her that someone had heard a tale about it from one of the thieves and several incidents had convinced her such men still were hunting it down.

It amazed him that Jane's husband had obviously fought off or eluded several attempts even though he knew he was dying. It was why she and Morgan had got off the train at the last stop to travel on to her mother, where she hoped to burrow in until she was no longer hunted. She was convinced the ones hunting her knew something about the chest. He prayed she would be proved wrong. If greed had driven her pursuers to hunt for it so hard, they would certainly not hesitate to hurt her and a child to get the chest of gold.

Sometimes tales about such things led to people being killed, but he had not heard of anyone who had actually found gold or some other treasure. Geordie had wished Jane luck and a secure, safe place to live with her mother. It did bother him that she was so pale and often rubbed at her middle as if she had some pain there. He had wanted to ask her about it but had never figured out how to do it delicately. Geordie could only hope it was something her mother could fix. The war had already collected enough dead.

James had allowed him to share his address with the woman. Geordie had also given her his home address, although he doubted she would contact him there, since it was so far away. Things she had said made him suspect the very last place she wished to go was anywhere in the west. Still, it eased his mind to know she could find them if she ever needed help. He hoped she could burrow safely at her mother's, but two women and a child would have little defense against men who wished to get rich without working for it.

As he counted out the money to have the horses stabled for the night, he tried to dodge the man's attempts to introduce him to his daughter. He had to laugh as he thought about all the single men who would be going through these towns for a while yet. The men drifting back home, the ones who had families they ached to reunite with, who thought they were safe now that the war was over. They were in for a big surprise.

Jane had gotten off the train in what had looked like a mill city, and he hoped she was not pushed to work in one. He had seen how it aged and wearied women workers.

They quickly went in search of a hotel. When Geordie had mentioned getting a room, both James and Robbie had readily agreed. It took several tries to find one that had a room at a price they thought reasonable, but soon they were settled. As Robbie sprawled out on the bed, he and James went on a search for some food.

Since they were still close to the train station, the crowds on the street ebbed and flowed, but Geordie just wanted them gone. By the time they got to a place that sold sandwiches and coffee, Geordie breathed a hearty sigh of relief. James went up to get their food, bringing mugs of coffee over as he waited for the rest. Geordie sipped the strong coffee and looked around at the people.

It was a working man's eatery, he decided. There were a lot of people who had just arrived on the train as well. That confirmed his feeling that it was the cheapest choice they could find. It was much like the kind of places they had gone to on occasion back home when they had briefly stayed in the city.

"Coffee is good," said James. "Hope that means the food will be as well."

"Look at the customers. Mostly working men. Often means a place that is reasonably priced, plain but good."

James nodded. "Same where I live. Go down near where the fishing boats dock and you'll find such places."

"My da used to tell us about the fancy restaurants. He went to them with clients who wanted to buy a portrait of someone in their family, and wanted to discuss it over a meal. He said he thought they took him to such places as a bribe, hoping he would lower his price. He didnae. Also said what ye paid for was fancy napkins and fancy plates and foreign food ye couldnae often ken what it was exactly."

"Rich people often prefer foreign food. Never figured out why."

"Maybe just to show people they ken more than the common mon."

"Possible."

The man behind the counter stepped up and bellowed James's name. Grinning, James went to get their sandwiches. Geordie hurried to finish his coffee. He frowned when James returned with a tray holding what looked like a small kettle of soup and three more mugs of coffee, as well as six sandwiches.

"The man asked where we were staying and I told him. Seems we can take this with us and leave it at the hotel. He will send a boy to pick it up late tonight. Guess it is a regular service between this place and the hotel."

Geordie collected their mugs and took them up to the counter to have them set on a small tray to carry them.

"Just try to keep people from bumping into me."

"Aye, sir." Geordie grinned, knowing by James's brief muttering that the man had an urge to hit him but could not do it while he had the tray.

James and Geordie walked slowly back to the hotel, careful that James did not get the tray knocked out of his hands. When they entered the hotel the man behind the desk showed them where to leave the things that would be returned to the eatery after their meal.

By the time they got to the room, Robbie was sound asleep. Geordie helped James set the food out on the rough table in the room. Whether it was the scent of the coffee or the soup which did it, Robbie started to wake up. When he sat up and rubbed his hands over his face, then looked over at him and James seated at the table, Geordie just smiled.

"Guess this is good coffee. It wakes the dead," Geordie said.

"Ha, ha," said Robbie. "So funny," he muttered as he stood up and walked over to the table.

"Coffee, soup, which I think is chicken, and a beef sandwich," said James. "One sandwich. I got the others for later."

"Ye were allowed to take these things out of the shop?" Robbie asked as he sat down.

"They have an agreement with this hotel. There's a spot in the lobby where we can put the mugs, tray, and other things."

"How long are we staying here?"

"Two nights," Geordie replied.

"That's nice. Then we ride, right?"

"Yup," replied James. "Figured a bit of a rest after riding the trains for so long would be good."

Robbie nodded. "I'll admit, it would help me build up a tolerance for the ride."

"Me? I just want a wee rest from traveling on a train," said Geordie. "A wee rest from all the people."

James laughed. "Not the friendliest fellow, are you."

"I am friendly, just dinnae like crowds."

"So, we will have a rest and then start riding up the coast. If the weather turns sour there are a lot of short rail runs we can catch a ride on. I have traveled on the Boston to Maine line, and it was fine." James frowned. "There are a few small ones up the coast, too. The one that goes from Lynn to Portsmouth gets up north and we can ride on the coast road." Noticing how Geordie and Robbie were staring at him, James asked, "What?"

"Did the East go mad for railroads?" asked Geordie.

"A bit, I think. We have a lot because once the first ones

were in, it seemed like every town wanted one, and then people wanted a way to travel to the coast with ease." He shrugged. "It supplied troops and all, and that impressed folk. Some say it is why we won the war."

"Probably, although I dinnae think anyone really won except the gravediggers."

Everyone went silent and finished their meal. Soon they moved to get ready for bed. Geordie let Robbie have one of the two beds. He figured he could toss a coin with James to see who had the other and who had to sleep on the army cot the hotel set up in the room.

To his dismay, James won. They then took turns using the washroom and toilet down the hall. When Geordie got on the cot after putting his bedding roll on it, he decided it was not so bad. Closing his eyes, he promised himself he would keep a close watch on Robbie. His brother would not speak up when he was wearied, so Geordie would watch and speak up when he saw the signs. He wasn't sure how it could make Robbie worse if he overdid, but Geordie did not want to be the one on watch if it was a possibility. And he did not want to watch his brother suffer.

As soon as James returned and put the lights out, Geordie wished a good night to his roommates and closed his eyes. Robbie did not reply and Geordie figured his brother was far more exhausted than he had realized and had already gone back to sleep. They would do their best to be sure tomorrow was a lazy day.

Morning arrived with the welcome scent of coffee. Geordie looked up to see James accepting the tray with three mugs from a blushing maid. They had been pleased that the place offered coffee with the room. Getting up, he put on his clothes and hurried down the hall to the toilet, then slipped into the washroom to have a quick wash. By the time he got back to the room, Robbie was sitting at the table sipping his coffee.

"Where did James go?" Geordie asked as he picked up his coffee and sat down.

"He went down the road to find us some breakfast."

"You didnae want to go?"

"Nay. A bit achy this morning. Rubbed some of the cream Emily made up for me on my leg and it has helped. James said it looked calm enough outside he didnae think he needed someone to guard over him as he came back with the tray."

"Ah, good, because I dinnae want to go either." He frowned. "I was surprised to see the morning coffee brought to the room by a lass."

Robbie chuckled. "So was James. He was bothered about how wee she was. Said they shouldnae be sending up such a wee bonnie lass, nay to the rooms they ken have only men in them. That is just asking for trouble for her. I got the feeling he may have a word with whoever is behind the desk, he was that bothered by it. Think he will say something?"

"Quite possible as I got the feeling it really irritated him, and James has never been too shy to let one ken why he is irritated."

"Weel, just so long as it doesnae stop the coffee from being delivered," Robbie said.

"Aye, cannae have that." He exchanged a grin with Robbie. "So, is there anything ye want to see in this city?" asked Geordie, glancing at the pamphlet Robbie held.

"Was wondering about seeing how far away some of the famous Revolution sites are. Ye ken, the ones Da told us about."

"Och, aye, he did love to talk about that. To hear him ye would think it had happened yesterday instead of nearly a hundred years ago." He grinned when Robbie laughed. "We need to decide what we want to see, and figure how far away they are." He nodded at the pamphlet. "Does that say anything helpful?"

"Tells me street addresses, but nothing more."

"Then we should see if they have a map, or the man at the desk kens where and how far."

Robbie frowned as he looked at Geordie. "Ye looked sad for a moment. Something wrong?"

"Nay. I just had the passing thought that Da would have loved being in this city, but he couldnae stop here for long. He would love to hear about what we might get to see."

"Ye ken it was just because they won, dinnae ye? They beat the English."

"Aye. He loved that."

There was a thump at the door and Geordie hurried to answer it. He let in James and put their mugs aside so he could put the breakfast plates down on the table. The scent of the food had his stomach growling.

"That is a lot of food," Geordie said as he looked at the ham, eggs, toast, and a small bowl of what looked like oatmeal.

"I looked at what they offered and asked for the full breakfast. This is what they consider a full breakfast." He set the tray aside and sat down.

For a while all was quiet as they ate. By the time he turned to his oatmeal, Geordie was not sure he had any room left for it. He almost smiled when he heard his mother's voice telling him to eat it, that it would stick with him for the whole day. He then wondered why, on this morning and in this city, memories of his parents were so close and so clear.

James piled the empty plates and bowls on the tray, then sat to savor his coffee. "Don't think I will be wanting more until supper."

"It was certainly a *full* breakfast."

"So, any plans for the day?"

"Nay sure. We need to find out how far away a couple of places are."

"I feel sure we can just ask the fellow at the desk."

"Aye, that is what we thought." Geordie looked at Robbie. "Maybe ye can write down what addresses we might be interested in."

As Robbie moved to do that, James asked, "What are you interested in?"

"He was thinking about actually seeing a few things that we always heard about when Da talked about your Revolution. Da just loved the stories about it. As I said, mostly he loved that ye won; ye beat the English."

"We did that. So we go to the guy at the desk and ask him. Maybe go see a couple places."

"Dinnae want to do too much walking around."

James glanced at Robbie. "I figured that was why you wanted directions. Not able to just wander around the city. That would be too much walking?"

"Och, aye. Leg is fine even though it does ache a lot from the long train rides. The pain I could deal with, but I cannae deal with it when my leg simply gives up, weakens so much it is mostly useless. So I try to keep my wandering to a minimum."

"Good idea." James finished his coffee and moved to put the mug on the tray. "If you have the addresses you are wondering about, give them to me and I will go talk to the fellow."

Robbie handed him the list, watched him leave and then looked at Geordie. "Do ye think he doesnae really want to walk about, so thinks to get it done and over with fast?"

"Nay. Matthew once said James is one of those who wakes up and feels he needs to do something right away.

He wakes up ready to go. Occasionally drove Matthew nuts." Geordie grinned. "Matthew is a let-me-linger-over-a-few-cups-of-coffee mon."

"Ah. Fine then. It works at times like this, when our only other choice is to just sit around in this room."

"True. Now ye are to be sure to let us ken if and when ye have had enough."

"Aye, mither." He ducked when Geordie tried to smack him on the head. "I will, as I dinnae want to push too hard when we have miles still to go."

"I am thinking James may want us to take a train for a ways. It will be faster and he does have to go to Maine, so that would suit him better."

"Got no problem with that. Now, I think I will see if the washroom is empty as I would like to clean up a wee bit."

Robbie went into the washroom, took off his shirt, and stared at the scars on his chest. For a moment he was back with those men who had beat him, wondering if he would survive, and then he shook off the paralyzing fear. It had taken him a long time to be able to do that, and he hoped that soon he could do the same with the stark memories that swept over him at odd times. He desperately wanted to forget it all.

As he washed up he wondered if he could at least soften those memories. It did not seem quite fair that he not only clearly remembered the abuse but also the pain of it, the feeling of deep helplessness, and the knee-buckling fear.

It was almost as bad as what Matthew sometimes suffered from, having been in the middle of a war. He had never been near the major battles, yet he suffered from memories, too. Robbie hoped the bloodletting of war would work to cure this nation of throwing its young men into another conflict, but, sadly, he doubted it.

Once his body was clean, he cleaned his teeth, rinsed out his shirt, and headed back to the room. It pleased him to see that James had returned. Grabbing a clean shirt out of his bag, he put it on and listened to James and Geordie talk about what they could look at in Boston.

They started out by going to the wharf where the tea was thrown into the harbor. It was busy there and hard to envision what it had been like all those years ago, but Robbie had a good imagination. By the time they wandered away in search of another site, he felt satisfied.

As they walked, James and Geordie remarked on the old houses they passed. To Robbie and Geordie they looked a lot different than the ones at home. Most everything he had seen west of this place was new, and it would be a while before they grew any character and gained any history. In the South, where there had been age and history, a lot had been destroyed by the war. Robbie wondered how long it would take for those scars on the land to fade.

By the time they got back to the room, his leg was beginning to twinge with weariness. He shed his trousers and rubbed Emily's cream on his leg, massaging it in as she insisted he do. It took a while, but he finally felt the ache ease and he idly wondered which was more effective, the cream or the massage. It was a question he asked himself more and more.

"Ye just going to lie there pantless?" asked Geordie.

"Aye. Cream needs to dry or soak in," replied Robbie. "Was just pondering which does the best work, the cream or the massage."

"Might be the massaging. The doctor who rode with us often spent time massaging wounds similar to yours, and he did not have any fancy cream. From what little I saw of the effects, it appeared to work. Do you massage your hand?" James asked.

"When I put some cream on. Why?"

"Well, if it doesn't hurt much, maybe you should do more of it, cream or not."

"There's a thought. Think it would work?"

"Might. Worth a try. Things stiffen up and become hard to work with if you don't keep them limber. Know that from the injuries round my father's farm."

"True. I will do that."

Robbie sat up to eat the sandwich James handed him. Once he had finished, he pulled up the sheet and closed his eyes. He wanted to be well rested when they finally headed out on the next leg of their journey.

Geordie looked at Robbie and realized he was already asleep. Setting down the book he was reading, he watched his brother closely, then turned to James, who was also reading. Glancing at the title he nearly groaned. The man was reading about bridges.

"Do ye think Robbie is all right?"

James looked over at Robbie and then looked at Geordie. "The walk around this morning probably tired him right out."

"I guessed that. Just wondering if he and I misjudged his ability to take this trip."

"No. I don't think it is a thing you can judge anyway. Don't think he ever pushed himself, so you have nothing to judge by. He's tired and he's resting. Best thing to do and he apparently has the good sense to do it. We'll keep an eye on him, but I think he will let us know when he has had enough, and then you both can take the trains home."

"True. Then all he needs to fret about is how annoyed I am to miss seeing the ocean because of him. And he will. He is very quick to blame himself and his 'infirmity,' as he calls it too often."

James shook his head. "He is not infirm. I have seen infirm. Lots of men missing bits of themselves after the war. Robbie is, well, bruised, shall we say. He has a limp and a weak hand. What was done to him probably gives him nightmares, if only because it was a senseless brutality, but those will slowly fade. We'll just keep a close watch on him. If he can make it through this, maybe it will give him a better view of himself."

"That is what I am hoping." Geordie stood up and stretched. "I want a drink. Have no idea why, but it just seems as if this day should end with a drink. Or two."

"Good idea," said James as he also stood up. "Should we wake him?"

He went to his bag and found a pencil and paper. "Nay. I will leave him a note so he doesnae wonder where we went. Robbie isnae much of a tippler. Likes his cider but not much else. And if he is sleeping while we talk, he obviously needs a rest."

Setting the note on the table, Geordie grabbed his coat and left with James. He hoped the man was right, that Robbie would gain some confidence in himself if he finished this journey. It would be good if his brother gained some benefit from it all.

Chapter Six

Mehitabel answered the pounding at the door, not surprised to see her neighbor and several of his men standing there. Her little dog was with her, so she knew it was not a complaint about him getting through the fence and harassing the cows again. Odin sat down by her feet looking cute and innocent, which he was this time. Mehitabel suspected Charles Bennet did not believe it any more than she usually did. But this time Odin really had been with her all day.

"Your damn goats have been at my fence again," Bennet snapped, and held his rifle so that it was more visible.

"I sincerely doubt that. They are over at my aunt Mary's. She needed them for some yard clearing."

"What good can they do?"

"Quite a lot, actually. They crop the grass down neatly and they eat all those things you don't want growing in your yard, like that vine that gives you itchy spots."

"Poison ivy?"

"That is the one. You have it all over your annoying fencing. It is one of the reasons I had to lend my auntie the goats. As the weather warmed she noticed it was spreading all over her grape arbor. They kept going over to the fence to try to get to the treat winding all over it." She tensed when he aimed his gun at her. "Now, Bennet, that will only cause you more trouble."

"It might be worth it. I would finally get this land, and I suspect your family would like the money."

"Then you would suspect wrong," she said as she pulled her rifle from where it was hidden by her skirts and aimed it at him. "My family does not want your money. They don't want money instead of the land. They might not be your kind of rich, but they have enough to get them through some hard times. They want the land. They have always wanted the land. That is why it is so protected in the will and in any other way they were allowed to protect it."

"So you're hanging on to it. Plan to give it to the Injuns. Yeh, I heard about that. Fine. We'll just take it from them."

"Not easily. They are Amplefords, and this is listed as Ampleford land." She watched the red flush of anger come and go in his face. "Aunty is an Ampleford, too. Pa made sure of it."

"Stupid cow. I need this land."

"Why? Appears your cattle have plenty."

He was breathing hard, which worried her a little, but then he started bellowing at her, calling her foul names and insulting her in some crudely creative ways. Mehitabel was sorely tempted to shoot him, but all his men were also armed and appeared ready to shoot her. She really did not want to die in a shoot-out at her own front door.

It puzzled her that he was so out of control. For a long time he had been unreasonably angry with her refusal to sell to him, but never this crazed with anger. Then he leaned a little closer to hiss a few insults and she caught the smell of whiskey on his breath. He was drunk, and she worried that could be enough to turn what was an old, and too frequent, angry confrontation into a deadly one. Drunken, angry men were dangerous creatures.

As she wondered if there was a way to calm things

down, to say something that might placate him, she saw movement behind him. Looking over his shoulder while trying to keep a close eye on him, she saw three men walking toward her house. She prayed they were not more of his men, most of whom were just local boys. The men approaching did not look like local boys.

Geordie took a deep breath and savored the ocean scent that was so special, that salty crispness. A train had brought them up to the northern coast. Now they rode calmly along the beach. He noticed Robbie was almost as enthralled as he was. It was sunny and warm and colorful, with the rays of the slowly setting sun brightening up the water. Then he felt a slight bite to the wind coming off the water and frowned.

"I am thinking the weather is going to turn on us," Robbie said as he looked up at the sky and rubbed his leg. "My bones think so, too. Especially the broken ones."

"Damn," grumbled James. "I was hoping a storm would hold off for a while."

"Ye kenned one was coming?" asked Geordie.

"Could smell it in the air, which occasionally has a telling bite to it. We should look around for a place to sleep. By dark I think it will be raining. At least, I hope it will be rain."

"Bit warm for it to be much else *and* too late in the year." Even as he spoke, Geordie felt another cold bite in the wind and he cursed.

James laughed. "You can never be sure of that in this part of the country."

"We didnae stay in this part of the country all that long, but I did notice that."

"Da called it temperamental," said Robbie. "Bloody

temperamental, just like home." He winced and shifted a bit in the saddle. "Mither liked it."

Geordie nodded. "I remember. She especially liked the rocky hills that rise up from the beach in so many places."

"So do I." James nodded toward one. "We can tuck in against some of the rocks to shelter from the rain coming."

"True enough," Geordie said as he moved closer to the rocks and guided his horse to walk along the base until he noticed something that looked like a staircase. "Someone wanted an easier way down."

James looked down the beach. "The rocky hills get smaller soon."

They kept walking until Geordie spotted another set of steps. This hill was low enough to see the grass growing at the top. He dismounted and sat on one of the steps and looked out at the ocean. The wind had definitely gathered some strength, and that bite of coolness still clung to the breeze, so he suspected the rain was rapidly approaching.

A strange moment of silence allowed voices to be heard. Geordie frowned. He heard an angry male voice. He listened for a while but could not hear any precise words, so he turned, secured his horse, and slowly climbed the steps. At the top he saw a long, low house with one section two stories high. Seven men faced a small woman standing in an open door. He saw the weapons they held and crouched down.

A moment later James came up and took a place by his side. "Trouble?"

"Sounds like it. Hell, looks like it, too," answered Geordie.

"Seven armed men, big fellows against one short female, also armed," said Robbie as he squirmed into place on the other side of Geordie. "Aye, I would call that trouble."

Geordie stared at a sign nailed to a post at the top of the steps. A road ran along the top of hills and he would wager the sign was clear to anyone riding by.

He sidled up to the verge and turned to see the sign more clearly. *Rooms to let. Clams. Anadama bread. Goats for rent. Nurse.* The sign gave them a good excuse to walk up to the house, if only to inquire what anadama bread was. Geordie got slowly to his feet and stepped off the stairs onto the grass.

"Planning to charge to her rescue?" James snapped.

Geordie ignored the voice in his head that told him to stay back, even to hide. He straightened up, grabbed his gun out of its holster, and started walking toward the house. Robbie and James hissed at him to get down. James cursed him for thinking he was some white knight who had to ride to a woman's rescue.

He had barely gone a few steps when Robbie and James stood up to follow him. The men at the house yelled at the woman when she leveled her rifle at them. He aimed his gun at her again. Geordie moved a little faster and got close enough to poke his rifle into the big man's back. When he heard the sound of two more rifles being readied to fire, he knew he was now flanked by Robbie and James.

The big man tensed as did the men with him. They all lowered their weapons, but the woman only eased her stance a little, still firmly aiming her rifle at the man. Geordie knew she saw him, but the tense silence continued and he began to feel uneasy.

When she glanced his way, Geordie was stunned, for the look from her wide golden eyes hit him like a hard punch to the belly. It was then that he took a good look at the woman. She was short, as Robbie had said, but she was also small in other ways. Despite her size, she stood firm, and her hands on the rifle may have been delicate but they held it firm and steady. Her gown was plain, but it fit well over some very tempting curves.

"Did you hire some new hands, Belle?" demanded the man.

"I think a better question would be why would I hire some hands."

"For the same reason everyone does, to do some work for you."

Geordie wondered if the man knew how his condescending tone put him in danger. He saw the woman's eyes narrow, and her grip tightened on the rifle. It was clear this confrontation between the two was not a new one, and he watched her struggle to fight down her anger.

"Working at what? Herding my four goats? Caring for well-caged chickens? Perhaps tend to my two horses and one donkey. Or my two milk cows. I suppose I could have hired some of them to dig my clams. Or, just maybe, I hired them to get the trash off my lawn." She spoke harshly and glared at him.

Bennet growled a little and stepped closer. The woman just smiled. "If I were you, Bennet, I would toddle home and leave me to talk to these men. Or, I can step aside and you can have a chat with Thor. Did you not hear him growling from behind me? I am the only thing holding him inside. Dogs don't forget the person who shot them. Not sure how much longer he will tolerate that."

"Ye shot her dog?" Robbie burst out. "Bastard."

"Aye, disgusting behavior," Geordie agreed. Now aware of the deep growl coming from behind her, he realized it was not the cute little dog.

"He leaps for my throat again and I will not miss," Bennet snapped, then marched off toward the back of the house.

Geordie noticed four of his men hurried after Bennet, but two gave the woman a grin and a wink and meandered after the man. He thought back over the scene and realized those two men had stood behind the others and he had not noticed their guns aimed at the woman.

"He does not realize those two fellows are relations of yours, does he?" asked James with a grin.

She grinned back. "Bennet never did pay attention to family lines. My cousins are Murphys, but Thomas Murphy married my aunt, who is an Ampleford. I am Mehitabel Ampleford. Everyone calls me Belle. How can I help you gents? Bread, clams, or goats?"

"Actually, miss, we have come about the bed you had to let?"

"All three of you?"

"If there is room. We want to shelter from the storm that is soon to hit. Maybe stay a day or two to see the ocean and all, if we can."

"Well, get your things and your horses, if you have them, and bring them up. If you go a short way farther up the beach you'll find paths you can walk the horses up."

"All right. Ye stay here, Robbie," Geordie said, then looked at the woman. "If that is all right with you."

"It is fine. Come up." She waved to Robbie to come up on the porch. "You can sit here or come inside. Thor looks mean, but he will not hurt you," she said as she stepped aside and a huge shaggy brown dog stepped out.

"That looks like a fine guard dog, but what kind is he?"

"A lot of different kinds. You are welcome to come in if you want. That rain is pretty well on the doorstep." She stepped inside and held the door open.

"Hope Geordie and James dinnae get soaked." He stepped inside and took his boots off on the rough square of carpet there, then put them on the wooden rack set to the side. "Fine house ye have."

"Thank you. Great-Grandfather built it. That is why most of it is only one story high." She flashed him a grin. "He did not like climbing up a big ladder. My great-grandmother preferred length instead of height, as well. My father added the second floor with the bedrooms. Where did you come from? I do not recognize the accent."

"Scotland."

"Did you break your leg on the journey?" She steered him toward a large, heavy wooden rocker when he started toward the settee. "My pa said this chair is better if you have an injury or pain."

"Nay, it didnae happen on the journey from Scotland, which was years ago. In the war some men took me and wanted me to join the Rebs. When I said nay they tried to convince me by bashing my leg and my hand. My brother Iain feels certain they were not trying to fix me when they finally patched me up, but hoped to make me useless to anyone else who might try to take me as a recruit."

"What were you? Ten? They should have considered you too young and moved on."

"Nay. I was of an age to join in the war. Didnae want to, but was certainly old enough."

"Only the ones with money and power should go fight. They are responsible for starting the war and they are the ones who gain from it, so they and theirs should be out there fighting."

"Ye have a verra cynical view of wars."

"I have a very cynical view of a lot of things. I'll get you something to eat and drink."

Mehitabel went into her kitchen and started to put to-gether a tray of food and drink for her guests. She thought about what else she needed to do to be ready for James, Geordie, and Robbie. It was early in the season so she doubted there would be others looking for a room now. If there was, any male could join them in the infirmary, which, with its beds lining each wall was much like a bunkhouse, and any female could pick one of the two remaining bedrooms. This was a profitable start to the season. She hoped it continued.

Bennet's anger troubled her. Her refusal to sell to him had always been a source of real irritation for him, but tonight his behavior was extreme. She wondered if he had some deal he could make if it included her land, too. The man had never really been happy with what he had inherited. For some reason he believed he deserved more.

She suspected he wanted to be one of those fancy-dressed men who strolled the streets of a big city. He wanted to be a big man of industry or something similar. There was no city near them where he could fulfill such a dream. If he had reached the point where his life displeased him so much, she should expect even uglier confrontations. Belle sighed with the weariness such a thought brought with it.

After starting something for a proper dinner, she got some linen out of the cupboard and went to make up the beds in the infirmary. The sound of a footstep made her look toward the door, and Robbie stood there. She was going to be nosy soon and find out more about his injuries, she decided, as she sent him a questioning smile.

"I came to give ye a hand," he said as he walked toward her.

"That is not necessary. You are the guest. Nearer to summer, these beds would be made up all the time for the guests. It is just a bit early for any beach hunters."

"It is all right. I do this kind of thing at home. Cannae expect Mrs. O'Neal to do everything when there are seven of us 'boys,' which is what she always calls us."

"Seven? You have *six* brothers?" she asked in shock as he helped her spread out the bottom sheet nicely.

"Aye. We lost our home in Scotland because the laird

decided sheep or cattle would bring him more profit than tenants, and so he threw us out. 'Tis a long story that many Scots are all too familiar with, and so we came here after a bit of trying to make a living at home. Sadly, my parents died when we went west, as so many others did, but all of the rest of us made it to the Ozarks, and my brother Iain thought it a good spot. We raise sheep."

"I thought sheep were not much liked out west of here."

"Nay, they are hated, but up in the hills, we arenae near people who are that rabid about them. We stumbled across a couple of Welsh shepherds and they watch the flock. Good fellows," he said as he helped her put the spread on the bed. "They were finding it hard to make a living as shepherds, so were happy to take over our flock. Built them some cabins and they went and found themselves wives and are growing families."

Plumping the pillow and moving to the next bed, she asked, "Who is Mrs. O'Neal then?"

"Our housekeeper. I gather that is what folk call them. Her husband got killed in the town near us back home in the Ozarks when some men wanted to take the money he had just received for the apples he grew. So she grabbed her kids and walked out of there. Saw our place, which has a stockade like a fort, and decided that was a safe place for her kids. She convinced Iain he needed to hire her. She became the one who cleans the place, cooks us meals, and nurses us. We built her a place, too, inside the stockade since she loved it so much."

"It is like you have built yourself a small village."

Robbie laughed. "Never thought of it that way, but it does, doesnae it." He smoothed down his side of the cover, then moved to the third bed.

"What are ye doing?"

Belle squeaked in surprise at the voice from the door, but Robbie just grinned and turned to look at Geordie.

"Making the beds. Just figures ye would wander in when we are almost done."

Geordie walked over and lightly slapped the back of Robbie's head before turning toward Mehitabel. "Miss Ampleford, we were wondering where ye would like us to put the horses."

"Any empty stall. You might want to avoid the ones next to the donkey's stall. He can get stroppy around an animal he does not know. The black horse doesn't care, just so long as your horse doesn't try to eat his feed."

"Thank ye." He turned to start out of the room.

"We can discuss what you pay and what you get and the few tiny rules I have when you get back."

"Ye have rules?" asked Robbie after Geordie nodded his agreement and left.

"Just a couple. Ye already followed one—took your boots off when ye came in and set them on the boot rack."

"What is this room?"

"The infirmary. My grandfather and my father were doctors. I learned a lot but not at a school, so that is why I put 'nurse' on my sign. I still get a lot of the folk in town coming to see me as if I am a doctor. No doctor has come to the town. Too small, I guess."

"I dinnae think we have one either."

"Maybe they will come now that the war is over."

Robbie murmured a matching hope, then Belle went into the kitchen to put dinner on. As soon as she had the meal started she put a bit more food and fresh drinks on a tray and took it in to the men; the two others were already back from tending to their horses. They were a handsome collection of young men, she thought, and smiled as she poured herself some coffee from the pot she had brought in.

"This is verra nice. Thank ye," Geordie said.

"Dinner will be ready in an hour and a half," she said. "We'll eat at the big table over in front of the fireplace. If you wish to do something, there are books in the room where you will sleep or in what I like to call the social room. It is the room with the carved wooden double doors. The social room also has cards, a chess set, and checkers."

He watched her walk away and then looked at Robbie. "She reminds me a bit of David's wife." Geordie looked at James. "He's one of the Powell brothers, shepherds we hired for the flock we have. Small, with a mile of hair, can do a lot of things, and will do every one to make a good living."

"I wonder where the growling Thor went? I want to see what he looks like," James said as he sat up straight.

Robbie replied, "Big, brown, and shaggy. Miss Ampleford says he is a mix of a lot of breeds. I saw him when she stepped aside and turned to go into the house, but he disappeared into the kitchen."

"So there is a little white dog called Odin and a big brown dog called Thor."

Geordie pointed to something curled up on the seat Belle had been in. "What is that?"

"I thought it was a pillow she was sitting on," said James as he studied the lump of gray and white.

Belle walked out of the kitchen and saw the three men studying her cat. "That is my cat, Loki."

"Those are all Norse gods, aren't they?"

"Yup. Read a book about them that they had in the lending library. Thought they were interesting." With a soft little grunt she picked up the cat, sat down, and the cat curled up on her lap.

"That is a big cat."

"I know. Thor is scared of him."

"Nay surprised. The size of those paws must give him a good smacking swing."

"Knocks Odin right off his little paws." She looked at Geordie and asked, "So why are you all up here?"

"I wanted to see the ocean. We were here for a while

when we first came over from Scotland, and I liked it, but my mother wanted a place with a wee bit of land and Da had heard about all the land west of here, so they headed out there. It was this year as the weather warmed that I started to get a real urge to see the ocean again."

"Yet you came east. There is an ocean on the West Coast, too."

"East has better train connections, and the West is also a lot more dangerous than people realize."

"And I am heading to Maine because my mother asked me to come home," said James.

"Ah, not a request one can ignore. She probably wants to see that you are fine," Belle said. "During the war, the list of our dead posted in the square from time to time must have frightened her half to death."

"Well, yes, that might be some of it, but my father hurt himself and can't finish some work he needs to get done."

Belle nodded. "Yes, this time of the year is a bad time to leave things undone." She carefully moved the cat and stood up. "Well, you are welcome to stay as long as you want and the ocean is right out there. Now I need to go and finish putting together the dinner."

."Need any help?" asked Geordie.

"No. Thank you. Things are just cooking and I only have to check. I'll call if something comes up. Over the years I have actually come up with a lot of things to help me." She picked up the tray they had put their empty dishes on and disappeared into the kitchen.

James stretched out his legs and sipped his coffee. "I think we were lucky to find this place. I will probably stay here for a day or two, then head home."

"Do ye want us to come with ye?" asked Geordie.

"No, wait until I have a better idea of what needs doing. I will contact you if I have a desperate need of a few extra hands." He looked at Geordie. "I think this is a perfect place to satisfy that craving you have to look at the ocean."

"Certainly is convenient. Right out the door and down the steps. Hell, can probably sit on the edge of the hill and just look at it whenever I get in the mood."

"Maybe that is one reason that man wants this property so bad," said Robbie.

"Possibly. It is not only high up but far back, so should be safe from the water rising. Very tempting property, depending on what he has in mind," said James.

"Cannae see him running a place like this."

"No, but the number of people coming to the ocean when the weather warms might warrant something fancier, and I can see him liking some fancy hotel with his name on it. It would be a shame to build something like that here."

"There is money to be had in entertaining visitors to the ocean?"

"It begins to look like there might be, and, if interest is building, it is always best to be one of the first to respond. Especially if the visitors tend to be wealthy. And most are. After all, who else can leave work for a few days to wriggle their toes in the water? And more trains run to the coast now."

"Then I had best get my fill of ocean-watching while I can," said Geordie.

"Good idea. I have been trying to think of how to warn my folks about what I think is coming. We are not right on the water, but we are very close and have a nice piece of land. I want to be sure they have all they need to prove the place is theirs, all theirs, with no debt owed anyone. Buying up your debt is only one way rich men manage to take your land."

"You've already looked into it all, haven't you?"

"Oh, yes. The ones who do underhanded things to grab

land can be found everywhere. The war was treated like a gold mine by some of them. Lots of land, papers proving ownership gone, and so on. I need to make certain my folks have good, solid proof."

They all looked toward the kitchen door when a soft thud sounded, and saw Belle rolling out a cart. They all moved quickly to give her a hand. Very soon they were seated around the table, trying to ignore her pets, which lurked around, attempting to convince someone to feed them or drop something.

It was a good meal, simple but filling, just as Geordie liked it. He smiled faintly when she offered them a fruit tart with heavy cream to pour on it. It all reminded him of home. Geordie decided James was right. They had been lucky to find this place. He was going to enjoy staying here to get his fill of the ocean.

Chapter Seven

"Och! I cannae breathe!"

Geordie sat up and rubbed his eyes, then noticed James trying to do the same. Then they both looked at Robbie, and Geordie had to choke back a laugh. Thor was sprawled on top of his brother. Robbie was trying to wriggle out from beneath the dog, interspersed with attempts to push the dog off the bed.

"Thor, I really cannae breathe," Robbie said. The dog just stared at him, tail wagging and his mouth open a bit.

Robbie stared up at the dog and decided he would try to speak calmly, but then he noticed the drool slipping from the animal's mouth. "Nay! Dinnae ye dare spit on me." It fell, hitting Robbie right on the nose.

Cursing, Robbie yanked on the sheet until he got enough of it free to wipe his face. Geordie started to turn onto his side, only to realize he could not. Looking down to see how tangled in the bedcovers he was, he found himself staring into Loki's eyes. The cat was sprawled comfortably between his legs. As he watched, the cat stretched out one front leg, spread apart the toes, and unleashed some very impressive claws. When the cat began to clean that paw, Geordie decided he did not have to move. He looked at James, who did not appear to be entrapped by any animal.

"How did ye end up all alone?" he asked James.

"I only have one pet left, and he always stays with me."

Geordie looked toward the door and fought the urge to grab the sheet and hold it up over his chest like some outraged maiden. Belle was dressed in another somewhat plain but well-fitted gown. This one was a soft blue. She had not taken the time to do her hair and he had to struggle to keep from staring at the long waves of black hair that fell to her knees. He thought of how he would love to feel it wrapped around him.

"Sorry, I forgot to tell you to shut the door tightly." She walked in, grabbed Loki by the scruff of his neck, and hefted him off the bed and put him on the floor.

Watching the cat march off, Geordie noticed the cat's huge plume of a tail twitching, and how his ears were a bit flattened. "I dinnae think he appreciated that."

"Never does. Like all cats, he dislikes being told no, silently or verbally." She turned to Robbie. "Sorry about him. He has no idea how heavy he is. Waving your arms about and gasping for air sometimes helps."

"He is holding the covers down too tightly."

"Well, that doesn't bode well for me." She poked the dog on the neck. "Thor, move. Get down. Now."

The dog stared at her and growled, but then slowly got down off the bed. He took little care about where he put his feet and Geordie could tell Robbie was struggling not to curse. When the dog trotted away, Belle looked at Robbie.

"Did the cream help?"

"Oh, aye, though I have begun to think it is the rubbing it in that helps as much." He frowned at his hand. "And just now I actually got a good hold on the sheet when I was grabbing it to wipe the dog spit off my face."

"That is very good. And, sorry, Thor can be a bit of a drooler. You should keep up with the cream and the massage."

"Oh, I will."

"When I was applying it to your leg, I noticed the bones had not healed right. The bones touched other bone, so some healing happened but it happened wrongly. That is what causes the pain, I fear."

"I have heard that, too," Robbie said.

"From a doctor?" When Robbie nodded, she sighed. "Did he tell you how he might fix it?"

"Aye, he said he would have to cut my leg open and break the bones again. Then he would set them correctly. He also said he didnae feel he had the skill to do it right."

"A shame. For a moment I was going to tell you to find him again and get it done. Sounds a good, honest man. I can't do it, although my da did it once. It didn't make it as good as new, for the man still limped, but most of the pain was gone, which suited the man well. He was pleased with that alone. So, if you can, you might want to hunt the man down again to see if he has gained some confidence."

She turned and started out the door. "Unless you require many hours to beautify yourselves, breakfast will be on the table by the time you are ready."

"A bit saucy this morning," James murmured as he got up, yanked on his trousers and headed for the washroom.

"I didnae ken ye had gone to some doctor and he'd told ye that," said Geordie, frowning at Robbie.

"Weel, it wasnae something I wished to talk about, disappointing as it was." Robbie sat up and rubbed his hands through his hair. "I actually considered for a moment to let him try, but the thought of my leg being broken again and that I still might have pain and a limp was more than I had the stomach to face."

"Did ye have him check your hand?"

"Aye, and he really had little to say about that except to call the men who did it a lot of names I was surprised a doctor kenned. Them being so learned and all. He did say he thought they had smashed it so badly they had damaged the muscles and nerves, and that was what was causing the pain."

"Being learned just makes them more creative when they want to insult someone. At least he gave ye the reasons it all stays a bit of a mess. Someday someone will have an answer. We will just keep hoping it will be in time to help you." He grinned when Robbie laughed, then got up and pulled his pants on. "Her cream works better than Emily's?"

"A bit, but I think it was the way she rubbed it in that really eased the pain. Haven't slept that well for a long time."

"Maybe that is some of the answer. Ye need to work it, massage it more."

"Hurts like hell to do that, but I do think it is better than it was. I actually try to use the cream at home before we make the cider."

"Well, I need to get into the privy. Hoping James will be out of the washroom soon."

As Geordie walked away, Robbie eased himself out of bed and tugged on his shirt but did not bother buttoning it. James came out of the washroom just as Geordie came out of the privy, and Robbie sighed as the two men switched rooms. He would have to wait a bit longer because he also needed to visit both rooms. Hopefully he would not have to wait too long, as he was hungry.

Breakfast was a hearty, satisfying meal. Geordie had to wonder just when Mehitabel had gotten up in order to cook so much food. He was also surprised the smell of it cooking had not dragged him from sleep.

He watched her as she asked questions about Robbie's wounds. Robbie spoke easily about it all, and Geordie supposed it was easier to talk to a woman who spoke knowledgeably about pain, broken bones, and all the things that troubled him. It was much like a visit to a doctor.

Once done with his meal and having his offer to help with cleanup kindly refused, he decided it was time to go and see the ocean. He had his coat on and was just reaching for the door when it opened and a small boy ran in. The boy halted so quickly he stumbled a little and then stared at him.

"Are you a paying guest?" the boy asked.

"Aye." He held out his hand. "I am Geordie MacEnroy."

"I am Abel Ampleford, Belle's brother." He turned and bellowed, "Hey, Belle!"

Belle came running. "Abel, we have guests. No bellowing. Why are you here and not at Auntie's?"

"She is sick and was wondering if you could come by just to make sure it isn't the plague."

Sighing, Belle shook her head. "I keep telling her she can't get the plague. There is no plague here." She grabbed her coat. "I will go and see how she is." She looked at Geordie. "Anything you need before I leave?"

"Nay, we are fine."

As she and the boy hurried off, James and Robbie stepped up. "Where are ye going?" asked Robbie.

"To do what I came here to do. I am going to look at the ocean. Ye coming?"

"Nay. I am going to read a book and sit in the sun."

"I'm coming," said James as he grabbed his coat.

Geordie left the house to walk down to the beach. He had only gone a few steps when James joined him. Once he reached the edge of the cliff he turned toward the path they had used to bring their horses up from the beach. He was just about to start down that path when he saw a man striding up the beach and he recognized the man as Belle's argumentative neighbor, Bennet, so he stopped. Signaling James to do the same, he crouched down, struggling to remain hidden behind a thorny, tangled bush while still keeping Bennet in view.

Bennet had the courtesy to stop where it was easy for Geordie to see him. His men gathered around him, except for the two James had recognized as having a familial attachment to Mehitabel. They sat on the beach a little to the side of Bennet, laying their guns over their laps and staring out at the water.

Suddenly one of them looked up the hill, stared right at Geordie, and grinned. He nudged the young man next to him, who also looked up the hill and grinned. Neither said a word and Geordie felt the tight knot of anxiety inside of him loosen and fade away.

"Perfect. Just perfect," Bennet said, revealing that he had the kind of voice that carried well.

"I wonder if the fool realizes secrecy will never be his friend," Geordie muttered, and James choked back a laugh.

"He has a general's voice," said James.

"Indeed he does."

"We will build on this end of the land," Bennet announced.

"She does not seem obliged to sell, boss," said one of his men, then cringed faintly when Bennet stared at him.

"I am working on some ways to persuade her. There are ways to push her into selling. Important men have found ways to slip around obstinate sellers. She is not putting her property to good use. Look at this cursed path. Wide stone steps would be better and safer, easier to bring in building supplies and materials."

"And for the ocean to wash it away," said one of the young men related to Mehitabel.

"What are you talking about? They would be made of sturdy rock."

"Uh-huh. Best if you get a good supply of rock then, as you will be rebuilding them a lot."

"Are you a builder?"

"Nope, though I have done some. Just know you don't build on sand."

Bennet waved that aside. "We will build access here and use the land up there for the rest. Get a lot of good lumber when we cut down those trees."

"Can't do that," said the other young man.

Geordie was amused by the way Mehitabel's kin kept calmly interrupting Bennet's grand plans, but he feared they would push the man too far and get shot. He was surprised the man had hired them. Geordie suspected they would be fired soon.

"What do you mean? No law against cutting trees."

"They are protected."

"Protected? No one protects trees. Even she cuts down a few trees now and then. I see her do it."

"Thinning them is allowed."

"Allowed? What nonsense are you spouting?"

"Thinning is allowed by Grandfather's will. Cutting the whole lot down is not. Breaking a will is a crime, I think. Most courts honor a man's last wishes unless what he wished is an illegal act."

"I have got to check that all out and see what can be done about it."

"You do that."

Fortunately Bennet was already walking away and didn't hear him. The pair joined the men who followed him. Geordie shook his head. He had the feeling those two young men would soon be out of a job. The moment they disappeared around a hill, he stood up and brushed the sand off himself. He shook his head again.

James did the same, then said, "Those boys will be out of a job soon."

"That's exactly what I was thinking. That or shot. They certainly won't help him build what he wants."

"The man says he is looking into all the ways he can take her land."

"Think the grandfather's will that the boys mentioned can protect her?"

"Yes, unless she is in a position where a man with money can sneak around her and snatch the land."

"Think I should say something to her?"

"Oh, yes, I would tell her all about what we saw and heard. That should impress her with the urgency of the problem. I get the feeling she thinks of him mostly as a bombastic nuisance."

"Maybe I will give her a hint of the trouble that will head her way soon."

"I think those boys will be sure to let her know."

"Ah, aye." He stopped and stared at the water carefully lapping at the shore. "Ocean is calm today."

"I like it best when a storm is coming in. It shows its power then. Very impressive."

"Unless ye are living on the low ground. Or near the marshes and bogs."

"Sadly true, but why would anyone build their home there?"

For a while they just walked along the beach. He had forgotten how invasive the sand was and soon took off his shoes and socks. James did the same and they continued their slow amble down the beach. Geordie wished he could have both—the ocean and his home in the hills.

Realizing it was nearing time for lunch, they headed back to the stairs they had first climbed. Just as they reached the top they heard the cowbell ring. A moment later, Abel ran out the door and ran over to them.

"Lunch will be on the table soon," the boy said.

"Aye, we heard the bell your sister told us about," said Geordie.

"It is to get people back up from the beach."

"Weel, it does its job, that is for certain."

"Where are you from? You don't talk like anyone I have ever talked to before, and Belle gets a lot of folk staying here in the summer."

"I am from Scotland. Robbie talks like me, although he has a lot more American in his speech because he was so young when we came here."

"I haven't talked to him much. He was in the social room reading a book."

"He appreciates that courtesy and he likes quiet when he reads, I am certain."

The moment they stepped into the house, the scent of food hit them. Geordie hurried to the washroom with James at his side. Once they had washed up, they headed to the table, where Robbie was chatting with Abel.

Mehitabel pushed her cart through the doors and set everything on the table. When she sat down and started to help herself, everyone followed her lead. As dishes were emptied, she set them on the cart, which she kept at her side. Geordie smiled faintly. The woman had figured out some very good aids for organizing all the work she had to do.

Geordie realized he admired the woman. She was young and alone, raising her brother, and she had figured out ways to bring in the money she needed. He frowned as he remembered the scene they had ridden up on when they arrived. She also had the courage to face down a bully.

As soon as conversation eased around the table, he took a deep breath and asked, "So have ye got this place free of debt and all that?"

She gave him a questioning look. "Yes. It has always been debt-free. Papa always stressed the need for that. Why do you ask?"

"When we were down at the beach earlier, we saw Bennet and he was pointing out to his men all that would need to be done when he got his hands on the place."

"Ha. Man is ever hopeful, but he is fated to be sadly disappointed."

"He claims he has ways to get it."

"No, he doesn't. He just refuses to accept the truth because he is a Bennet. No debt he can buy up, no violations of local laws, and all the other sneaky ways some men use to gain land. We know all about those. My father, his father, and right on back to the beginning made sure of it. They always checked any new laws passed in the state, town, and county. Told every one of us we had to keep informed of such things or someone could try to cheat us. Trained all the males then in line what to look for and ways to fight it. We don't even have to worry that the fool will try to kill us and then try to claim the house from the people running the town. The will has a long, long line of heirs, and if we run out of them it goes to the Pennacooks, part of the Abenaki Confederation, and whoever gets to be the executor of the will has to do all he or she can to find an heir or make a deal with the Abenaki leaders. There's some more in there, but nothing that will help Bennet get what he wants."

"Huh, so they made it very elaborate. Tried hard to cover all problems that might arise. Clever. Obviously had the wit to see that the women could carry the weight too, if needed. But how about if one of the heirs is made to believe all the talk some people use to belittle the natives?"

"My da said it has been written to make sure a very long time is spent finding an heir. Great-Grandfather wanted to be certain it stayed in Ampleford hands and, if not theirs, then it definitely goes back into Pennacook hands. Our grandfather made a very precise will to ensure his wishes were fulfilled. It was a promise he made to the man whose daughter he married. That is one reason the women have some protection, too. They are allowed to be heirs and the decision-makers if needed. Great-Grandmother insisted on it. Bennet doesn't like the idea of anyone with Native blood living near him. He really doesn't like, and doesn't believe in, all the rights the women have been given in this will."

There was a mischievous glint to the smile she gave him. "I believe Bennet is feeling very much put upon, thinks the world is being unduly unfair to him. The state chased away or killed many of the Natives, but he has to live next to some. Even more unfair, no one shares his outrage about that. And no one has ever argued against the women having some say."

And even worse, Geordie thought with an inner grin, the one Bennet got stuck with was bitingly saucy and did not cower before his bellowing. He found that slightly naughty look on her face intensely attractive. Her golden eyes shone and her full mouth had a tempting curve to it. He was suddenly grabbed by the urge to lean closer and kiss her, but stuffed a forkful of potato in his mouth instead.

"Is my bedroom still open for me?" asked Abel.

"Yes, but I thought you were going back to Auntie's because you didn't bring your clothes back with you."

"They needed washing, so Auntie says she will wash

them and bring them back here tomorrow. She is hoping she will have a chance to visit with Gabe and Rafe while she is here."

"She'll have to figure out how to do it without being seen."

"She already has."

"Are ye talking about the two young men who work for Bennet?" asked Geordie.

Belle looked at Geordie, noting out of the corner of her eye that Robbie and James were looking at her, too. "Yes. They are my cousins."

"Well, after what they did today, they may not be working long for him."

"What did they do?"

"They just informed Bennet that he couldnae do what he planned. Couldnae do the steps on the sand and couldnae cut the trees. I gather there are restrictions on some things in that will or, as with the stairs, nature makes it impossible. Bennet wasnae happy. Why are they working for the mon?"

"They got it in their heads that someone in the family should keep an eye on him." She shrugged. "I couldn't see how he would even hire them, but he did."

"Maybe the same idea they had got into *his* head."

"Oh. Oh! Could he do that?" She frowned. "I just can't see him performing such a deception well, certainly not well enough to fool Gabe and Rafe." She rubbed her cheeks as she thought it through. "If he is playing the same game, what does he intend to do? There is no way to get this property from us."

"Weel, maybe we can all think on it tonight and see if anything comes to us by morning."

She nodded and picked up the rest of the empty and used dishes, taking them into the kitchen, her mind fixed on the problems with Bennet. She had never believed it would get as bad as it had. It was as if with every disappointment, he got more determined to get her land, more angry that she had the audacity to refuse him, and more rabid with the surety that she was wasting or misusing her land and it needed a better steward. He believed a man would be better and that he was that man.

Shaking her head, she began to wash the dishes. Looking out the window, she saw Bennet riding along his fence. Geordie, Robbie, and James showed up on their mounts and kept pace for a while, trying to engage him in conversation then left. Bennet looked as though he had not enjoyed the chat at all and she smiled. She was going to be sorry when they left, she thought, and ignored the sharp pang in her chest that told her she would be very sorry indeed when Geordie rode away.

Geordie helped Robbie exercise his hand and gave it as good a massage as he could manage. He told himself he would be sure to find out what he could about massage, because he could already see improvement. It was doubtful his brother would get the full use of his hand back, although he hoped he was wrong, but even the small improvement he saw gave him some hope. He did not share his opinion because Robbie had been so thrilled when he had been able to grab the bedsheet in a proper grip to wipe off Thor's drool.

Once done with his brother's hand, Geordie rubbed Belle's cream onto Robbie's leg. He could almost see the pain that constantly assaulted him fade a bit. It was going to anger him beyond words if these simple things really helped him, because that would mean they had wasted a few years, while Robbie suffered and they had done little for him. The doctors Robbie had seen should have told them. The only thing the doctors had told them with utter confidence was that both the hand and the leg should be amputated.

Done with tending Robbie, he left his brother, cleaned the cream from his hands, undressed, and got into his own bed. James was already sound asleep. He had announced that he was headed home soon and needed the sleep. Geordie had actually considered accompanying James rather than waiting for word from him after he returned to Maine, but just could not motivate himself to leave. He told himself it was the ocean holding him, but a little voice that became louder every day kept whispering that it was the hostess who held him in place. Determined not to pay attention to that voice, he closed his eyes and welcomed sleep.

Chapter Eight

James packed the last of his belongings and closed his bag. He did not really want to leave, because he was enjoying his stay, but, on the other hand, he was eager to see his family and they needed him. The longer he waited to get to Maine, the closer they drew to storm season and the more agitated his father would get, which he also knew would make his mother crazy. James did not want to have to rush to finish a job in order to beat the storms.

Picking up his bag, he went outside to where Robbie and Geordie sat on the front porch. They had brought his horse to the door, saddled and ready for him. The animal was shifting around in a way that told him it was more than ready for a ride. Belle came out as he secured his bag to the saddle and she handed him a small sack.

"Food for the journey," she said. "Hope your parents can get the house readied for the storm season."

"They always do, although there are times they really have to push hard to get it done in time. Think their luck will hold this year, too. Are *you* ready?"

"Yes. Will be checking the storm shutters soon. Da got them when they tore down an old garrison house in town. Fixed anything that was broken, and then painted them to suit the house. He was highly amused to be able to put

'Indian shutters' on our house and worked hard to make it easy to shut them from inside the house. Of course, everyone else calls them storm shutters now, including me, and they certainly did their job well in the storms of the past."

James thanked her. He then told the MacEnroy brothers he would definitely send word if he needed their help, but he was hoping to stir up some relatives to do some of the work, and assured them that there were more than enough relatives to get everything done. Mounting his horse, he started on his way. He waved once before he turned his full attention to the road he had to travel. After being away from home for so long, he was eager to see his family.

Geordie stood up and gave Robbie a hand to get to his feet. "Hope he gets his kin rallied like he thinks he can. Or gets there and finds them already at work. I suspect his father helped a lot of them when they needed it."

"Hope he does, too, but, as he said, those kin might have their own work to do," murmured Belle. "Everyone tends to do some tightening and strengthening of their home at this time of year."

"Is this 'storm season' ye keep talking about, a real problem?" asked Geordie as he held the door open for Belle "We didnae stay in this area long enough to even hear about it."

"It varies, but you soon learn to get ready for it, just as if it really was just another season. Sometimes it doesn't seem to come this way at all. Later, one reads, or hears, that it stayed south of us. Other times it is mostly just rain and some wind. Then there are the ones that bring on floods and flatten houses. But it always happens at the same time of the year, so at least one can try to be ready for it. So we always fret and moan and prepare. Now"— she stopped to remove her shoes—"I have to go and dig some clams." She tugged on some high black boots. "Got some orders to fill." She grabbed a straw hat off the rack of hooks set on the wall over the boot tray.

Geordie watched her walk out the door, grabbing a couple baskets to hook onto her belt as she went, one of which held a small spade. "May I come along? I have no idea what ye are going to do, but I do want to see." He glanced at Robbie to see if his brother was also interested.

"Well, I am staying inside," said Robbie. "Maybe Abel will feel like playing checkers with me. I admit to a touch of curiosity about clamming, but then I remember the smell of the flats when the tide goes out and it is nay a fond memory." He turned and walked to the social room as Geordie hurried out the door to catch up to Belle.

"Did you never dig clams when you were here years ago?" Belle asked when Geordie joined her.

"Nay. Cannae say we were ever tempted by that food. We were just passing through, anyway, looking for a place to live. My parents couldnae agree on any of the places we saw and couldnae afford the ones they did, both fancy. Then my da heard all the talk of going west and how that land was cheap, even free in some places, but, sadly, he didnae get there. He was killed, along with my mither, about half the way there. The wagons were attacked. The attackers clearly intended to kill everyone, but we had Iain." He grinned. "He got us all to safety, hid us. That seems to be his gift, keeping people safe. Oh, and convincing adults we can do for ourselves, which we did by taking the wagon and continuing on."

"Oh, I am sorry."

"Long time ago, but thank ye. But, as I said, my brother Iain stepped up and took us all. And there were days when the rest of us would have happily banded together and beat him senseless. Then we got to the Ozarks and as we made our way through them, Iain decided to see if he could get some land there. He said it had the look of home. He got as much land as he could and, over the years, has added some to it. The first acres we got were from a mon headed to California, thinking he would get rich; we never heard from him again. Then we built our house and the stockade."

"A stockade? You were just boys and you built a house plus a stockade?"

"Aye. Iain wanted us safe. That is how he looks at everything. Is it safe or will it keep us safe? Can we make it safe? Every time we stopped the wagons to set up camp, he went and found a good place for us to hide if we needed to. He even thoroughly checked the house Matthew built for his family, then tested how long it would take him to gather up his family and get behind the stockade. Same with our shepherds and their families. Over the years it certainly proved it was worth the work, though we often cursed him heartily as we worked on it."

She laughed softly as they went down the steps to the beach and walked over to some mudflats. She took a rolled-up mat that hung from her belt and laid it out on the ground. Next she took the baskets off her wide belt, which, he realized, had a lot of ties, loops, and hooks that carried the tools she needed for her job. She kilted up her skirts and knelt on the mat to gather her clams.

"Do ye have a spare digger on your magic belt?" He grinned when she laughed.

"No, but I will be certain to carry one next time I am ready to harvest."

"Is this worth the trouble and mess?"

"It is, but I always wait until I get a few orders for them first. If I have got to go and dig in the mud, I want it to be for a good reason."

"Tried one when we wandered through the area." He shuddered. "Couldnae understand why anyone ate them."

"Ever had chowder made with them?"

"Nay. What is it?"

"A creamy soup made with clams."

"Cooked ones might be better."

Belle laughed. "You don't sound all that sure." She noticed one of her baskets was full, and asked Geordie, "Could you take this basket down to the water and dip it in and out so the clams are cleaned off?"

"Aye." He took off his shoes and socks and folded up the legs of his trousers. Then he studied the water. "The tide is coming in."

"Yup. That is why I have to get to the next bed."

Geordie stood up, picked up the basket, and began walking toward the water. He did not really like the feel of the mud under his feet, not like he had as a child. When he reached the water, he dunked the basket and swished it around several times. He then reached into the basket to turn the clams and swished it in the water again.

He headed back to Belle and smiled as she stood up and stretched, rubbing her back and smearing mud on the back of her dress. She was a bit of a mess. Pulling up her skirts had not saved them from getting a lot of mud on them. Despite having a tool to dig out the clams, she had mud covering her arms up to the elbow. As he got closer, he saw that she also had streaks of mud on her face. He reached her and took the other basket, now full of clams, while handing her the one he had dunked in the water.

"Maybe ye should come down to the water, too. Wash some of the mud off." When she stared at him with narrowed eyes he shrugged and headed for the water. A moment later she was walking by his side. They walked to the water in silence and Geordie fought the urge to chuckle. He suspected that would truly annoy her.

"This is the one thing I hate about digging clams. We have a shower on the back porch, but by the time I get to it and get everything all set up and running, the mud has dried on me and that always feels horrible."

"Ye have one of those shower baths?"

She sighed as she cleaned off her arms. "Yes. We also use it to rinse off after a swim. My father studied one, then made one. It took him a while because he had to get the water to it, but he did it. It is on the back porch because that's where the water comes into the house, and he fixed it so it drains into the kitchen garden. Which leads us to the only drawback—no soap. You cannot use soap in the shower because it would harm the plants in the garden."

"Test some soaps. There are ones made of stuff that isnae harmful."

"I think my father did that with the soaps we use. But, it is a thought. Plant something and water it with the slightly soapy water and see what happens." She picked up one of the full baskets. "Well, best to get these up to the house and sort out who gets what."

"Who do you sell them to?" he asked as he fell into step beside her.

"Mostly just folk who want some to serve guests and a few people who need some for the foods they sell in their small cafés or at the market."

"Do ye get a lot of visitors up here as the weather warms?"

"Enough that my rooms to let make a nice profit, as do others around here. And they come mostly from the bordering states. Bennet thinks that business is going to grow. Not sure I look forward to that. And I am not sure I understand why people from bordering states come. They have their own beaches and hills and all."

"It is a change of scene, and some may come because they dinnae have the funds to go far and stay fancy."

"Still don't see the why of it, but it makes me enough money to stay here, so I guess I welcome the madness."

He laughed as they reached the stairs and started up them. Although he would not say so, he rather agreed with her. After all, he had traveled a long way just to see the ocean, but there was nothing like it near his home.

When they reached the house, Geordie decided he had to try the shower. While Belle went into the kitchen to tend to the clams they had dug, he went out on the porch and prepared the shower. He drew the curtains draped around it and closely inspected it as he cleaned up. He had a passing thought that he could make one of these. It would take a lot of work, and a lot of cursing, but he was sure he could do it. When he finished washing, he reminded himself to make a few sketches of it to take home with him. Getting out and drying off, he wondered what they did with it when the weather turned cold. Then he quickly dressed and went inside to let Belle know it was free.

"Did you like it?" she asked as she collected up towels and her clothes in preparation for taking her own shower, then set them aside as she remembered something else she should do that would add to the dirt she wanted to rinse off.

"Immensely. I am going to make some drawings of it and all its works so I can show it to my brothers. Thinking we might be able to set one up. Maybe even inside the house. I can definitely see my brothers loving it."

"Father would have been so happy about that. He really loved it when people liked the things he made. He was always tinkering."

"Everyone likes approval for their efforts."

"My father was always careful to let people know it wasn't his idea, that he had just made something he had seen elsewhere."

Geordie followed her as she went back outside and started walking toward the trees on the land where Bennet dreamed of putting a fancy hotel. "What are ye doing now?"

"Time to check on the fruit trees."

"Too early for there to be fruit."

"I know, but one needs to keep a watch on them. They get attacked and chewed up by a lot of things."

"True. Robbie often complains about things eating his apples."

"Well, we have apple trees, pear trees, and peach trees, plus a lot of beach plum bushes. Also some quince bushes to the left. And wild blueberries in the woods there. A true buffet for the deer and other creatures. I throw netting over them and it may be getting near the time to do that. Have already got it over the grapevines on the back porch. I sell a lot of the fruit, and the things I can make with it, on market day, but when it is hot and I am climbing a ladder to drag a net over the top of one of the trees, I find myself doing the math to remind myself it *is* worth it."

"Robbie finally put up a fence to protect his trees. Took several tries until he got it to the height where they could-nae just leap over it." He grinned when she laughed softly.

"I doubt I will go that far, although we put up a fence of sorts between the orchard and the other trees so the deer could not sneak up from the far side where we would not spot them.

"Oh, hell," she muttered and tied up her skirts again. "Can you give me a boost up?"

"Ye have to climb the tree?"

"I do. I hope I am wrong, but I think I see something that needs to be dealt with soon. I can go get the ladder. It is just tucked in the barn."

Geordie shrugged, then lifted her up until she could grab a branch. She appeared completely unconcerned by the fact that she was showing her legs and giving him the opportunity to have a look up her skirts. He crossed his arms over his chest and watched her scramble up the tree with true skill. Even he could not climb a tree with such ease and grace. Then she studied a number of apples, putting several in her pocket, and he was pretty sure that muttering she was doing included a lot of swearing.

She started to climb back down and when she got within his reach he grabbed her by the waist and helped her the rest of the way down. Then she put her hands on his shoulders to steady herself, so he tugged her close against him and held her there. She tensed slightly and narrowed her eyes. He just grinned.

"You can let me go now."

He smiled. She sounded so prim and proper, a bit like his brother's wife, Emily, when she got cross with one of them, but actually a bit primmer. Belle sounded much like a queen ordering her subject, despite the fact that she had just been climbing a tree with her skirts hiked up to her knees. He was just going to have to show her he was neither a subject nor very obedient.

"Why? I think I deserve a reward. I did all the heavy lifting."

"Heavy?"

He had never heard a woman growl like that, he thought, fighting not to laugh. She felt good in his arms, and fit perfectly. Leaning his face a little closer to hers, he brushed a kiss over her mouth. She did not jerk away and she tasted sweet. Her kiss also stirred his manly appetites in a way none had before. Then she sagged a little in his arms and he went down with her as he deepened the kiss.

Mehitabel held on tight as she savored his kiss. She had been kissed a couple of times and, ignoring the youthful ones that had been awkward and were never repeated, there had been one or two that were unwanted and forced on her until she struck back. Yet she had heard enough women rhapsodize over a man's kiss that she had remained willing to try. This man made her understand why people kissed. She finally glimpsed why it could make a woman sigh.

The way he was stroking her as he kissed her only added to the strong mix of emotions she was experiencing. Her father had firmly believed that women should not be kept ignorant of things that concerned them, and freely told her whatever she wanted to know, as well as things he felt she really needed to know as she grew. Belle knew what her body was becoming interested in, but could not fully understand why she should feel that way. He was handsome and pleasant, but that alone did not seem like enough to stir anything wanton in her.

Yet she was feeling a bit wanton and increasingly so, she thought as she tightened her hold on him. For some reason this man was making her think of learning if what her father had told her was actually right. Then she decided that was a dangerous, perhaps even foolish thought, as he was her guest, a paying customer. The very last thing she needed was him talking and spreading the idea that she came with the rooms she let. He did not strike her as a man who boasted and bragged to any who would listen, but she did not need that trouble. Being a lone woman renting out rooms had always caused her enough trouble without her adding to it with her own thoughtless actions.

Then he moved his mouth down and kissed the side of her neck. She shivered and he kissed her again, even as he lay down and pulled her firmly into his arms. She felt good there, he thought, and held her a little tighter. He was just sliding his hand around to touch one of the full breasts pressed into his chest, tempting him, when a sound ripped through the air. It sounded like a scream caused by pain, a lot of pain.

He kept a hold on her as he listened for the sound to come again. Geordie had the odd feeling that he should recognize that voice, despite how the voice was changed and twisted in a scream of pain. Then he decided that no matter who it was, they should go have a look. Someone had been hurt. By the look on Belle's face, she thought the same.

Chapter Nine

Belle pulled away and stood up to stare in the direction the sound had come from. Geordie sat up and looked as well. He was still wondering who or what could have made such a sound. It had definitely sounded like a scream of pain, but he could see no sign of a fight or anything else as he also stood up and looked around. Then he saw a small figure appear at the top of the steps leading down to the beach.

"Abel," Belle gasped, then waved her arms. "Abel! Abel, what has happened?"

The boy stopped, then turned and began running toward her. Belle brushed off her skirts and began to run to meet him. Geordie did up his shirt, idly wondered just when it had become undone, and hurriedly walked over to the two of them.

"What has happened?" Belle asked when she reached Abel. "Was it you who screamed?" She patted him on his arms and back, then reached down to pat at his legs.

"Not me," the boy gasped as he struggled to catch his breath and tried to wriggle out of her grasp. "Not me. Robbie fell on the steps. You have to come, Belle! I think he broke his leg, the bad one. There is a bone sticking out! I think it is more than one, so it is a bad, bad break," he added in a soft, panicked voice. "It is bleeding a lot. You have to come now."

Belle grabbed Geordie's arm as he started to move. "I need you to get my bag. I will need to tend him some, if only to stop the bleeding, so we can move him. My bag is just inside the front door, on the right, on a small table. The bag is black leather with blue trim."

Geordie ran for the house. He looked back to see Mehitabel and Abel racing toward the stairs. Once inside, he found the bag easily. It was a large, well-used bag and had probably been her father's. The blue trim was something lacy that had been knitted or tatted.

Picking up the bag, which was surprisingly heavy, he headed out the door only to nearly walk into a tall, black-haired woman. It took only one good look to guess that she was probably related to Mehitabel and Abel.

"Ye must be Auntie," he said.

She smiled, transforming her stern face into something beautiful. Geordie saw the future Belle in her sparkling silver eyes and finely drawn features. The woman's long black hair was only lightly streaked with gray. She was much taller than her niece as well, plus had a lusher figure.

"Yes, I am Mary Magdalene Ampleford-Murphy, hyphenated name like the rich." She grinned when Geordie couldn't stop his eyes from widening slightly at her name. She then nodded at the bag. "Is someone hurt?"

"Aye. My brother. It appears he fell and may have opened an old wound."

"Best get going then. I will follow with the body cart."

"The what? Robbie is still alive."

"Not that kind of body. It is for ones who should not be up and walking around."

"Oh, all right then."

He waited as she dashed into the house. He could hear

her moving things around in the infirmary. Thinking he should get down there to Belle, he took a step just as she came out the door pulling a large cart. He helped her get it off the porch, then turned to make his way down to the beach.

As they started on their way, moving at a brisk pace, Mary said, "My brother Noah put this together so he could move his patients around more easily. He needed it, as he was not some big, strapping fellow like you. My brother was constantly putting things together to make life easier." She shook her head. "Then he is taken from us because his heart fails." She shook her head and sighed, a sound weighted heavily with sorrow.

"I am sorry for both you and Belle. From what little she has told me about him, he sounded like a verra good mon."

"He was. And he was too young to collapse like that. Where do you come from? I have been trying to place the accent since I met you at the door."

"Scotland. Lost our croft when the laird got too English and decided sheep would bring him more money, so why keep his promises to his clan. They let us take only a few things. So after a sad time spent wandering, doing what work we could, and living in whatever hovel we could find, we came to America like so many others have."

"But you didn't stay here."

"My folks wanted a piece of their own land, and most of the tales they heard about America implied it was a place where that could happen. But what we could find on the shore that we could afford wasnae what they were looking for. They were farmers and shepherds and wanted enough land to plant some crops and run some sheep. My da heard about all the folk going west and he wanted to go too, was sure we would find a good place. So, he got a wagon and supplies and packed all seven of us up, grabbed my mither, and hit the trail. Then we got attacked and my parents were killed so we, my brothers and me, went on despite the reluctance of the others in the wagon train to take us with them, and we found a good place. Iain and Matthew went back, found where our folks were buried, and brought them back to the place we had found, to bury them proper and near to us."

They reached the stairs and Mary stopped to take a look behind her. "You go on. I see my boys coming around the house, so I will wait for them and we'll deal with this." She slapped her hand against the cart. "I will need them to help me get this down there. Just give us a yell when you need us."

Geordie hurried down the steps to where Robbie was sprawled. His first look made his heart skip with alarm as his brother was linen white and sprawled across the steps. Belle was bent over his leg, so Geordie could not immediately see the injury. Abel sat with Robbie's head cushioned in his lap. Belle turned when he reached her and handed her the bag.

"Your aunt is here and said her lads can bring the cart down when ye say ye need it."

"Oh, good. Robbie will need to be carried back to the house."

When she sat up straight and began to search through the bag, Geordie finally got a look at his brother's leg, but it was heavily wrapped in what Geordie suspected were strips torn from Mehitabel's petticoat. It was his bad leg, and Geordie could not even imagine how much worse this would make it for him. He feared this time it would have to be cut off, quietly muttering it to himself and hoping Belle did not hear him.

"Well, there *is* a bit of good news," Belle said when she

saw the despairing look on Geordie's face. "You remember that business I said I did not think I could do?"

He struggled to clear his mind of all the fear and worry for Robbie and suddenly recalled her speaking of a procedure she knew of but was not sure she could do, one that might help his brother. "Aye. Ye cannae do it now, can ye?"

"Well"—she bit her lip and looked at Robbie—"he has done most of the work for me. He has opened the wound and broken the bones. It looks as if they broke right in the same places they had been broken before. Proof that the bones had not really healed well. It was the weakest spot. At least I can now set them right, and that might be enough. It is going to pain him. A lot, I am sorry to say. But, unless some horrible infection sets in, I don't foresee any need for hacking his leg off."

"Sorry, didnae realize I had said that loud enough for ye to hear me."

"Just muttered it, but since I am sitting right next to you." She shrugged. "But I am serious when I say this will pain him a lot."

"I can help with that," Mary called down the steps.

"Thank you, Auntie." Belle looked up at her and smiled. Then she said to Geordie, "I would much rather that than me trying to use some of my father's potions. I always fret about how much I am using, how long to hold the cloth over nose and mouth, and then start fretting over silly things like can I put myself to sleep as well by using this. Auntie uses unusual methods, but nothing that might cause a fatal mistake."

She worked on wrapping Robbie's leg for a few minutes longer and then yelled up the steps, "Ready to move him, Auntie."

Mary and the two young men he had seen with Bennet came down the stairs with the top of the rolling cart. Geordie realized the clever doctor had made it so the top could be easily removed from the cart. Then he began to think that the man's death was a true loss to the world, because he had obviously been an extremely clever man.

They carefully picked Robbie up, Geordie and Gabe both steadying Robbie's leg as they moved him to the board. Mary put the straps attached to the board securely around his brother and then he and the others walked back up to the cart. Once the board was secured back on the top they easily walked back to the house. It was good his brother remained unconscious because Geordie knew that calm would shatter loudly when the real work on his leg began.

Once inside the infirmary they settled him in a bed as Belle spoke of readying a meal for them. Robbie woke up enough to ask Geordie what had happened, but fell back asleep, or passed out again, before Geordie had been able to explain it all. Belle convinced him to leave his brother and come get something to eat. She promised to thoroughly explain what she would be doing for Robbie, so he finally got up and went with her. He savored the smells seeping out of the kitchen and ruefully accepted that despite what had happened to his brother, his appetite was still strong.

Finally, when everyone was seated around the table, Gabe said, "Abel keeps saying your brother broke his bad leg. What's that mean?"

"Robbie got hurt by some Rebs who felt he was old enough to get involved in that cursed war. They tried to beat him into joining with them," replied Geordie as Mary put a slice of roast beef on his plate and he softly whispered his thanks. "By the time he came back to us they had smashed his leg and his hand. Both have caused him a lot of pain since then.

"All of us tried whatever we could think of to make it better, maybe improve his ability to fully use his hand, but we never got any results. Finally, he got a little better and took some short trips. He claimed they were trips to try to get some buyers for his cider and we were pleased he was getting back to his business. We didnae feel so guilty once we found out he had actually gone to see doctors and they hadnae kenned how to help, either, but one still wonders from time to time."

"Of course you do. No one likes to see a family member suffer," said Belle. "Well, unless it is Auntie and she has finally, really got herself the plague." She grinned when Gabe and Rafe laughed, then ducked when her aunt tossed a roll at her. "Bad example for the boys, Auntie."

"Bennet is a bad example for the boys," Mary grumbled, then frowned at her sons. "Can you not quit now?"

"Not yet," said Rafe. "He is plotting ways to get his fat, greedy hands on this land and we really need to find out how he thinks he can do that. There is always the chance he has actually thought of something clever, and we should be ready to fight it."

"That could be years from now."

"No. I think he is intending to act soon. As you saw"—he nodded at Geordie—"he has reached the point where he is planning out what he will build on the land, and I caught him figuring out what money he could gain from it quickly."

"Lumber," Belle said.

Rafe nodded. "He actually stands by his fence now and then and just stares at your woods and grumbles about stupid women who don't understand how to make good use of what they have."

"What? By chopping down every damn tree I have, like he has on his land? He's left his animals without an ounce of shade."

"Yup. He figures there is enough pine, maple, and oak

there in your wood that he could build his fancy hotel just for the cost of getting it milled."

"All those lovely trees," she murmured.

"Belle, trees get cut down all the time. We need wood to build houses and furniture and all that," Rafe said and rolled his eyes.

"Not my trees."

"They won't be your trees if he gets this property or if he figures out something he can tell the council that would make them believe the trees need to come down. Ow," he said, and scowled at Mary, who had thrown a roll at him, which smacked him in the forehead. "Ma, stop throwing food at me."

"Stop arguing. She has more important things to fret about than that old fool." Mary looked at her niece. "Belle, do you think you can put that boy's leg back together?"

"Yes, I do. It is going to be tough, if only because it will hurt him a great deal. The ones who did this also did not bother to set the bones correctly. They didn't know how to doctor his wounds or simply didn't care to do it right. There will be a week or two of bed rest after that is done, which no male seems to tolerate well. I will accept your offer to help me with his pain."

"Good. Glad to help."

"So, we will be starting on him soon?" asked Geordie.

"Yes." Belle looked at Geordie. "We will need some muscle to hold him still on the bed. We can strap him down, but sometimes you need more than that. And having friends and acquaintances holding patients down appears to make them fight much less than they might otherwise."

"Then I will help hold him still, if needed." He smiled sadly. "I have had to do it before."

"Are you going to need us?" asked Rafe.

"I might. It is very important at times that he stays as still as possible. It can be tricky trying to set those bones correctly, and they have to be set correctly this time or the damage to his leg could become permanent."

"Then we will stay right outside the infirmary and you can call us when you need us. We don't have to stand right near and watch, do we?"

Belle smiled. "No, you can keep your weak little tummies out of the room."

They just smiled, finished off their meal, and Belle helped her aunt with the cleanup, then went to change her clothes and scrub her hands clean. She slipped on the thin cotton coat she wore over her gown and headed to the infirmary. Hearing someone speaking softly, she hurried into the room and saw Geordie talking to Robbie. Belle cursed softly when she saw that the young man was awake. When her aunt came in she breathed a sigh of relief, for the woman had a true skill with keeping a patient calm and easing the pain, even putting them to sleep. Some people called it witchcraft, but she knew it was just the woman's voice. It was as if she mesmerized the patient a bit.

"Robbie? You are going to need to be calm and still now," she said as her aunt gently rubbed his forehead. "I have to put the bones back together and stitch up the break in your skin to help hold them in place. I will try to work as quickly as I can. I am just going to give you a little morphine. Needle or spoon?"

"Spoon," Robbie said quickly, and Belle saw her aunt nod slightly.

She suspected her aunt, who had her hand over his heart, had felt an alarmed reaction to the mention of the word *needle*, so she poured a spoonful of morphine and, gently raising Robbie's head, gave it to him, silently praying she was giving him enough to help. The face he made as he swallowed it made her smile. Now she just had to give it some time to work. As she waited, she gathered the things she would need and tried to keep them out of Robbie's sight.

"I think it is hitting him," Geordie said.

Belle looked at Robbie, who was heavy-eyed, his lids close to closing but he fought the need. Her aunt kept softly stroking his head and singing softly, so she fetched the hot water she needed to clean the wound. She carefully removed the cloth on his leg, ignoring Geordie's soft gasp as he finally saw the wound. She then gently washed his leg all around the wound until he appeared to fall asleep. Her aunt's nod when Belle looked at her let her know that he was actually asleep.

Next, she very gently washed the wound itself. Robbie flinched now and then in his sleep, even cried out in pain. She took a deep breath and applied a salve she hoped would hold off any infection. He cried out once more, but he must have slipped deeper into unconsciousness afterward because he did no more than moan occasionally after that.

Taking a deep breath, she prepared to set the bones. With the help of Geordie and her cousins, who held the leg as steady as they could, she worked as quickly as she dared to set the bones. She gritted her teeth, and with her helpers holding the sticks in place around the bones near the break, she stitched his skin back together. It was a relief to get to the point where she could just wrap the injury as tight as she was able. Finally, with Geordie's help, she placed stabilizing boards on each side of his leg and wrapped them on.

Stepping back, she asked her aunt, "How do you think he took it?"

"Very little agitation. The only time I sensed any was when you put the bones back together, but that was the most painful thing you had to do. Oh, and a bit when you mentioned a needle. I think he may be one of those who reacts strongly to morphine, so you should probably keep a close eye on him until he wakes."

"I'll do that, but now I need to go wash up," Belle said.

"I'll stay and watch him for a while," said Geordie, moving to take Mary's seat when she got up. "Thank ye. All of ye." He looked at Mary and said, "That is a verra impressive and useful skill ye have."

"Thank you. Women having a babe think so too." She smiled when he laughed, and then walked away.

Belle also made sure to thank her relatives before she went to clean up, change her clothes and put them in a bucket of soapy cold water to soak, then dressed and went to get a drink. With a tall glass of cold lemonade, she sat in the kitchen and sipped it. After a moment she said a quiet prayer that she had done everything right and he would be better. She was just realizing that the major reason she wished for that was that she did not want to disappoint Geordie when the man himself strolled into the kitchen. He stopped by her chair, bent down and kissed her.

A little breathless from the kiss, she asked, "What was that for?"

"For fixing him."

"I can't promise I have fixed him. He probably won't get up and start dancing when it has healed."

"A good thing, as the lad cannae dance to save his life." He grinned when she laughed. "Nay, ye fixed what he did this time, and I think ye have fixed at least some of what he suffered from. I could see the bones were wrong before, could even feel that they didnae sit under his skin right, but ye put them together nicely this time. I have hope that at least some of the pain he suffered will be gone."

"So do I. It did look straighter, more as it should look,

and it could well be that the odd fit of the bones could have been a source of his pain."

"It was. Now I have to go and think out what I should say to my family."

"You are going to tell your family all about this?"

"Aye, or I will be thoroughly thrashed when I get home," he said as he walked off.

Belle sighed, then finished her drink and went into the infirmary to sit by Robbie's bedside. She was just getting comfortable when her cousins dashed into the room and told her Bennet was coming. Then she heard the banging on the door and her cousins slipped into the washroom. Sighing in exasperation over the man disturbing her now, Belle got up and went to the door. She opened it and stepped out on the porch after grabbing her gun, not wanting one of his bellowing arguments inside her house.

"What is it now, Bennet?" She frowned at him standing there, flanked by four of his men.

"What have you planted near my fence? My cows are getting sick."

"I have planted nothing there. Never have. Waste of time as they'd just eat it. You've obviously ignored some nasty weed and let it grow up there."

"You probably planted it so it would be easier to steal my cow."

"What?! Why on earth would I take one of your cows? I have two milk cows and goats. You put your cow in there so you could cause trouble for me."

He grabbed her arm. "We'll just wander over to your barn and see."

"No, we won't, because it is a stupid accusation and now you try to use me to help make it stronger." She tried to pull free of his grip, but he kept yanking her toward the steps leading down into the yard on the barn side.

At some point he decided it would be a good idea to

disarm her and tried to yank her rifle out of her hands. Belle fought that, and when Geordie stepped outside, he began to fear they'd manage to fire it off soon. He also did not like the way the man was so roughly handling her. Just as he began to step forward, drawing the attention of the four men Bennet had brought with him, Bennet grabbed her gun and yanked again.

For a moment they participated in a childish tugging battle with her gun and he grew nervous. It was a dangerous thing to do. He watched her hand slipping as she tried to get a firm grip on the trigger guard. Then Bennet suddenly yanked her close to him and they both released the gun, but before Geordie could relax, it hit the porch and went off. One of Bennet's men cried out and fell, clutching his leg.

"You old fool, you shot one of your own men."

"No, I didn't. You had the gun."

"Of course, let us blame it on me. That was probably your plan all along. Let go, so I can tend to your man."

Bennet released her and she hurried over to the young man who was holding his leg and moaning. Not one of the other men stopped her. They did not even look concerned by her tending to the young man, who had quietly passed out.

"I need one of those neckerchiefs you all wear to tie on his leg, a tourniquet to stop the bleeding."

Geordie reached for his, then stopped and nearly laughed when Bennet's men all shed theirs and put them in her outstretched hand. She snapped out the occasional order and they obeyed without question, fully trusting in her skill. He suspected that irritated Bennet a lot, but he would be willing to wager the man always brought his men here when something was wrong with them.

"I need to take him into the infirmary. The bullet is still

in there and must be removed." When the men around her stepped forward and reached out for her patient, she warned, "Try to make sure his leg is kept up and straight so that he doesn't lose too much blood."

They all headed into the house, the men carrying the wounded fellow following her, Bennet marching behind them and Geordie bringing up the rear. The way the men moved into the infirmary and sought out an empty bed told Geordie that, for all his rancor, Bennet's men obviously trusted her doctoring skills. She worked fast while Bennet's men quietly talked to a very groggy Robbie. Everyone ignored Bennet's constant grumbling that it wasn't his fault.

When his man was fixed, Bennet was sternly informed that he was staying for at least a day or two, maybe longer. His other men, who were not all that far out of boyhood either, followed him when he left, murmuring farewells to Robbie and thank-yous to Belle. Geordie wondered what the man planned to do now.

"He never used to be an idiot," Belle said as she washed up. "He will be back with the sheriff."

"Why?"

"He will still try to claim I stole his cow, and I should go check the barn myself and see if he managed to get one of his in there. He may also try to blame me for his boy being shot."

"He doesnae have any pull with the sheriff, does he?"

"Not in this nonsense. Fact is, I think the sheriff would like to shoot Bennet at times."

"I am sorry I wasnae more help."

"Nothing you could help with. You certainly did a good thing by not getting into the middle of the squabble over the gun. I was surprised he didn't end up shooting himself in the belly." She looked down at her dress, shaking her head at the bloodstains there.

"I need to clean up before he drags the sheriff here. If either of you boys want anything, just ask Mr. MacEnroy."

"Boy?" said Bennet's man. "You are only about a year or two older than me."

"True, but I am still older," she replied sweetly as she left.

Chapter Ten

Robbie collected the cards he and Geordie were playing with. "Ha! Beat ye this round. So, think I will get some sleep now before I start to lose my magic touch."

Geordie laughed as he stood up and put his chair back against the wall. "Ye never had a magic touch, just occasional flashes of luck."

"It was all a ploy to make ye believe that and let down your guard so I could swoop in with my skill and thrash you." He smiled when Geordie laughed, then he yawned.

"Get some sleep. Boasting has clearly worn ye out."

"I cannae wait until this heals enough so I can sleep on my side," Robbie grumbled.

"Try to grasp some patience. It has only been a night and a day. Even in that time, ye have done a lot of healing."

"I ken it. She did a wonderful job. I barely feel the stitching she had to do. Aye, I have moments where I could scratch the skin right off my legs, it itches so fiercely. Fortunately, it is so well wrapped I cannae do that."

"Good. Rest now so we dinnae wake up Will with our chatter. Want me to rub cream into your hand before I leave?"

"Sure."

"Is it hurting?"

"Nay. It just aches a bit, probably because I was exercising it some."

He massaged the cream into Robbie's hand and Geordie wondered if he just imagined that it actually felt better beneath his fingers, felt less tense, less withered. He prayed he was not letting hope make him imagine it.

As he finished massaging the cream into Robbie's hand he began to wonder why Bennet had not returned. He could not believe the man had simply given up on his accusation or that he would not still try to make some crime out of Will's being shot. Perhaps he had finally figured out that the only crime committed had been his idiocy in fighting with Belle and trying to yank away a loaded gun. As he paused to wipe off his hands, he caught the scent of food and was sharply reminded that he had not had any breakfast. Concern for Robbie had woken him up early and he had come downstairs, to find that his brother wanted to play a game of cards.

"Sleep for a wee bit now, Robbie," he said, and hurried off toward the kitchen to share a hearty breakfast with Belle.

"If ye fill two plates I can take some food into the infirmary for the lads," Geordie said as they finished their breakfast.

Belle nodded as she finished and swallowed what was in her mouth. "That would be good. Thank you. You will have to help both of them to sit up. Will should not be here for long unless an infection sets in. That bullet came out easily and he is sewn up tight. Slept well, too, and that is always a good sign. As long as Bennet doesn't force him to work too soon, he should heal up well."

"Do you think Bennet might do that?"

"It is very possible. He is one of only a handful of

employers who does not give his workers at least part of the Lord's Day off, not even half a day so that they can go to church. Because of that I may well keep Will longer than I would if I knew he was going home, where people would care for him."

There was a banging on her front door and Belle sighed. "That'll be the sheriff."

"The fool really dragged the law into this? Or is he still after the cow he tries to say ye stole?"

"He usually does keep the nonsense going for a while. He is very much like a dog with a bone. I am surprised he gave it a rest for the night." She stood up, quickly rinsed off her hands, and wiped them off as she walked to her front door.

Geordie moved to stand in the kitchen doorway and watch her answer the door. Bennet stood there scowling. Beside him was a slightly shorter, much thinner man with thick, dark red hair that badly needed a trim and who looked as if he had just been dragged out of bed. He wore a star pinned to the front of his jacket. It was difficult to read the expression on his thin, finely carved face, but Geordie would be willing to wager that the man was not happy. Fearing he might have to give Belle some help, he hurriedly moved to bank the fire.

"Hello, Sheriff Woods," Belle said. "I am sorry you have been dragged out here yet again. What is he claiming I have done now?"

"Just whining about how you shot one of his men. Wounded the boy. Says you tried to stop him from looking inside your barn. Although I was curious about what he had done to make you feel compelled to shoot."

"Well, William was shot, in the leg. No doubt about that. I have tended to it. I also did not do it, and we were not headed to my barn but standing here at the front door having an argument. It happened because Bennet grabbed my rifle and was trying to wrestle it out of my hands."

"It was your hand on the trigger," accused Bennet.

"Actually, my hand was caught in the trigger guard."

"Belle didn't shoot me," said a slightly weak voice.

Belle turned and frowned at Will. "You were told to stay off that foot."

"I did. I hopped."

Geordie nearly grinned when she growled softly, then said, "I told you not to put any weight on that leg. It would have been very easy for you to wobble or stumble and hop on the wrong leg. Now get back in that bed." She glared at him until he did as she ordered.

"There, you saw the wound, Douglas. She shot him. Arrest her."

"She didn't!" yelled Will from inside the infirmary.

"Get in bed, Will!" She heard him muttering, the sound fading as he did what she asked, and then she looked at the sheriff. "So what happens next, Sheriff Woods?"

"Well, since the one who got shot is set in his mind that you didn't do it, nothing happens."

"Woods!" shouted Bennet. "You saw that he was wounded."

"I also heard him say Belle did not do it. I'm going home now and have my damn breakfast. Sorry to trouble you, Belle."

"It was no bother, Sheriff."

She shut the door on Bennet arguing with Woods. The tone of Woods's soft replies told her that he was really annoyed. She hurried back into the kitchen to make up plates of food for Robbie and Will. Setting them on a tray, she let Geordie pick it up and they walked into the infirmary. Geordie helped each young man sit up, then moved to sit with Robbie in case he needed a hand.

"Ye *have* improved," Geordie said as he watched Robbie

spoon up his stew. "Ye are having nay trouble with the fork or the spoon."

Robbie smiled. "Dinnae curse me. Yes, it is better. I can actually feel that I have a good grip on them."

"Good. We'll keep up with rubbing that cream in then."

"Aye, but I truly think it is the massage as it is rubbed in that helps the most." He put his empty plate on the tray and set it aside, then picked up a ball from the small table by the bed, holding it in his weak hand. "Belle also gave me this before she retired for the night. Several times a day I just squeeze it a few times. Seems silly, but I think it is helping too."

"Anything that works. I wonder where she got such ideas?"

"Helping her da nurse her mum when she fell sick. They were trying to help the woman get strong again. Unfortunately, she died. Some sickness had felled her, sucked all the spirit and strength out of her, but it didnae go away when the sickness that hit the town did. Belle's da didnae want her to get near her mum, but finally gave in. Needed the help, I suspicion. But she remembered that this had worked for her mum until the sickness got worse."

"Well, she has been right about the other things she has dealt with, so best we trust her on this. I also think I need to send a letter to our family."

"Aye, it would be good to tell them we got here and all."

"True. I also thought I would mention some of the things that have gone on with ye."

"Are ye sure ye should? I am nay fixed up fine, just a wee bit better. We cannae ken how much better until I can actually get out of this bed. Dinnae want to raise false hopes."

"I plan to be verra cautious in what I say."

Robbie nodded. "Aye, best to give them a soft warning in case this all turns out better than we hoped it would."

Geordie went and collected Willie's plate. He picked up the tray and hurried to the kitchen, reaching it just in time for Bella to add them to the washing. He took a towel and wiped the dishes that had been washed.

"Ye may be interested in kenning that the ball ye gave Robbie is working to strengthen his hand. It is becoming clear that it might weel heal his hand until it is actually useable again."

"That is wonderful! I had hoped it would help my mother, but the sickness took her too soon."

He reached out to rub his hand over her shoulder. "Some sicknesses are stealthy. They fade away enough for ye to think things will be fine and then rush back to claim their victim."

"I know. Have seen it too often. I much prefer mending a wound to nursing a sickness."

"Especially since few of us are good patients when we are ill. So what happens next with the sheriff? Will he be back?"

"I do not think so, but there is no telling what Bennet might try to blame me for next." She moved away to grab a pot off the stove and put it in the washing water. "I need to make something sweet."

"Why?"

"Abel will be back from Auntie's soon. I also have two wounded young men stuck in their beds."

"Ah, ye want something to quiet the whining that is sure to come."

Belle laughed. "Something like that. Or a bribe."

"Bribes are always good. Do ye need my help with anything?"

"Well, could you come to the barn with me so I could see if the fool's cow is in there?"

"I can do that. He didnae take the sheriff in there to

look, did he? Odd, when he was acting so upset over his cow." He held the door open for her.

"Not so odd if he knew it was not there. I keep the barn latched most days since the last time he accused me of stealing some of his stock."

"He does this often?"

"Not really. The last time he did not pay attention to the fact that I was not here but was at my aunt's for the day and the previous night because she was sure she had the plague again. So I could not have stolen his stupid cow. And no one had the backbone to try to accuse my aunt of lying for me, not even Bennet. I suspect this time the sheriff just did not want to bother looking."

Geordie just shook his head and followed her to her barn. He scolded himself for behaving badly, yet still watched the gentle sway of her hips as she walked, but it took him a long time to stop it. He did manage to step forward fast enough to help her pull open the barn doors.

It was well lit, the scattered openings letting a lot of light in, and surprisingly tidy and clean. Four young goats hurried up to the edge of their stall and tried to call Belle to them. She gave them some attention, then slowly walked down the line of stalls and turned to walk up the other side before stopping in front of him.

"No strange cows in here," she said.

"Dinnae ken which animals are yours, but I'm seeing only what ye mentioned to him. How does he think accusing ye of theft will work with the sheriff?"

"I have no idea. I think he just gets frustrated and jumps out with a mad idea. I also think he drinks too much."

"Has he always been this way?"

"Yes, in a way, but it became a problem after my father died. And I think something happened between him and my aunt about then, because he got worse then, too."

"Perhaps you should ask her if there were some harsh words between them, or something else."

"I should, and I just might be annoyed enough at the old fool to get up the courage to do it when she brings Abel home later."

"Weel, might as weel go back inside and I will keep a watch on the barn to make sure no one tries to slip a cow in there." He took her hand in his and, ignoring the way she briefly tensed, walked them back to the house.

Once in the kitchen he helped her prepare for their next meal. He briefly gave thanks for Mrs. O'Neal's instruction so that he did not make a fool of himself. Belle was just sliding the meat into the oven when there was a banging on her front door.

"Bennet again?" he asked as they headed to the door.

"Probably. Auntie would just walk on in." She opened the door and sighed when she saw Bennet and the sheriff. "Thought you had gained some sense during the night, but, no, here you are."

"We didn't get a look inside your barn," said Bennet.

"That is your fault. It was sitting right over there"—she pointed at the barn—"doors open and all. You could have walked over and looked, but you were too busy arguing with Sheriff Woods."

"And I think you should still be charged with shooting Will."

"Damn, will you just shut up," grumbled Woods. "Or I will charge *you*."

"Me?!"

"You're the fool who tried to wrestle a loaded gun out of her arms." The sheriff looked at Belle. "We will just take a quick look in the barn, if you don't mind, Belle."

"Go ahead. I have nothing to hide."

She watched the two men walk to the barn, obviously

still bickering. "I think the sheriff is definitely fed up with Bennet."

"Certainly sounds that way."

"Doesn't help that he keeps yanking the sheriff away from his meals," Geordie said.

Belle hurried into the infirmary. She stopped by Will's bed and frowned down at him. "How is the leg?"

"Hurts like the devil. Just a constant throb though."

"Weel, I will just have a look. Not a real warning sign but still ought to peek, maybe put some more medicine on it."

Will made a face that caused Geordie to smile. He looked when she unwrapped the wound and saw nothing that could be called a warning of infection. He suspected it was a deep hole and that was why it throbbed.

"Looks fine, Will," Belle said. "It is still a very fresh wound, deep too, because it went all the way through, and that is probably why it still throbs. But so far it seems to be healing." She put some medicinal cream on it and wrapped it up again.

"What is that idiot Bennet doing with the sheriff at your barn?"

Belle turned and smiled at her aunt as the woman walked in. Abel ran over, gave Belle a quick hug, and then hurried over to speak to Robbie. The boy seemed quite taken with Geordie's brother, she decided, and wondered how he would feel when the MacEnroys left.

"Bennet made him look in the barn for the cow he claims I stole," she replied. She turned to Will. "As I said. An idiot. Why are you still working for the fool?"

"Only job I could get."

"Your father has his fishing boat."

Will sighed heavily. "I know. I can't do that job. I get sick on a boat. Don't do much work when you're spending the whole time on the boat hanging over the side emptying your belly."

Mary clapped her hand over her mouth, but Belle could see by her eyes that the woman was trying not to laugh. It was obviously a bit of embarrassing truth the family had kept quiet about. By the look on his face, it was obvious Will could also see how badly her aunt wanted to laugh, but he looked more resigned than insulted. Belle moved to her aunt's side and took her by the arm to hurry her out of the infirmary. She got her all the way to the kitchen before her aunt started to giggle. She stumbled into a chair as Belle made some coffee.

"Just a little mean, Auntie."

"I know and I am very sorry for it but can't help it. The boy comes from a long line of proud fishermen. I bet his father is sorely disappointed."

"I hope he is also understanding."

"I am sure he is. He adores all his children and he has two other sons who love the boat and water. I also thought of your father. He was afflicted in much the same way." She sighed as Belle set them out a cup, spoons, and cream and sugar. "Fancy. Sugar is dear."

"I know. I get it for the guests. If I run out I use honey."

"Is that one of the reasons you raised the cost of a bed here?"

"Yes. Things like sugar make it feel special and fancy to the guests, but as you said, it is dear." She moved to check the coffee in the pot. "It will be ready very soon." Belle sat down and clasped her hands together on top of the table. "I have something I would like to ask you."

"What? Can it wait until we get our coffee?"

"Sure. Very soon is about now." She smiled faintly and went to get the pot of coffee, pouring some in each of their cups.

Putting the pot on a trivet in the middle of the table, Belle added cream and sugar to her cup. Stirring it slowly, she asked, "Have you and Bennet had some argument I don't know about?" She noticed her aunt blush a little. "Auntie, I only ask because I thought it might help explain his persistence here."

"After my husband died, he came calling quite often. After a decent interval, of course. Then he asked me to marry him."

"And you said no."

"Oh, I said yes. It was quite nice for a few days, and we didn't tell anyone, but then I noticed how he always asked questions about this property, this house. I finally got snappish and told him to forget about this place as it is yours and Abel's. He then went on about how he was sure we could convince you two to sell it. Went round and round on that for a while and finally I took back my yes because it became clear exactly why he wanted to marry me."

"I am sorry, Auntie."

"Don't be. I actually felt relieved and soon realized I had said yes because I was lonely, not because I was in love. It was actually a close escape. But why do you ask?"

"It is just that he is persistent to the point of being obsessed, and it just doesn't seem right. He offered money to start with, and I said no. Then he just pestered, causing constant minor annoyances. Now it appears he would like to get me in legal trouble, and I suspect he already knows of some way that could aid him in getting his hands on this house if he accomplishes that."

Mary shook her head. "I don't know what to say, or even what to do."

"We'll have to think on it. Now that there appears to be a growing interest in going to stay by the ocean when the weather warms, he will only get worse. Geordie actually overheard the man laying out his plan for some grand hotel, and he obviously plans to add this to his holdings."

"Fool. This summer there may be people all eager to go stay by the shore. Next summer they will want to run to the hills. The summer after that? Who knows."

"I know. People with the money for such things can be fickle in their choices." She sipped her coffee. "I was hoping I would see some way to fight him, but no, nothing comes to me."

"Nor to me either. Shall have to think on it more."

"And I should try to get something together for the midday meal."

"I can give you a hand."

They finished their coffee and then got up to sort out what they could serve for a hearty lunch. Mary checked the icebox and set a lump wrapped in paper firmly on the counter. "This should do. Salted beef."

Belle got out some onions and began to peel them. They soon had the meat boiling and the vegetables readied to be added when needed. It would not be done until a little later than she usually had lunch, but she had the roast she was cooking to make up for it, Belle decided.

She and her aunt had just sat down to have some more coffee when Geordie walked in. He nodded toward the coffeepot and Belle nodded back, so he poured himself a cup and sat down.

"Something smells good," he said. "What are ye making?"

"Corned beef. So, lunch might be a little late. Ever had it?"

"Aye. Mrs. O'Neal has made it at times. Salted beef, she called it."

Belle nodded. "I have heard that name. Salted beef is what Auntie calls it. It certainly is more fitting. I have a weakness for whatever is left over. Chop it all up and fry it. Good for breakfast the next day."

"Like that at our house, though there is rarely much left over. Lots of times Matthew and his family join us. Then there is the ever-growing crop of children. And the three orphans who were taken in, one being Iain's wife's nephew and the two Matthew's wife collected from the war. Then there are the Powells and their growing families. Huh, ye were right when ye said we are building a wee village."

Mary laughed. "Not so 'wee,' is it?"

"Nay"—Geordie grinned—"and I suspect it has more growing to do."

Chapter Eleven

Geordie built a fire in the fireplace in the sitting room, hoping it would ease the damp in the house. Mehitabel sat on the well-cushioned settee in front of the fire and picked up some sewing out of a bag next to it. Geordie sat down beside her, looked at the badly torn small shirt she held in her hands.

"Abel is a little rough on his clothes, aye?" Geordie asked, and winced a little as he thought on what Mrs. O'Neal would have to say about that.

She smiled. "Very rough on his clothes. He got caught up in a tree when wearing this. He was climbing the tree and ended up hanging from a branch by this shirt. Auntie stood under him in case the shirt finished ripping while I climbed up to get him." She shook her head. "And I hate heights. Fortunately, Abel is a skilled clinger, so once he had a good grip on my back there was no trouble getting him down."

"How old is he?"

"Almost nine. Small for his age, but my father was short and slight of build."

"He spends a lot of time with your auntie."

"I know. At times like now, that is actually a help but it is mostly because the school he attends is nearer to her home than mine and, well, I think she is often too aware of how empty her house has become. Uncle died several years ago when his fishing boat went down, her youngest sons now work for Bennet, her daughter got married last summer, and her eldest son is at Harvard. She claims Abel gives her something to do other than sitting in a rocker and knitting."

Geordie laughed. "I only talked with her for a few minutes, but I just cannae picture her doing that."

"Neither can I, especially because she doesn't knit. She does tat, make lace, though." Belle pointed toward the long, low table in front of them with a lovely cream cover on it. "This cloth is some of her work."

"Verra nice. My mither occasionally did some, but mostly before she had so many boys running around. Robbie did weaving before he got hurt. He made most of the carpets in our house. He loved doing it and he was verra good."

Belle put her hand on his arm and, moved by the sadness in his voice, gently rubbed it. "I never make promises about healing, but I do believe his hand will be greatly improved. I did nothing to fix it as he was not wounded there, but my cream seems to be doing better than I ever expected."

"Robbie actually thinks it is the way you have it rubbed into his hand, so I have been doing the same."

"Huh." She sat back and thought about that. "I will have to see to that tomorrow."

He turned so that he faced her, and settled his arm along the back of the settee behind her. "What will ye have to see?"

"Just if massaging his hand really helps in some noticeable way. If it helps it regain its limberness and strength."

"He says it does, and he would know." He kissed her ear and felt her shiver.

She briefly eyed him with suspicion, which increased a lot when he just smiled. "He would know if it felt better, yes. But I want to see what I feel as I do the massage."

"Ah, weel, it is true I dinnae ken what is what under the skin, but it felt more normal to me than it has since he got hurt. He also held his spoon and fork more firmly than he has since he was hurt."

"A good sign. But, since I *do* know what is under the skin, I still think I will check."

"Weel, if ye must, I will allow it," he said as he tightened his hold on her and tugged her closer.

"You will *allow* it?" She glanced at his arm. "And just what are you up to now?"

"Weel, I have been thinking about the day Robbie had his tumble, the day I helped ye down from the apple tree. That was almost a week ago."

He could not tell if the look she was giving him was one of annoyance or amusement. She put her hands against his chest but did not push him away. He could remember the sweetness of her kiss and how right her slim body felt pressed against him. Alert for any sign of unease or rejection, he kissed her.

As before, she softened against him, her body relaxing in his hold. When he ended the kiss and turned his head to kiss her neck, she slid her arms up and around his neck, bringing them even closer together. He nipped at her lips, and when they parted a little, he deepened the kiss, slipping his tongue into her mouth. Geordie could tell she was new to such kisses, so proceeded gently until she began to mimic him.

Her body began to go down beneath the gentle press of his weight. Geordie savored the feel of her slender warmth beneath his body. She even shifted as he moved over her so that he was nestled very comfortably between her thighs.

He had to grit his teeth to push aside the strong urge to rub against her.

"What are you doing?"

Belle had to bite back a screech and fight the urge to shove Geordie away as she heard Abel speaking right near her ear. She calmly pushed Geordie aside and pushed herself up until she sat with her back against the arm of the settee. "Where did you come from?"

"Auntie's. School ended early today because our teacher got sick. She threw up right in front of the class," Abel said gleefully and smiled. "I thought we could put the boat in the water today."

"Ye have a boat?" asked Geordie, pleased to hear that the fierce need he had felt had not roughened his voice.

"Just a small boat with oars. To save having to pull it in or out of the water because of the weather, we have a post and anchor we put with it. Used to just pull it up on the beach but it's been floated off by waves before and was hard to drag into the water on many days. Why? Do you like boats?"

"Dinnae ken. Have not really been on one save for the trip over here and I dinnae e'er want to do that again."

"We only use the dingy to travel up and down along the beach, maybe do a little fishing."

"Weel, I rather like fishing. Certainly like eating fish."

"Then perhaps we can do that before you head home." Belle looked back at her young brother. "Why do you want to do that now?"

"It is nice out and summer is coming, so why not get it done? Then the next time it is nice and sunny we don't have to bother." Hands on his hips, Abel stared at the front door as if he could see right through the wood to the boat waiting for them. "We can just go and use the boat."

Belle sighed. "I suppose we can." She stood up and

took the boy by the hand. "We will get that done now then. Coming, Mister MacEnroy?"

"I believe I will."

They were headed for the front door when Belle heard a sound as they walked by the infirmary and she abruptly stopped. She let go of the boy's hand, whipped toward the door, opened it, and marched in just in time to find the two young men in there trying to quickly hobble back to their beds. Belle put her hands on her hips and glared at them.

"What the devil are you two fools doing? Was there a word in the order 'Do not put any weight on that leg!' that you did not understand? I am sure Abel here would be happy to explain it all to you." She ignored Abel's giggles.

"We hobbled with skill," said Will as he settled down on his bed and pulled the covers over himself.

It was difficult but Belle bit the inside of her cheek to banish the urge to laugh as she went and gently pulled Will out of his bed. "No, you will now sleep next to Robbie, as it will be a shorter distance for you to hobble. But, do try to stay in the bed. You are slowing your recovery every time you try to walk around. Or feel the inclination to 'hobble with skill.' I will be back soon to check over your wounds." She ignored their groans as she marched out. "Now we can go out in the boat and put Abel to sleep."

"He sleeps when you go rowing?"

"Almost always. Even when he was a baby, my father would bundle him up when he would not sleep and take him for a little ride along the shore."

As soon as they were back inside she ran up to her room to change into a dress. When she went back down the stairs she realized she did not smell coffee. She quickly hurried into the kitchen. Geordie was already placing their cups on the table.

"I hope ye dinnae mind but I made cocoa instead," he said as he pulled out a chair for her to sit in.

"Oh, no, I don't mind at all. I never say no to a cup of cocoa. Best you have it now, you may not be able to lift the cup after you have tried your hand at rowing."

"That bad? I cannae believe ye do it regularly come the warm weather."

"I am not sure I would say *regularly*, but a lot, I suppose. I also like to eat fish," she added with a smile.

"Should I have made some for Robbie and Will?"

"Might be something they will appreciate."

"I would appreciate some, too," said Abel.

"Should probably take them some cookies or a piece of cake, too."

"Ye have cookies?" asked Geordie.

"I do. I always have some. Young brother, remember? I also have some blueberry cake. I made those sweets I spoke of."

"A berry cake but not a pie?"

"I can make a pie, too, but I didn't this time." She got up and went to the stove to heat some more milk. "Just not sure which to take into my patients."

"Which one will make more crumbs?"

She laughed as she took a few plates out of the cupboard. "Good thinking. Don't really want to hear the whining if their beds end up full of crumbs. I just hope they are awake." She set pieces of cake on the plates and set them on the tray with the cocoa she had made, then made some for Abel and also got him a few cookies. After tossing napkins and some tableware on the tray, she took it out of the kitchen and headed for the infirmary.

Geordie got up and followed her, wanting to have a look at Robbie. Will was seated on Robbie's bed as they played cards and Geordie thought the young man was fortunate he was quietly handed his cup of cocoa. The look on Belle's face made him think she would have liked to

pour it on his head. Will at least had the grace to look
properly abashed.

Standing back, she crossed her arms over her chest and
asked Will, "How is that throbbing in your leg?"

"Not bad," he mumbled in response.

"Well. Let's wander back to *your* bed and have a look."

She held his arm as he hobbled back to his bed, taking
note of every badly hidden wince and every grimace,
thinking it had been a very good idea to place him closer
to the other patient occupying a place in the infirmary.
She was not terribly angry with him but annoyed by this
I can take it male attitude that seemed to make him think
he could just ignore her advice. It would make her truly
furious if she thought there was any of that *she's a woman,
what does she know?* attitude, but she had never gotten
that feeling from any of these young men.

Once he was back on his bed, she unlaced the leg of his
pants, rather sorry she had taken the time to add the lacing
to save him embarrassment over having his pants yanked
down by a woman, and opened it to look at the wound.
The wound did not show any signs of an infection, although it was red. She suspected that was caused by stress
on the healing wound, but she would not let him go back
to work yet.

"Still doesn't look infected but it is looking stressed."

"Stressed? How can a leg be stressed? It has no emotions, no feelings."

"Really?" She put one finger on his wound and pressed,
causing Will to suck in a breath and push her finger away.
"Punished and irritated by all the skillful hopping around
you have been doing. You could pull out the stitches,
and you are definitely making it struggle hard just to stay
together." A bit more gently she felt all along his wound.

"So, if you don't want to be hobbled for life, do try to do as I ask." She turned and started to walk out of the infirmary.

Geordie looked at Robbie and raised his brows before looking back at Will. "Have ye kenned her for long?"

"Since I was seven. We walked to school together. Actually, about five of us walked to school together. She was bossy back then, too," he finished in a loud voice.

Geordie grinned and turned to walk out of the infirmary, only to have to step aside to let Belle walk back to Will's bed. "Might be wise to listen to her. If nothing else, she has the knowledge to cause ye a lot of pain without causing another injury."

"And embarrassment," he muttered as she struggled to lace his pants back together.

Belle nodded. "That too. Doctor's orders. Try to follow them."

"I can see those two are going to try to be a lot of work," she added as she headed back out with Geordie.

"I can have a talk with Robbie."

"Thank you. If you think it will help, have a nice long talk. Might knock some sense into his noggin."

"Might. No promise of it. The trouble is, he feels little pain after years of having constant pain."

"And that pain could return if he is not careful to obey instructions."

"I will try to stress that. A brother is often ignored when he gives advice, especially an older brother."

"Huh. Well, that does not bode well for anything in his life, does it, especially since he has six of them. All older?" She sighed and shook her head when he nodded. "Maybe you shouldn't waste your breath."

"He might listen."

"Or he might not. I'd lay money down on the latter. Younger siblings don't often obey older ones." She raised her voice so it would reach the boy skipping ahead of them, now wide-awake and dressed to go out in the boat. "Not even when they have been told to do so."

"Depends on who gave the order," said Geordie, grinning at the boy who was so blatantly pretending not to hear what was being said.

"Our father when he was sick for a while. We thought he had caught what our mother had, so he was setting the rule for the future to help me. Auntie says the same thing. And she agrees with me when I say I think Dad did get what our mother had and, although he improved and seemed well for a while, it left him with a weakened heart."

"Quite possible," he said as they went down the steps. "Where is this boat?"

"Just down the beach a little ways, tucked up against the dune. We hid a small shed there."

He was surprised by how well the boat had been hidden, tucked in a small shed well sheltered by the hill. He helped them drag it out and down to the edge of the water. Abel brought the oars, one at a time. Then some time was spent checking the boat for leaks that might have developed while it had been stored for the winter.

Belle put an odd, brightly colored vest on Abel before he climbed into the boat. He and Belle then pushed it farther into the water, hopping in before their clothing got too soaked. She sat and grabbed the oars. He studied what the boy wore, a vest that buckled on and had a lot of cork on the sides and front.

"I have never seen one of these." He reached out to touch the cork he could see.

"Da saw a cork jacket in a magazine and tried his hand at one so we could take Abel out in the boat. It will keep him mostly above water if he falls in. He is learning to swim. When he feels confident, I may have trouble getting him to wear it," she added softly.

"When I learn how to swim I will be a man and won't need this," Abel said and shot his sister a firm scowl.

"No. You will just be a little boy who was clever enough to learn how to swim *and* one who will be clever enough to know he should still wear it."

When Abel folded his arms over his chest and stared out over the water, Geordie leaned closer to Belle and whispered, "Weel played, Miss Belle."

"Thank you," she replied as softly as she picked up the oars and began to row. "Now I just have to hope he likes being thought of as clever more than he wants to be considered a man. Do you want to try your hand at this now?"

"Aye." He waited as she moved out of the way, then took her place.

"Nay as elegant but a bit like the punts on the Thames."

"Just in the fact that they are wooden boats needing muscle to move them. You saw those in your travels?"

"Aye. Just for a few minutes as we were headed to the ships. The ship we had taken out of Glasgow was not strong enough to cross an ocean, so they took us to a port near London that had ships sailing to America."

"I had no idea it was such a convoluted thing."

"Aye, and with a lot of men along the way trying to get their hands on the funds ye saved up for the trip."

"Of course. You'd find them here, too." She grabbed the edge of her seat as the little boat swerved sharply then was righted. "Need to use the same force on each oar."

"I can see that." He sent Abel an exaggerated glare when the boy giggled.

"We can turn back and pack it in for the day in a little while."

"I think I can keep it smooth now."

"Actually, I wasn't thinking of that, I was thinking about the strain on your arms. It doesn't matter how big and strong you are," she continued when she saw the hint of insult in his face, "if you are new at rowing you will feel it after even a short trip. You can end up weakened and shaky."

He had to admit there was a powerful pull on his arms each time he used the oars, but could not really see how it would suck all the strength from his arms. Nevertheless, grudgingly accepting that she might know more about this than he did, he carefully turned the boat so it was headed back to shore. It was not done smoothly and he ignored the giggles from his passengers.

Despite having enjoyed the small trip in the boat, he felt relief when the boat bumped into the shore. At Belle's instruction he gave one last push and the boat slid up onto the beach a bit. She showed him how to put the oars down and then how to lash the boat to the anchoring post.

He helped Belle out and then collected Abel. Belle was right about the boy. He was indeed small for his age and was a very good clinger. He was beginning to think he would have to pull the boy's arms away from his neck, when they reached the top of the stairs and Abel's grip lessened, and he breathed easier. By the time they reached the house, he was very happy to put the boy down onto his own two feet.

Watching as Belle shed her coat and went into the infirmary, he rubbed his arms. They were already making a small protest about what he had just done. He hoped they did not get worse because he would have to go to her to give him a hand. That would be more humiliation than he wanted to suffer from.

He made his way to the settee and sat down. It took effort not to groan as he leaned back. Halfway up his arms, across his shoulders and a short way down his back it was already starting to hurt. He was going to have to soak in a hot bath, which was ridiculous as it was too hot for one of those. Then he heard Belle return and struggled to sit up straighter.

Belle sat down and fought the urge to grin. He was hiding it very well, but she could see he was already starting to ache. Without saying a word she held out the tub of ointment he could use.

"What is that?"

"Ointment that will help sore muscles."

He took the tub and took off the top before taking a sniff. At least it was not made with a strong floral scent. Looking at her again, he sighed. He could not wriggle his way out of this and he had to admit, he really wanted something to ease the growing ache. He knew enough about sore muscles to know the ache would only grow worse before it eased on its own.

"It works?"

"Oh, yes, and very well, too. Unfortunately, I don't think I can put it on here, and you cannot do it yourself. Trust me on that."

"Then where am I to go?"

"The infirmary for now. I will rub it in there and we might even be able to get you up the stairs to a bed. If not, there is still one in the infirmary."

"All right." He sighed in resignation when she had to help him stand up.

Belle helped him into the infirmary, where he was quickly the victim of teasing by her other two patients. She told them to hush and was not surprised when they did not stop. She glanced at Geordie, who was muttering, and shook her head as she helped him lie down on his stomach on the bed, then worked on taking his shirt off.

The sight of his bare back made her uneasy. She was not sure she could massage the ointment into that smooth, tanned skin without revealing how much she was going to enjoy it. That could prove very embarrassing with the audience she had. Taking a deep breath, she pushed that concern aside and decided to ignore all the watching eyes and do what needed to be done.

The first touch of Belle's hands on his back shocked Geordie. They were a bit cool and so soft, yet she massaged in the ointment with a gentle strength. He felt most of the tightness and ache fade away. He also began to feel relaxed, too relaxed, he thought as he closed his eyes.

By the time she was done, Belle knew he had fallen asleep. She was shocked by the urge she had to crawl on the bed and curl up beside him. Getting up, she closed the pot of ointment, and as she went to put it away in the pantry, she decided to just ignore that strange urge. Work was what she needed now, good hard work to push aside the strange, wanton thoughts in her head. But then she felt Geordie standing behind her.

Chapter Twelve

He slid his hand up her ribcage and over her breast, his body tensing as it filled his hand. Geordie heard her breath catch, revealing that she was feeling the same heat. A small voice in his head whispered that this was not the place, that he needed to get her somewhere more private. He slipped his hands around to her back and lifted her up with him as he sat up. Still kissing her, he attempted to keep his eyes on where they were going as they stood to climb the stairs and he began to lead her down the hall.

Several times he paused, pressing her against the wall to tease her more as well as give her a chance to push him away. By the time they reached her bedchamber, he had little doubt she was willing. She had wrapped herself around him and was pushing his shirt off his shoulders, and he was not even sure when she had undone it. He settled her down on the bed and carefully came down over her.

"This is not right," she murmured as she ran her hands over his chest.

"Ye can say nay," he said, not surprised at how hard it was to say those words.

"I know. Not going to do it though."

Thank God, he thought as he began to undo her gown. She was as quick to help him shed his clothes as he was to tug hers off, assuring him that she was as willing as he was eager. Finally they were skin to skin, and he sighed as much with relief as with pleasure.

He desperately wanted to go slow, to give her as much pleasure as he could, but he feared it was all going to be fast and furious. They were panting and stroking each other. He moved to kiss her breasts.

Belle clung tightly to Geordie as he covered her breasts with kisses. His skin felt taut and warm beneath her hands. Her body ached and she had enough knowledge to guess what it ached for. Then his hand slid over her stomach and continued down until it slipped between her thighs. She cried out at the strength of the pleasure that went through her.

Geordie groaned as he felt how wet she was. He kept stroking her as he kissed her, then settled himself between her shifting legs. Each step of the way he waited a moment in case she decided she should push him away. Taking a deep breath, he cautiously entered her, feeling only the slightest resistance before he was fully seated.

The shock of him being inside her faded fast and Belle clutched Geordie tightly. She wrapped her legs around his hips and he began to move. After that, all she was aware of was how he made her feel. Then that feeling he stirred with every thrust of his body condensed into one sharp pulse, and seemed to explode inside her, her whole body shuddering as it swept through her.

When she came back to her senses she realized she was lying beside him, turned into his body. They were both a bit sweaty and still breathing too hard. Geordie was lightly stroking her back and gently kissing her face. She was a bit shocked that she had done this, and she hoped he would say something that would reassure her.

He kissed her briefly, then got up. Belle felt the desertion for only a moment before he was back with a damp cloth that he used to clean her up. Embarrassed yet strangely touched, she tried to fight back the blush heating her cheeks. Then he crawled back into the bed and held her close. When he said nothing she lifted her head and sighed. His eyes were closed and she thought of the women who talked to her when she was caring for them in child-birth, and how they often complained about their man just going to sleep afterward.

"Are you sleeping?"

"Nay. Just resting my eyes."

Belle laughed and slapped his chest. "I wish I had thought of that answer when the women would complain to me about their husbands."

He looked at her. "Why would they complain to you about such things when they came to you to birth their babies?"

"No idea, except they were usually trying to push out a baby and just wanted to complain about the fellow who put it there."

Geordie fought to hide the sudden panic that swept through him at the thought of a possible pregnancy result-ing from what they had shared. "I suppose. But what else is he supposed to do? He's in bed after a long day."

"Talk? Cuddle a bit? Now that you ask, I really have no idea."

"There ye go then."

"What?" She pushed herself up a bit and stared at him. "What does that mean?"

He laughed. "I have no idea. Ye arenae sleepy at all, are ye?"

"Doesn't appear so."

"Weel, I need to go shut the fire down. Shouldnae keep it going during the night."

"No. I could go."

"Nay. I lit it. I should make sure it is out," he said as he got out of bed and yanked on his pants. "Be back in a moment or two."

Geordie carefully made his way down the stairs. He suspected he should have said some love words, but he was not a good talker. Obviously he should try to learn. He did not want Belle to step back from him because he lacked the sweet words she might want to hear.

Once he was sure the fire was completely out, he made his way back to her room. He stepped inside, walked to the bed and sighed. All the sweet words he had been practicing in his mind had been wasted. Belle was sound asleep. Worse, she was sprawled on the bed in a way that did not really welcome anyone to join her.

Determined, he sidled in beside her and got as comfortable as he could. As he settled down, wondering if he could get to sleep, she shifted as if to accommodate him, and he sighed with relief as he turned to hold her close. Geordie closed his eyes. He hoped he would recall the things he had thought of to tell her, in the morning.

Belle woke up and tried to stretch, only to feel a weight around her. She turned her head to the side and her eyes widened as she recalled what had happened the night before. As slowly as she could, she eased out of the bed. After quickly throwing on some of her clothes, she stopped and looked at Geordie sleeping peacefully.

She sighed as she yanked on her gown. A large part of her wanted to crawl back into that bed and curl up next to him. He was handsome. Even better, he would be warm. That made for a temptation it was hard to resist. She shook her head and left to go downstairs and start breakfast.

It bothered her that she expected him to speak of something, maybe of love. She had given in to passion, so why should he offer her more than that? It was something she really needed to think about. Belle was not even sure she wanted love from Geordie. There did not appear to be any future for love between them. He was going to return to what sounded like a large, loving family, and she had to stay where she was.

Walking into the kitchen, she decided to turn her wandering mind to the importance of feeding her guests. She started to wonder what would happen next between her and Geordie and forced the question out of her head. She was an adult woman who made her own living. There was no desperate need of a man in her life. Then she realized she was wearing the same clothes she had worn yesterday, and put aside the batter she had been whipping up to race back upstairs to change her dress.

Geordie woke up in time to see Belle slip out of the room. He cursed. He had thought to woo her a little while they cuddled in bed. Getting up and yanking on his pants, he headed to the washroom. He knew he had to do something, or he might as well just leave for home soon. He just was not sure what he wanted or needed to do. One thing he was sure of was that he did not want to leave Belle thinking he had just used her.

They ate breakfast in the infirmary with the young men, so there was no chance to talk. Geordie watched as Belle got Will up to walk. She refused his offer to help, and he briefly thought of how she had felt when she had wrapped her body around his. There was a lot of well-toned muscle in that slim body. When Will settled back in his bed, he groaned softly and Belle assured him he just needed to build up some strength in that leg, then she walked over to him.

"I want Robbie to try standing up, and could use your help. I want to feel his leg and see how the bones are doing as he tries to stand, so it would be best if someone strong can hold him steady."

"How is Will?" he asked as they moved toward Robbie.

"There was some damage to his muscle and it will need building up. He cannot regain what was taken by the bullet, but he can definitely build up all the rest to make up for what was actually a small loss."

He urged Robbie to try to stand on his foot. He was as tense as Robbie felt as he stood up and slowly put weight on his bad leg. Geordie closely watched the expressions on his brother's face as Robbie stood straighter. His body trembled, but Geordie did not think his brother shook from fear or pain. He got the distinct feeling his trembling was from the hope and happiness that swept through him as his leg held. As he adjusted his hold to make sure Robbie stood straight, he realized he was not doing all the work, that Robbie himself was managing it. Geordie was just a support in case he was needed. He looked at Robbie's leg and could not be sure if it was the boards or the wrapping that made his bad leg look so normally straight.

"All right," said Belle. "That was good." She helped Geordie get Robbie back in his bed. "Did it hurt?" Robbie shook his head. "Any pain now that you are off it again?" Another shake of his head. "Okay then, tomorrow we take you out to start some swimming in the ocean. It will build up the strength you need. You too, Will. Maybe you can improve in the skill. Can you keep yourself afloat now?"

"Never go to a doctor whom you knew when you were a little kid," Will told Geordie as Belle laughed and left the room.

Geordie laughed and then sat down on the edge of Robbie's bed. "No pain?"

"No," Robbie whispered. "As I let my weight rest on it, I kept waiting for the pain, braced myself for it, but nothing. Just the discomfort of the wood and wrapping. And after? Not a twinge to tell me I was doing something I haven't done for a long time. It is hard not to just bellow with joy because I think she did fix it. Feels strange to be grateful one fell and broke one's leg, but I do feel that way."

"It seems as if it was just what it needed."

Abel ran into the room and stopped beside Robbie. "Have you already stood up?"

"I have."

"And it didn't hurt or anything?"

"Nope. Not even a pinch."

"So now you go swimming. I will come with you."

"You can swim?"

"I can, but Belle will probably make me wear my cork vest."

"Well, your da did, didnae he?" said Geordie.

The boy let his shoulders slump. "Yes. But I can swim pretty good even when I wear it. It will be great. I'll go tell Belle." He ran off.

"He really has taken to ye," Geordie said.

"Probably because I let him tell me stories and read his kid books to me. He actually tells some truly fantastic stories, has a very inventive imagination."

"Oh, Lord, yes, he does," said Will, and then he laughed. "Very fond of dragons, too."

"Sorry I missed that," said Geordie.

Belle walked in with Abel and looked at Robbie. "I think we will not be trying swimming out tomorrow as it will be raining, according to Auntie's bones and her headache. So later today I will take out your stitches. Just thought you might want a warning."

"Thank ye," Robbie said, then sighed as she left.

"Dinnae ye want the stitches out?" asked Geordie.

"Oh, aye, fair sick of them but"—he took a deep breath—"it is a foolish thing, but I just cannae shake the fear that something will go wrong when they are finally taken out."

"What, like your bones will fall out once she unties the stitches?" Will asked, and then shook his head. "Nonsense. What Belle stitches together stays stitched together."

"As I said, it is a foolish worry. Unfortunately, I looked at my leg before she stitched it and it is hard to get that image out of my head."

"Yup, I can see getting upset at that sight, but it isn't going to open up. They don't open when they are in, and she seems to know just when they can come out. None of us have had the wound break open after." He smiled a little. "Of course, Belle usually tells us very firmly what we can or cannot do once those stitches come out and no one ignores her rules."

"Ye make her sound very fearsome," Robbie said, and grinned.

"Like Emily or Mrs. O'Neal?" Geordie asked wryly. He laughed when Robbie just frowned, then grimaced.

Will laughed. "Strong women, huh? Yup, that's Mehitabel Ampleford."

"Have any of you with Bennet done this swimming thing? Does it work?"

"Worked for me a few years ago when I broke my leg. Hoping it will do as well this time. If I remember right, it worked just fine for Jonas. I have no idea why it works, though. You can move easier when in the water as it carries some of the weight, and some say the ocean water has some healing quality."

"Well, I hope it works again," said Geordie as he stood up. "Ye do need to build your strength. That leg hasnae even let ye try. I'll come back when she takes your stitches out." He started out of the infirmary and added, "So I can be there to pick up the bones that fall out." He grinned when Robbie cursed him and Will laughed.

"What did you do to get them stirred up?" asked Belle as he walked into the kitchen.

"Just a little joke. Calming Robbie down as he was getting nervous. Lad has little idea about doctoring and actually worried about what could happen when his stitches were taken out."

"You mean he thought it would all fall apart?"

"Ah, ye have heard that worry before."

"I have. I calm myself by recalling what my father always said, that no one bothers to give folk even a tiny bit of knowledge about wounds and their bodies. He was always amazed and amused by what people would ask him. Not long before he died he told me some of their questions, thinking it would help me to be ready to answer with a straight face. He always believed most people round here would start coming to me when they had a problem."

"And they did." He walked up behind her and put his arms around her, then rested his chin on her shoulder to look at what she was mixing up. "What are ye making?"

"Mixing up some biscuits for supper."

"When is supper?"

"Not for about three hours. A beef roast."

"I can make some gravy for it if ye like."

She turned to look at him. "Really?"

"Really. If ye have what I need. I often make it when I am home. Mrs. O'Neal is one of those cooks who has a plan and schedule when she is cooking a meal. She allows others to help, but only if she is not using the kitchen. My contribution is usually gravy. The wives do a dessert or peel the vegetables."

"Have a look in the cupboards to see if anything you need is up there. I will be certain to call you when it gets closer to mealtime."

He found enough to start the gravy and they worked together in a comfortable silence. When he could do no more, he peeled some of the vegetables she needed. Then he asked her about the use of swimming to improve Robbie's leg. It sounded promising and he felt his hope for a good recovery rise. If, by the time they headed home, Robbie had lost the worst of his limp and regained some strength and agility in his hand, he would consider their trip a huge success.

Chapter Thirteen

Mehitabel stretched as she stepped out on the back porch. It was sunny and the sky was clear. Even better everything had dried out after the heavy rain they had gotten a week ago. She suspected it would be a warm day and there was a nice breeze. She looked over at the fence marking the boundary to Bennet's property and saw one of his cows standing there staring back at her, lazily chewing her cud. Behind that cow were half a dozen others, also staring at her.

"The man's damn cows are as arrogant as he is," she muttered and turned to go back into the house, planning to do a few chores before making breakfast, only to walk into Geordie.

Geordie caught her by the arms, looked around, and then looked back at her. "Who are ye talking to?"

"The cows," she muttered, knowing it sounded ridiculous, and shrugged her shoulders when he just stared at her.

"Ah, of course, and did they answer ye? Oof!" He rubbed his belly where she had just jabbed her elbow into him. "Vicious wench. What was that for?"

"Being saucy so early in the day. Some of us are slow to wake up in the morning. I certainly am not awake enough to make clever quips or attempt a joke, especially not on such a too bright day with a long day of cooking ahead of me."

He put his arm around her as they walked into the house, through it, and went out the front door. "Attempted and succeeded." He bit back a grin, but the way her eyes narrowed as she looked up at him told him that she was fully aware of that. "So, what is the chore for the day? Checking on the trees? Weeding the garden? Fixing something?"

"Why does the 'fixing something' sound so hopeful? Have you seen something broken?"

"Nay. It is just a chore I would have the most interest in doing."

"Well, I am sorry, but the chore for the day for me is baking some anadama bread. I sell some to the bakery, and some at the town market, which is tomorrow."

"What is anadama bread? I saw it on your sign but forgot to ask."

"Old New England recipe my mother taught me. A round yeast bread made with flour, cornmeal, molasses, and butter."

"Oh. And people like that?"

"Yes. It is simple but a bit sweet. Suspect that is why people like it. But first, I should at least have a look at the garden and see how it is doing before that rain falls."

They walked to the back of the barn, where the tallest plants had been put in with a good fence around them. After a quick walkthrough with the occasional pause to yank a weed, Belle moved on to the garden behind the house. After another walkthrough and some weed-pulling, she decided it was also doing well and headed off to the orchard.

They soon returned to the porch. Geordie found the

curry brush and went to tend to his horse, leaving her to bake her bread. As he entered the barn his mount loudly greeted him. Geordie decided he should probably take the poor animal for a ride. Back home he would ride at least once a day. He did not know if animals could get bored, but if they could, he was sure Romeo was getting there. After grooming Romeo, he saddled him and led him out of his stall.

For a while he just rode around Belle's land, admiring how tidy the place was kept. He had to wonder who kept the grass cut and why she did not just let it grow in a lot of places. He would have to ask. If she did it, it was a lot of work, and if she paid someone, he had to think it was a fee she might struggle to pay at times. Then he saw the goats and grinned. Belle clearly knew someone else who had goats, because eight of the animals cropped the grass today and he knew she owned only four. He turned and took the path down to the beach, passing Thor, who was sprawled in the grass keeping a close eye on the goats.

A strange choice for a herd dog, but he suspected the animal did very well. It certainly had the size and strength to protect the goats. Once he reached the beach he started to ride in the opposite direction from the one he had taken on his last exploration.

It was not long before the high ground disappeared. The number of houses also increased and he decided he was probably headed toward whatever town was in the area. In the distance he could see a lot of farmland beyond what appeared to be marshlands. Curious to see what a town looked like in this part of the country, he rode on, looking for a path up to the road he could see running along the coast.

Once up on the road, he could see the farmland more clearly. It looked a lot easier to farm, or use as grazing land, than the rocky patch of land they had had in Scotland. Places in the Ozarks looked similar but still had the hills and rock to deal with. Geordie idly wondered if there were many places where everything was perfect or if he would even want to find such a place.

He approached the town and looked for a place to tie up his horse. Once his mount was secure he began to wander the street, looking into several stores. He bought some cider for Robbie to try and something called maple syrup, which the lady running the store said was very good on some of the things Belle made them for breakfast. Then he found himself wandering through a store that offered things he felt comfortable buying for the women in his family.

By the time he returned to his horse, his arms were full of packages and he spent the time to fit them all carefully into his saddlebags. He mounted his horse and started on his way back to Belle's. It was not until he turned up the path to her property that he began to get a little nervous about the small gift he had bought for Belle. He was not sure what had made him buy it or how he would give it to her. He had seen it and thought of her, which puzzled him. He had never spontaneously bought a gift for a lover before.

After he settled his horse back in its stall, he felt the first touch of rain as he walked to the house. His plan had been to get to his room and put away the things in his saddlebags, but he met her just outside the infirmary. He felt a light blush touch his cheeks when he looked at her as they walked into the infirmary. It made him feel like a young boy caught out in some mischief.

"You found our little town?" She flicked the top of one package with her finger. "Been shopping?"

"Just for a few things. Something to take home." He

looked at Robbie. "Got ye a bottle of some locally made cider and a few names of places ye might want to visit before we head out."

"If he is not up to walking around much when you think you want to go, you can use the donkey cart and maybe take a cane." She smiled when Robbie groaned, then she tugged Geordie out of the infirmary. "I am going to test him on his feet again tomorrow, and will want you close at hand in case he needs a steadying hand or he stumbles and needs someone to catch him."

"Does he ken that? About the testing?"

"He does. He knows it will just be a short test, only a bit more than just resting his weight on that foot, followed by a round of swimming, so your gift of cider may well prove very helpful."

He nodded and went back in to place his saddlebags on Robbie's bed, then searched out the bottle of cider he had bought him. He also took out the ones he had bought for Will and himself. After handing the drink to Will, he carefully sat down on the edge of Robbie's bed.

"What are ye watching me for?" asked Robbie.

"Waiting to see what ye think before I take a drink."

"Ah." Robbie took a sip, swished the drink around his mouth and swallowed. "Good, but what is that other flavor I taste?"

"Peach."

"Huh. It is good, but maybe too sweet for drinking more than one or two."

"Ye can try mine. It is a mix of apples, a tart one most people use for cooking and another usually used for eating. Will is sipping one that has a berry of some kind added to it."

"Cranberry," said Will. "Sharp, rather sour berry that

grows in bogs round this part of the country. It actually blends in well, but I don't usually like sweet drinks anyways."

"And nay an ingredient we can get easily in the Ozarks, I suspect," said Robbie as he switched his bottle with Geordie's. "This is good." He looked at the label. "And we have both of these apples."

"Time for a swim," Belle said as she walked into the room. "No more of this," she said, and took Robbie's bottle of cider away. "You too, Will, Geordie."

"Dinnae we need something else to wear?" asked Robbie as he sat up and slowly swung his feet over the side of the bed.

"I brought some things, if you choose to put them on, but you could swim in what you have on, and I will wash them after."

"I'll help them," said Geordie.

Belle went out and waited by the door. She felt a little awkward in her bathing costume, which was little more than a short dress with short puffed sleeves, and stockings. When the men came marching out she almost grinned. None of them looked comfortable in the men's swimming costumes she had dug out for them, but she picked up the sack with the towels in it and helped them all get down to the beach. She was glad Geordie had not protested coming along as she really needed his help.

She noticed that Robbie kept watching his leg as he moved, as if still worried that somehow all she had done would unravel, but he did not hesitate to get in the water. His brother helped him remain steady as he moved his legs while she stayed near Will. He needed little help, so she occasionally took a little swim around on her own and just kept a close eye on him.

By the time they left the water and made their way back to the infirmary, she could see that both Robbie and Will were tired yet obviously felt pleased with their own progress. She wrapped a towel around herself when she caught Geordie studying her in her bathing costume and feared that it was showing too much. She helped a little in getting Will and Robbie into dry clothes, then warned them supper would be brought in within the next hour as she hurried off to change.

She changed her clothes and went down to the kitchen to finish working on the evening meal. She was just taking the meat out when Geordie came into the kitchen. He came over to the stove when she set the pan down, and spooned up some of the juices.

"The last and most important ingredient," he said, spooning some of the meat juices into the pan holding the rest of his makings for the gravy. "What do ye usually do with the meat juices?"

"Use them as gravy and just spoon them on what I want."

"Simple and efficient."

"Most of what I do falls into that style."

"Easiest way when ye have to cook for a crowd every day."

"True. Would be nice if I could figure out how to do a few fancy things more simply and easily."

"Why do ye think ye need fancy?"

"For the guests. They are paying for a special holiday. Special holidays should have meals that are not just plain old meat and potatoes."

"Most people like plain old meat and potatoes. Ye will satisfy most of your guests with that. Ye dinnae want to get into menus or the like, as then ye will never get out of the kitchen."

"You are probably right. I give them the necessities. A clean bed, three satisfying meals, and drink. I set up the social room two years ago and that seems to be working well. And when the season for visitors really gets going, I also make sure there are always some snacks at hand."

"Sounds like a decent boarding house to me."

"And that is really all I want. Some call them bed-and-breakfast places. Bed and breakfast would look good on a sign. I shall have to look into that."

He nodded as he stirred the warming gravy. "This will only take a few minutes. Did ye want to get a tray ready? I can take it to the boys."

"Yes, thank you, and I will set ours out while you do that."

Mehitabel put the plates on a tray and began to fill them. She fetched some glasses and filled them with chilled lemonade. Then set out the cutlery and napkins. She handed it to Geordie and he went off to give it to the boys in the infirmary. She turned her attention to setting the table for her and Geordie.

She was just about to sit down when Geordie returned. He stopped to push her chair in, then bent down to kiss her neck before sitting across from her. For a few moments they did not speak as they filled their plates. He then reported on Robbie and Will.

"So they suffered no ill effects from their little swim?"

"Nay. They are tired out though."

"For a little while, everything they do will tire them out."

"I recall that with Iain, and he was not pleased." He had a drink of lemonade and then said, "He got shot by some fool that was hunting his wife."

"Why was someone hunting his wife?"

"She held part of an inheritance, and her nephew had even more, so this mon wanted them dead. Then he would get it all."

"It's always the money, isn't it."

"Seems to be, but to hunt down a woman and child and kill them to gain an inheritance?" He shook his head. "That I will never understand."

"How did Iain get mixed up in that?"

"We found her cabin burning, then found the bodies of her sister and brother-in-law. Buried them and found a locket that showed they had a child. So, we went looking, followed a trail, and found her hiding in the hollow of a tree with her nephew hidden under her skirts. It was not until later we discovered she had also been injured. So, we got Emily and Ned and now are friends with her grandfather." He grinned at Belle. "A duke from England."

"You have met him?"

"Aye. Nice fellow, although it took Iain a while to warm to the man. Iain has a dislike for English aristocracy, which was why he was so slow to understand that he wanted to keep Emily. At least we didnae have to suffer that ridiculous confusion with Matthew and Abbie."

"Matthew met her in a more normal fashion, did he?"

"Nay. Met her during the war. Rebs had attacked her house and killed her parents and we arrived to find her fighting them. So he, James, and their men took her back to the town they were stationed in and put her in what they called The Woman's House. It was a mansion, and the woman who owned it allowed them to take in orphans and women widowed or lost in the chaos of war. When Matthew brought Abbie home with him, she brought two orphans with her. Noah and a bairn." He frowned. "We seem to have gathered ourselves up a crowd of children. Not sure why my brothers feel compelled to add to the mob."

"Nature."

"What about nature?"

"Nature is why, even if they have children, they will work to have children of their own blood. Nature demands that."

"Not sure I like the idea of some unseen force making me do something."

Belle laughed. "Sorry."

"So you should be." He pushed his empty plate aside. "Excellent, as always."

"Thank you, kind sir." She stood and picked up their plates to put them in the sink.

"I'll get the dishes from the infirmary." He grabbed the tray and left.

In the infirmary, he collected up the empty dishes. "Want me to rub your hand?" he asked Robbie.

Robbie pushed himself into a more seated position and nodded. "I have decided it is something that should be done every night. Should be able to do it myself soon."

"So how does the leg feel after your attempt at swimming?"

"It did not make it hurt, not really. A hint of an ache, no more."

"Good. I suspect ye will be doing a lot more of it."

Robbie sighed and closed his eyes. "If it helps I will do it, don't worry about it."

"I wasnae worrying about it. But it will help if ye want it enough so we have your help in getting a place to swim set up nearer to home."

"Sneaky," Will said.

"Aye," agreed Robbie. "It was, but I will use my poor battered body to get ye a place to swim."

They talked about where they could make a swimming hole as Geordie massaged his brother's hand. He stopped when it was obvious Robbie was going to sleep. Geordie cleaned off his hands and headed to the kitchen.

Belle scrubbed the roasting pan as hard as she could and finally decided it was as clean as it would ever be. She sighed. It was probably time to get a new one. She knew it was clean despite what marks remained, but if a guest saw it they might not. Belle decided she would find out what Auntie thought about it.

Wiping it off, she put it on top of the stove and then stared at it. Then two strong arms wrapped around her. Belle sighed again and leaned back against Geordie. She felt a soft kiss on the top of her head.

"That was a heavy sigh," he said.

"Heavy decision to make."

"Oh, aye?"

"Aye," she said and briefly grinned up at him. "This pan is showing its age and I am trying to decide if it should be tossed out or if I should keep using it and hope I don't get any very fussy guests who would be horrified by it."

Geordie looked at the pan and shook his head. "I dinnae see any reason to throw it out. It is clean, just has a few cooking scars."

"Cooking scars." She laughed as she took the pan and shoved it into a cupboard. "Like that one."

"Do ye really get guests that choosy?"

"Oh, yes. There is always someone who thinks they should be treated like royalty. Why they would think that, at what I charge for a bed, I don't know."

He put his arm around her shoulders and started to lead her out of the kitchen. "There are always people like that." He grinned. "I am a bit surprised ye put up with it."

"I try, but am not always successful." She realized he was leading her upstairs but said nothing. "Fortunately, so far, just as I was about to give my opinion, something interrupted me. Quite often, it was the husband. I think some of them can just tell when their wives have pushed someone too far. Where are we going?"

"Your room. Or we could slip into mine."

"Being a little presumptuous, aren't you?"

"I dinnae ken. Am I?" He turned into her room and nudged her up against the edge of the bed.

"I will have to think about it," she said as she fell back onto the bed.

He settled himself over her and grinned back at her. "Think hard."

"I think we need to get our shoes off before we soil the bedspread."

He laughed, then sat up and took off her shoes before taking his own off. Slowly, he crawled back onto the bed and began to undo her gown. Belle felt drugged by his kisses and the stroke of his hands as he undressed her. She briefly thought that she ought to stop him, but she could not really convince herself to do it. A voice in her head told her she was getting in too deep, but she decided she did not need to think about that right now.

Geordie kissed her as he finished easing off her clothes. He sat back on his heels as he stripped off his shirt. There was the soft touch of a blush on her skin as he studied her. Turning a little, he yanked the rest of his clothes off, tossing them to the floor. Then, slowly, he settled his body over hers, savoring the soft, trembling gasp she made when their skin touched.

Belle smoothed her hands over his back as he kissed her. She really liked the feel of his skin, taut and warm as it stretched over firm muscle. The crisp hair on his legs rubbed against her in a way that stirred her blood. He slowly kissed his way down her body, teasing her stomach with kisses and light nips that made her shiver.

The heat and need building inside of her waned just a little as he slid down her body even further. Startled, she was about to say something when he spread her legs then lifted them onto his shoulders and kissed her there. Belle clutched his head, threading her fingers through his hair.

She loosened her grip on his hair as he teased and tormented her with kisses, the play of his tongue on the sensitive skin, and the gentle caress of his hands on her legs. Then something inside her began to wind itself tighter and tighter. Belle was both fascinated by it and a little afraid. She shifted a little in an attempt to move away from what he was making her feel but he just moved his tormenting mouth to her inner thighs.

Geordie began to slowly kiss his way back up her body. Belle wrapped her arms around him, stroking his back as he kissed and suckled her breast. Then he kissed her, a hungry, demanding kiss that clouded her mind. He softened the kiss even as he joined their bodies.

Belle clung to him tightly with her arms and legs. The tightness returned and, again, grew tighter and tighter. It had just grown rather uncomfortable and she was about to push him away when it snapped and a feeling she could only call delicious flooded her body. She tried to stay still and just savor it, but her body refused to be still.

Then Geordie thrust hard inside of her and stilled. She could feel tension in his muscles and he held himself still, then lowered his head enough to give her a slow, heated kiss. His body jerked a little a few times before he slumped down on top of her. Before she could complain about his weight, he rolled onto his side and pulled her close to him.

She thought about making a comment on how he was going to sleep, but she yawned. Biting down a laugh, she snuggled closer to him and closed her eyes. They were going to have to talk about what was happening between them. She had avoided such a talk, for she did not want to hear him say there was nothing between them save passion.

Yet, there was a part of her that believed they should stop being lovers if that was all he wanted. She admitted she wanted something more from him, yet if there was more, there would then be a lot of things that would need sorting out for it to be worth anything. Belle was reluctant to admit it, even to herself, but she was becoming certain she was falling in love with the man. She feared she was going to find herself alone and deeply hurt when this affair ended.

Chapter Fourteen

Walking into the kitchen, Geordie was surprised to find Mehitabel standing by the stove and staring at the coffee-pot. "Um, Belle? I think ye need to turn the flame on under the pot before it will make the coffee. I wouldnae mind a cup myself."

After watching her fumble to light it, he nudged her aside. "I will do it, lass. I am thinking ye need to get more sleep."

"Have to dig clams this morning," she said. "Tide is out, so I have to get out there."

He looked at her and shook his head. "Ye will just end up facedown in the mud."

"Got orders to fill."

"I will get her to the table," Abel said as he walked into the kitchen and looked at his sister before grabbing her by the arm. "A couple of cups of her morning potion, which is what Auntie calls it, and she will wake up." He led her to a seat at the table. "She can be like this when the tide is out too early," he said as he turned and came back to the stove.

Geordie watched as Belle placed her arms on the table and put her head down on them. He shook his head, not sure coffee was going to help her this time. He would not even be up if he had not found her gone from the bed when he had reached for her.

"Oh, no," Abel said and started back to the table.

Catching the boy by the back of his shirt, Geordie stopped him. "Nay, lad. I will dig the clams for her this morning if we put the coffee in front of her and it doesnae make her stir."

"Do you know how?"

"Weel, I have watched her do it."

"Do you know which beds to dig in?"

"More or less."

"I best come with you then."

He opened his mouth to tell the boy not to bother, then changed his mind. The boy had come home yesterday and, for the first time, he and Belle had to be a bit sneaky to be together. Now it would help if the boy had something to do. The last thing Geordie wanted to do was dig in the wrong bed. "Thank ye. Is she going to be all right there or should I tote her back to her bed?"

"I will leave her a note in case she wakes up and looks for us, but she will be just fine sleeping there. She has done it before."

Placing a cup of coffee near her brought no reaction, so Geordie resigned himself to digging clams. Collecting her tools for the job, he headed down to the beach with Abel. By the time he and Abel returned Belle was gone when he did the evening harvest of clams. He checked her bedroom, then his own, finding her sprawled across his bed.

He bit his lip to suppress his laughter and gently moved her until he had her settled beneath the covers. Then he sighed, knowing he could not crawl into that bed with her as he would like to. Abel was waiting for him downstairs. Brushing a kiss over her cheek he went to join the boy and maybe make them some breakfast.

* * *

Although he did not like working in the mud, Geordie enjoyed the time he spent with Abel. The boy was smart and good company. He even had a keen wit that made an occasional appearance despite his young age. By the time he had rinsed off the last basket of clams and they headed back to the house with their harvest, he thought on the inheritance the boy was due one day. Abel would be a very good caretaker of the Ampleford property.

Abel, only partially cleaned off, skipped along by his side, dashing off now and then to look at something he had glimpsed on the beach. He was a happy boy, he thought, even though he had lost both of his parents. He had a sister and aunt who cared for him and a lot of cousins to play with. Geordie suspected whatever scars the boy carried from the loss were not too deep.

When they returned to the house Belle was there to take the clams and quickly began to sort them out. She also murmured an apology for sleeping past the time she had needed to get out there to dig the clams herself. He took Abel by the hand, intending to take him to the upstairs bath and rinse him off.

As they started out the door of the kitchen, he said, "Nay sure sleeping is the word ye want. It was more as if ye were unconscious yet still able to stand, even said a word or two. Interesting skill."

Mehitabel spun around to answer him but he was already gone. She had the suspicion he had picked Abel up and dashed right up the stairs, because she could hear the echo of the boy's giggles. Shaking her head, she went back to sorting the clams, needing to get that done so she could begin the evening meal, and hoped Geordie would get Abel cleaned up well.

* * *

Geordie laughed when the moment he got Abel dried off, the boy ran off to his room. Standing up, he looked at how his own clothes had gotten wet and quickly went into his room. Using his slightly dampened clothes to wipe himself dry, he put on dry clothes. By the time he stepped out of his room, Abel was waiting for him. Geordie crouched down to redo the buttons on the boy's shirt. Then he looked at Abel and, knowing he was a bright boy, had to wonder why he always seemed to do his shirt up wrong.

"Abel, why are your buttons always buttoned up wrong?" he asked.

"Dunno," muttered Abel, smoothing his now neatly buttoned shirt.

"Perhaps it would help if you looked at the buttons as ye did them up." He had to bite back a laugh when the boy's eyes widened a little and he just nodded.

"That's probably a good idea," Abel said calmly.

"Probably. Ye should practice it."

"All right. Think the food is ready now?"

Standing up, Geordie took the boy by the hand and led him down the stairs with him. "I suspect if it isnae, it will be soon."

When they walked into the kitchen, Belle was busy frying potatoes while ham slices sizzled in the fry pan. He got the plates and cutlery out, he and Abel setting the table as she cooked. As he sat down, Abel fetched napkins for each of them before sitting down across the table from him. Geordie glanced down, and on the floor at the end of the table sat all Belle's pets. Staring at her. He was not surprised when she put a little meat and egg on three small plates and set them down for the pets before bringing the rest over to the table.

"You dug a good crop," she said and then grabbed the

pot of coffee and set it on the table. "I will be able to make all my customers happy." She poured a glass of apple juice for Abel and, after serving it to the boy, sat down and poured herself some coffee.

Between discussing the crops she had, how they were doing, and eating their food they soon finished breakfast. Abel gulped down the last of his drink, leapt up to put his dishes in the sink, and announced that he was taking the dogs out. He then ran off and the two dogs were close behind him. Geordie heard the boy say good morning to the patients in the infirmary and get a cheerful answer. A moment later the front door slammed.

"Can Abel manage Thor?"

Belle smiled and nodded. "Thor behaves very well with Abel. It is as if he knows he is bigger and stronger and just doesn't bother to show it off to the boy. One time Thor ran off and dragged poor Abel along after him, and it upset him when he stopped and saw the boy crying, so he now behaves."

"Dogs are loyal, and Thor has decided Abel is one he will be loyal to."

"Well, I will just wash these dishes and then we can take the boys out for a little swim."

Geordie helped Belle with the dishes by wiping them dry and putting away the ones that he knew where they went. He leaned against the edge of the counter, crossed his arms over his chest, and watched her as she emptied and cleaned out the sink. Just as she was wringing out the washing rag, he suddenly felt a need to at least attempt to get an answer to one of the many questions crowding his mind.

"Belle? Do ye ever think of living somewhere else?"

Belle frowned. "Now and then, but not with any fierce need to go. It is a lot of work to run this place, but I can make a living here. I don't have many animals, but I like having a place where I can keep them."

"Aye, ye do have all those things."

"And I don't really know if there is a place I might like better than this." She turned toward him, crossed her arms, and studied him closely. "Why do you ask?"

"Just curious. Ye have relatives all round but ye live alone. Most women dinnae seem to much like that."

"I have Abel."

"Most days, aye."

The front door slammed open, then shut loudly. Belle frowned as she heard someone come stomping toward the kitchen. When her auntie marched in and hurled herself into a chair, Belle tried not to look too startled by the woman's arrival. Something had really upset her aunt and Belle was not sure she wished to know what it was.

"Something wrong, Auntie?" she asked as she put a pot of coffee on the stove. "Where is Abel?"

"Your cousin Rafe came by and they are out riding. They are not the problem. Your uncle John has arrived with his whole family."

Things became a little clearer then, as her aunt really did not like her brother-in-law or his wife. "Has he come for his usual summer visit?"

"No. He has come to claim the house." Mary nodded at the stunned look on Belle's face. "Fortunately, he announced that after Rafe and Abel left. Seems my Thomas never made a will or changed his father's. Since Tom has died, the will still states the house and land pass to his brother."

"But he left a wife and sons."

"Should have written a new will, his own will. I talked to someone who deals in such things and he says that without a written record changing it, the will is still in effect. I suspect John discovered that and knew his brother had not made a will. So he grabbed his prissy wife and his four sullen children and came right on over. Brought all their belongings too. Cluttered up my barn with them. I was, of course, expected to provide food and drink while they all rested from the ordeal of traveling ten miles."

"What about his own home?"

"He is already trying to sell it. Even suggested I might want to buy it since I will now need a place to live. I was still in shock, watching his wife inspect my home, but even then, I knew I never would. He has priced it three times higher than what he paid, yet I know for a fact he has not put any money into it."

"Ye need to find a good lawyer," said Geordie.

"I suppose I should. They might be able to find something that will block this move. Waiting until he dies won't help. If he still claims my house and has written a will, it will go to his wife and kids. I cannot abide sharing a house with him and that woman."

"Then come stay here. Just make sure your leaving the house will not cause you to lose ground in an argument over the place."

"It appears most everyone in the area kens the rules of the will for this property and all about the Amplefords, as well as how all the properties are connected. Does that nay aid ye in your claim?"

"It might, but John may well plan to fight it out in a higher court, and that would be in a town where people don't know about us. And he never really showed that much interest in my house but coveted this one."

"Which, from all I have heard, is verra weel protected."

"My home has many of the same protections, but this comes down to what happens now while I and the boys still live. That requires the will Tom ne'er wrote."

"Well, you can come here every single day so you don't have to deal with him and we will find you a lawyer. You might also look through any papers Tom left behind. There might be something in them that will help you, maybe even show what his ideas on the matter were." Belle briefly hugged her aunt, then sat back. "And if things get particularly bad, you can even stay a night or two."

"That would be good. I will have to tell the boys before they stop in and find John and his family settled in. That could bring on a fight I don't need. And it is *her* I cannot deal with. I really believe it is her who is pushing this. John knew exactly what Tom wanted. That woman just wants to be closer to the town and have a chance to be part of the society."

"We have a society?"

Belle smiled when her aunt laughed, and then moved to pour the woman a cup of coffee. She set it down in front of Mary and pushed the jug of cream and pot of sugar closer to her. Then she filled up her cup again and served Geordie before sitting down.

"I think I put a box of Tom's papers in the closet," Mary said. "I didn't look through them, just packed them. Tried to do it neatly and go drawer by drawer, but never looked at them. At the time it hurt just to look at his writing."

"Would they have exchanged any letters about this? Ye live so close to each other, I cannae see why they wouldnae just visit to talk, but ye can never be sure. Some planning for it could have been done."

Mary frowned in thought and nodded. "Tom would have consulted with my brother. He saw Noah as so much smarter than him. He would definitely have discussed it with him. Unfortunately, I forget much of the year before Tom died as he required so much aid, and all of my days were taken up with nursing him and knowing none of it was going to help."

"So, we go through all of my dad's papers. There is a big desk upstairs in what he called the study room. Then there is a smaller desk in the infirmary along with a small filing cabinet. A lot of paper to go through, though we can set aside the patient files."

Mary nodded. "Which do you want to start with?"

"I think the study. You and I can plow our way through all that."

"I will do the paper in the infirmary, if ye want," Geordie said. "And if that doesnae give us much, I can wander into town and see who ye have there for a lawyer. My brother has one, Harvard-educated, and I have talked to him a lot, so might have a feel for who would be the best choice."

"You have a Harvard-educated lawyer in the Ozark hills? Why would he open shop there?" asked Belle.

"Where he lived before there were too many people, and I think he may have had a touch of wanderlust. Iain hired him, was his first client, because the bank was trying to trick him into losing his lands when he got a loan. Fortunately, he had a bad feeling about it and hadnae signed the papers. Fellow not only fixed that but got the head of the bank booted out. Then his wife and Iain's wife became friends, so we are kind of stuck with him." He grinned. "Shame he is so far away."

"Well, if you haven't sent that letter yet"—Belle smiled when he hastily had a long drink of coffee—"maybe you can just ask if he knows anyone in this area who had knowledge of wills."

"I could do that."

"Best we get going on slogging our way through my father's papers," she said as she stood up. "He had very tidy handwriting, so it should not be too hard."

Geordie watched the two women head up the stairs and then made his way into the infirmary. He hoped she was right about her father's writing because his reading ability faltered over handwritten things far too often.

He found Robbie and Will very interested in what he

was doing as he started to pull the papers out of the desk. Seeing an opportunity to cut down on the tedious work he faced, Geordie carried two chairs over to the desk for them to sit in and explained what he was looking for.

After sorting out what were obviously patient files, they each began to carefully read over the rest. Will found one file that had a list of things Noah and Tom had obviously decided needed to be put in a will, but no signatures or directions. Geordie doubted it would be enough to help them, but they set it aside so they could at least show Mary her husband had given the matter some serious thought.

As they began to put the files back, Geordie found himself staring at the patients' files already returned to a drawer. One of them caught his eye and he frowned. He pulled it back out.

"What do ye want with that? It is a patient," said Robbie.

"Is it? Who? After reading over so much of what the mon wrote I find it hard to believe he misspelled Bill. This says BIL, all capitals. Rather implies it is an abbreviation."

"Short for some family names, like Billings?" asked Will.

"Or, just a thought, the abbreviation for brother-in-law."

"Only one way to find out."

Geordie took a deep breath and opened the file. He slowly flipped through a collection of letters. The ones that had come to the doctor were still in the envelopes and the ones he had answered were neatly copied onto a sheet of paper. A quick look did not show him a signed legal paper, but the correspondence between the Tom and Noah might contain all they needed.

"I think this might be some help." He stood up. "Thanks for the help. If it does nothing else, it will ease Mary's upset over the thought that her husband had not done anything to protect her and his kids. He had obviously begun and tried, but time caught up to him."

"I can't believe anyone could take her house. Everyone in town knows the story behind all the properties. Maybe you should have a close look at the old will."

"A good idea. I will tell Belle."

He made his way up to the room called the study and thought over what they had found. He had not looked carefully at what was in the file and really hoped they would find something that would provide more than a little ease of mind for Mary. He could not understand how a relation could do what this John was doing to his own brother's wife and children.

When he stepped into the study, he stopped. The women sat on the floor with papers spread all around them. Both of them were reading papers. He was pleased that he and the boys had been so much better organized.

"Found something?" he asked, and both women startled in surprise.

"No. Not yet, anyway. I had not realized how many people my father had corresponded with."

"Anyone important or famous?"

"No, sad to say. It appears he was keeping in touch with the Native side of the family. He often visited them to offer his doctoring skills. Then, when he got them a doctor who worked close by, he just answered any questions they had."

"That was good of him." He held out the file folder he had. "We think we found something. It was in the patients' files because one of the boys thought it said Bill, but it was BIL, brother-in-law. It is correspondence between your da and Tom. We looked at some of it and it does appear that Tom was making plans for his will. We just didnae read enough to ken if he had anything legal done."

"It is the same with all of these. There are some letters either to or from Tom about the need to make a will and answers from Da. A few others as well. We are hoping to find a lawyer in this mess."

"Need a hand?" he asked as he sat down.

Belle put a couple folders in front of him. "We are obviously not as quick as you."

"I had your patients to help me. Something to do to break their boredom."

"Huh. Never thought of enlisting their help."

"As I said, we did not read each letter, so there could be something of import there, something to lead ye to a lawyer."

"Well, I need a cold drink," said Belle as she stood up.

They all went down into the kitchen and Belle poured out three tall glasses of lemonade. Then they sat and spread out the letters, each taking one to read through carefully. Geordie noticed a suspicious shine to Belle's eyes on occasion as she carefully read each one.

"Well, a few lawyers are mentioned, but they were not hired to work on this," said Mary. "I do not understand why it was such a problem to find someone."

"There are a lot of people who do not like how so much land could end up in the hands of the Natives. And any one of the learned men who would be lawyers may have aspirations to run for office sometime, and would not want to be connected to any of it," Belle said.

"Does that feeling run strong here?" Geordie asked.

"Not as strong as it might out where you are, but there are some who can be very pig-headed about Natives owning land. We don't have much trouble, except from what considers itself society here, because we are Amplefords and that name has always been here, from the first settler on."

"We also marry and have kids and so still live on that land."

"You mean as long as we keep producing satisfactory heirs, they can rest easy?"

"That seems to be it." Mary smiled at Geordie, who was laughing quietly. "People in a small town can be unending entertainment."

"Oh, I ken that. Unfortunately, they can sometimes be dangerous. We pushed our luck a bit by hiring the Powells, shepherds, and running sheep on our land. Then the Powells married sisters who are Natives, half, and are now having babies. We are so out of the way, tucked up in the hills on our acres, that society can ignore us. I think the sisters get lost in the Scots, Welsh, and Irish up there, too. And one very English lady."

"Good Lord." Mary shook her head. "I mean, we are all countries mixed nearly everywhere here but most of us don't sound like it like you do. I suspect the others do, too."

"Mrs. O'Neal just sounds like she's from New England, which is not much of a saving grace. We supported the Union. Didnae flaunt it but didnae keep it a secret either. That causes some tension still." He politely ignored the somewhat profane opinions of the war muttered by the two women.

"Well, I think going through all these letters will take some time and we will probably need paper and pen to make some notes. I'll just pick this stuff up, or one of the furry gang might play with it all and leave us only shreds of paper."

It was late before Geordie had an opportunity to sit alone with Belle. She was studying the information she and her aunt had compiled from the many letters and papers they had gone through as she sipped her cup of hot chocolate. They had proof of what Mary's husband had wanted in his will, but little else.

"Only one lawyer mentioned in all of that paper," Geordie said. "I asked Iain to see if George, our lawyer, recognizes the name, and my letter will head out in the morning."

"Well, at least Auntie found some comfort in seeing that Uncle had tried. His time simply ran out."

"Will any of the other information help?"

"That will all depend on if the case ends up in court, where, and how the court sees it."

"When do ye think he will try to act legally to take her house?"

"I fear it will not be long. He wants it and has already put his house up for sale. And from things Auntie said, his wife really wants the house."

When she put her empty mug down, he wrapped his arms around her. "We will do all we can to help her sort this out. Her husband started the process of preparing a will, we have the proof of that, and we have proof of the things he wanted in it, right down to a list of who gets what. There may be more to find." He kissed the top of her head. "Why dinnae we just go and sleep on all this?"

He took her by the hand and pulled her to her feet. Geordie swung her up into his arms, ignoring her soft squeal of protest. "I am carrying m'lady to our bedchamber. It is supposed to be romantic."

Belle sighed and shook her head. "Whatever lady said it was romantic was obviously tall, one of those stately ladies who would never feel as if she was teetering precariously on some ledge."

"Ye climb trees with ease and show no sign of fear."

"Because *I* am the one doing it; *I* am the one in control. Here?" She waved her hand to illustrate her position. "No control at all. The best I can hope for is that, as I fall, I can grab hold of your shirt and it will not rip. That is just luck. Again, no control. Afraid I don't like what that feels like."

He walked into his bedchamber, walked up to his bed and, smiling at her, tossed her down onto it. While she was still held silent by shock, he settled his body over hers. He kissed her and began to undo her gown, kissing every patch of skin that appeared. He sat up when the gown was completely undone and tugged it off, pausing to tug off her shoes and toss them aside as well.

Sliding his hands under her petticoats, he untied her garters and rolled down each stocking, settling them more carefully on the floor. He dealt with her petticoats even quicker, leaving her in only her shift and her pantalets as he began to shed his own clothes. The way she stared at him, the blush on her cheeks deepening, made him smile. He kissed her, and she quickly wrapped her limbs around him.

They both struggled to shed the last of their clothing as quickly as possible. When their skin finally touched, Geordie sighed with pleasure and held her body close to his. He enjoyed her soft sigh of enjoyment as he stroked her.

Belle slid her hand down his belly and tentatively grasped his erection. When his body jerked she stroked him and he made no complaint. She decided she had just startled him with her boldness and grew more daring in her touch.

Geordie enjoyed her touch and the way his body hardened and grew needy. Then he decided he was getting too close to the edge and moved her hand, then slowly began to join their bodies. For a short while he moved slowly and gently but soon began to move with all the hunger and need of an untried boy. When her body tightened on his in release, it was all it took to take him over the edge.

He rolled onto his side and lightly petted her as he

thought over what they had yet to talk about. At some point they needed to have a serious discussion about where this affair should go. It was going to be a difficult thing to sort out as they both had close-knit families they would be loath to leave. But now there were trains, he thought, as she turned on her side and snuggled up against him.

"It was probably good that ye didnae let your auntie stay the night. Ye screamed."

"I did no such thing, and I don't know how you could have heard my ladylike cry over your roaring." She patted his hip. "Like a lion on the hunt."

He just grinned as he felt her relax in sleep. Kissing the back of her neck, he decided to go to sleep as well. They would face that difficult talk tomorrow, he decided.

Chapter Fifteen

Geordie was bringing coffee to Robbie and Will while he struggled to think of how to describe Robbie's injuries in a letter to his family. He wanted to explain the possibility of his leg improving as a result of Belle's treatment, but he did not want to give his family too much hope, nor did he want to be too pessimistic and make them worry.

He walked in and served Robbie and Will their coffee, then sat on the edge of Robbie's bed. Taking a drink of coffee, he pulled the letter he had been writing out of his pocket. His brother sat up straighter, looked over what he had written, then frowned at him.

"Why are ye showing me this?"

"I am stuck. I dinnae want to sound too hopeful, raise their hopes and all, but I dinnae want to be all dark and gloomy, either."

"Just say exactly what is happening. After all, I havenae really tested it out yet. Still too weak to try walking around on it. It doesnae sit there aching like it used to, and thank God for that, but who can say what it will do if I start walking on it regularly? Just say that. My leg is fixed, because it is straight again, but not really tested."

Geordie laughed. "Aye, I suppose that will do. Do ye ken when we might have a better idea?"

"In a few days," said Belle as she walked up to stand at the foot of Robbie's bed.

"Hey! What about my leg?" said Will. "I didn't even break mine, but I am still stuck here."

Belle sighed. "Such whining. No, you didn't, but you did get a great big bullet hole in your thigh and that needs to close up nice and tight. I also didn't want you going back to work until it is completely healed. I have the feeling Bennet would be putting you right back to work if I sent you back."

Will sighed and nodded. "Yup, he would do that. Been surprised he hasn't come round to yell at me for malingering or something like that."

"Oh, he has. Says how I need to hurry up and fix what I did to you because he has some cows nearing their time to calf."

"Damn. I wish he had never found out Uncle Ben was an animal doc."

"Has you taking care of them all the time, does he?" she asked as she began to carefully remove the stitching in his leg, pleased to see that his short time in the water had not damaged it badly.

"He does, but he doesn't pay me like I really am the animal doctor. Sometimes he says things that make me think he has been watching me for a while. He knew exactly what he was hiring."

Belle murmured in agreement as she worked out a particularly difficult stitch. "I suspect he did, maybe even got your uncle to talk about your work so he would get an even better idea of how good you are. Him using you as his assistant so much only confirmed all Bennet had seen you do. Why didn't you become a horse doctor?"

"I don't like cutting into living flesh, or the smells, or the cries of pain one too often hears."

"That is a problem. Pretty much covers the whole business."

"I don't know how you can abide doctoring people."

"Mustn't say *doctoring*, Will. Upsets the ones who have their papers from some school. *Nursing* is a better word. Doesn't sting their overweening pride so badly." Once the last stitch was out, she wiped the area down and studied the wound. "This has healed well and sealed nice and tight. We'll take you down to the water again today. It is time to get some strength back into that scrawny limb."

"Hey! That is a manly leg," Will protested as she pulled him up until he could put his feet on the floor. "Now what?"

"Now you carefully put weight on your feet and see how that leg feels."

He did as she asked so slowly and carefully she nearly snapped at him to hurry up. He gave only a soft hiss of discomfort. "Not bad, but it is weak. I am not sure that swimming we did before helped it much."

"As I believe I told you, I think the bullet stole a bit of the muscle in there and that *will* be helped by swimming. The swimming builds up the strength of the muscle, limbers up any stiffness caused by resting it so long during the healing. Could you help them ready themselves for a short paddle in the water, Geordie?" She smiled her thanks when he nodded.

She gathered up the swimming costumes for the men and hurried off to her bedchamber to put her own on. As she changed, she mentally tried to allocate the hours of the day to all the chores she had to get done. It was going to be a full and busy day.

* * *

James yawned and walked out onto the front porch. As he sipped his coffee he thought about what he was going to do. Stay or wander some more. Then a carriage pulled up and he stood up straight. His family did not expect anybody to arrive, and he started to get a bad feeling.

The driver of the carriage got down, looked over the house, checked the numbers James's mother had put up very prominently over the door, and then started toward him. James stared into the carriage and thought he saw movement, but then looked back at the man coming toward him. As the man stepped up on the porch, James heard a sound behind him, which let him know his mother was there and she had set the shotgun right next to the door. The man was slightly overweight and his tidily combed hair didn't hide the fact that his hair was getting thin.

"Are you James Deacon?"

"I am. What are you wanting?"

"I am Mister Harold Hobbs, a lawyer. Just one more question—did you come to know a Jane Benson Haggert on the train to Boston? Her and her daughter?"

"I did. My friend Geordie MacEnroy, his brother Robbie, and I sat near them and had a chance to offer a helping hand." James stepped to the side as his mother came out to stand beside him. "Geordie had a chat with them both. Has something happened to Mrs. Haggert?"

"I'm afraid so. She is dead, as is her mother. Some men broke into the elder lady's home, and after they killed the old woman they tried to beat the truth out of poor Mrs. Haggert."

"Morgan?" he asked.

"The child lives. The elder lady hid her under the stairs before she was caught and killed. For a while, Mrs. Haggert lived, but the beating was too harsh and she died of her wounds. She knew it was coming, for it took several days, and she called me in to handle the estate and told me what to do with her child. I was to bring her here to a certain Geordie MacEnroy. Your letter gave me the direction I needed. Is he here?"

"No." For just a second, James felt a pinch of anger that the woman had not chosen him, but it passed quickly. "I know where he is though. I can see that the child gets to him."

"Is he far away, as I should have a few words with him as well?"

"Not quite a day's ride."

"Well, I suspect we can arrange something." He turned and walked back to the carriage to open the door. "Miss Haggert, could you step out, please?"

James heard his mother make a soft sound of sympathy when little Morgan stepped out, dressed in full mourning and clutching her wooden doll. The child took the man's hand and allowed him to lead her over to the porch. She looked all round until her eyes fixed on him and he sighed at the sadness he could read there.

"Geordie?" she asked in a small voice.

"He isn't here, Morgan, but I know just where he is staying, and it is not too far away."

Mrs. Deacon stepped closer to the girl. "Would you like to come in for something to drink and a little food?"

Morgan glanced at the man with her and he nodded slightly, so she said, "Yes, please."

James walked with the man as his mother took Morgan's little hand and led the way into the kitchen. Once they were all seated around the table, James talked with Hobbs but kept an ear open to how Morgan was doing as she talked to his mother. He paused in his conversation to help his mother remove the mourning coat that completely enveloped the child.

"This is very fancy, Morgan. A lot for a little girl to wear," he said.

"It was my mother's when she was small. She wore it when her papa died."

"Ah, a sad tradition to carry on."

"I don't mind. Do you know if Geordie found someone to help Robbie get better?"

James shrugged. "I fear I don't know. I was soon going to see them, as I seem to have decided to stay here for now. It would be good if he did find someone. Robbie's family has worried about him."

"Because he hurts."

"Exactly."

"I hope he found someone who could end that, at least."

"Yes, that would be good. You should try one of my mother's wild blueberry muffins. Very tasty."

Morgan nodded, and he placed a muffin on her plate. He cut it in half and pushed a small plate of butter near to her. Morgan carefully ate, and took the occasional sip of her apple juice, as she sat listening quietly to James and Mr. Hobbs talk. She really did not understand what was to happen to her, but she knew she had to be brave.

"Well, Morgan," said James, "I think you are going to have to be patient a little longer. We will leave to get Geordie first thing in the morning. It is a bit too late to head out today, and considering how far the carriage team has come, they could do with a bit of a rest first. Is that all right?"

"Yes, thank you. So, we will stay here for the night?" She looked at Mr. Hobbs and then at James.

"Yes, dear," said Mrs. Deacon. "I have room, and I suspect you could do with a bit of rest yourself."

"Thank you, ma'am."

"Well, when you are done with your muffin I will show

you the room you will have, as well as some books you might want to read or toys you might want to play with."

"Why do you have things for little kids?"

"Because some of my children have done as they should and found a mate and given me grandchildren."

Seeing the way James ignored his mother, even though the woman was frowning at him, Morgan said, "James hasn't done that, has he?"

"No, but he keeps telling me there is time, that he isn't in his dotage yet."

"No, he isn't," Morgan said quite seriously, then smiled faintly. "But, I think he might want to hurry up."

Ignoring his mother's laughter, James got up and grasped Morgan by the hand. "Come along, Miss Sassy, I will show you where the toys are."

As soon as the pair disappeared into the room that served as a library, a den, and a play room, Mrs. Deacon looked at Mr. Hobbs. "Why has a lawyer come with the child?"

"Well, someone had to come with her, and she does have a bit of an inheritance to be dealt with. Since her mother chose Mr. MacEnroy as her guardian, I need to sort that all out with him."

"An inheritance? Not a really big one, I hope."

"Not sure what you would consider big, but it is not tiny. There is her grandmother's house in Boston and some savings. The property is the big thing, and it needs to be sorted out fairly quickly. Sold, or rented so the taxes on it are paid up."

"There is no one else in the family?"

"No. It was just the woman and the child. There are a few distant cousins, which is probably another good reason to get it sorted out."

"Get what sorted out?" asked James as he returned to the table.

"Her inheritance," answered his mother.

"Oh, hell, it's not a big one, is it?" James asked Mr. Hobbs.

Mr. Hobbs laughed. "I have never met people so dismayed about a possible large inheritance but, no, it is not large. It does, however, need guardianship and attention paid to it. There is a bit of property, you see. Nothing to worry about."

"Isn't me I am worrying about, it is the MacEnroys," James said.

"I am only interested in Geordie MacEnroy."

"Sorry, you have something that involves one, you get all seven of them."

"Good heavens, seven?"

"If you don't count the wives or their shepherds or their housekeeper." James grinned, then sighed. "And I should try to remember them as well."

"Do you think they will have a problem taking in a child that is not theirs?"

"No, not at all. They already have three orphans. They seem to have a soft spot for strays as well. Housekeeper and shepherds are some. No, they'll be just fine with another addition, not that they will have much to do with her, as I am not so sure Geordie will be returning home, at least not for good."

"You think he is serious about that Ampleford girl?" asked his mother.

"Yup. I think he is very serious about her, though doubt he has had the sense to face it yet. I wasn't there long enough to get a good sense of their relationship, yet they looked right, if you know what I mean."

"I do. Like your sister and her man."

"Exactly, which is why I didn't just knock him out when he sat too close to her." He grinned at Mr. Hobbs when the man laughed.

"So you think he will be willing to take on the care of the girl, and that this woman he is with would be willing as well?"

"I can't speak for them, but my gut says they would be willing. We can get an answer tomorrow. If we get as early a start as possible in the morning, we should reach him in the early to middle afternoon."

"I will show you to the room you can use, Mr. Hobbs," James's mother said as she stood up and moved to his side.

"Are you sure this will be no trouble?"

"No trouble at all. We have a couple of rooms we always rent out in the summer."

James watched his mother lead the man away, then got up to go and see how Morgan was doing. He cautiously entered the playroom, not wanting to startle the child. He frowned when he did not see her immediately, as he had expected. Finally, he saw her seated on the floor by the bookshelves that held the books for new readers. She held one open on her lap, but was not reading and did not seem to notice that she was no longer alone. Morgan was quietly grieving. Hurting for the child, James went over and sat down next to her. He put his arm around her small shoulders, tugged her close, and kissed her on the top of her head.

"It is hard, Morgan. Best not to hold it in."

"I'm not. They beat Mama, you know. They beat her bad. And they killed my nana. That was very wrong of them to do such mean things just for a chest with some coins in it. Mama would have given it to them, I bet, but they didn't even really ask. Just killed Nana and demanded Mama give it to them even as they beat her. I could have helped, you know, except Nana fell on top of the door to the hidey hole she had put me in."

"Don't think like that, honey. There was nothing you could have done. You are only a little girl."

"My nana died on top of the door of the place she put me in."

"And it kept them away from you, didn't it?" She nodded and he hugged her. "That's how you want to remember her, saving you. She would like that." He looked at the books she had pulled out. "What were you reading?"

She wiped the tears from her cheeks and carefully showed him the books. James did his best to keep her talking and smiling a little as she told him about each book. He hid his sorrow from her, not wanting to stir up her own.

His mother soon came in and took over the job of keeping the child company and James went back to the table. Mr, Hobbs had returned and was sipping a cup of coffee as he looked through some papers. James got himself some coffee and joined the man.

"These are the papers concerning her inheritance," Mr. Hobbs said.

"Why so many for what you said is a small inheritance?"

"There are requests about what might be done with things and what choices there might be for the child if Mr. MacEnroy cannot take her."

"I really do not think you will have any trouble with that. Hope the instructions about what she gets are not too complicated though. I don't know for certain, but Geordie may want to return to his home and family in the Ozarks."

"That would make things much trickier. Unless, does he have a lawyer out there?"

"I believe his family has one. Some fellow from Harvard."

"Then something could be arranged. I have done such things before, communicated with a distant lawyer over an estate."

"Calling it an estate makes it sound like a big inheritance," James muttered.

"It really isn't. There is enough money in the accounts to help in supporting Morgan, but not much more than that. A few stocks and bonds from the grandmother. As I said, the biggest part of it is the house in Boston. She is too young to make a decision about that."

"Well, Geordie can decide for her if that is allowed."

"Oh, it is. He was listed as one of several approved guardians. If he accepts he will have full control over the estate, and complete say in what is to be done with it. Morgan's mother lived long enough to write that down and sign it plus get it cosigned. She also made sure to tell the child and try to make her understand what it all meant. I am just not sure how much of it Morgan understood since she was very upset and frightened at the time."

James nodded. "Then we will definitely head out as soon as possible in the morning. I can show you the horse you can ride if you want to inspect it now."

"Actually, I was hoping we could travel there in the carriage. I am not that skilled at riding."

"Fine. Probably be a much more comfortable trip."

Chapter Sixteen

Geordie frowned as he slowly woke up. He immediately wondered what had pulled him out of his comfortable sleep. He looked at Belle, who was burrowed under the covers so only the top of her head was visible. Two days of searching through papers and worrying about her aunt had left her exhausted.

He moved closer to her, wrapped his arm around her waist and was just closing his eyes when he suddenly realized what had woken him up. Geordie took a deep breath and cursed. The smell of smoke had ended his gentle slide back into sleep and he sat up. As he got up and moved to the window, Belle sat up and pushed her hair out of her face.

"What is it? What's wrong?" she asked. "Something is wrong, isn't it?"

"I think someone has set your barn on fire." He started yanking on his clothes. "We need to get your animals out fast."

He yanked his boots on and hurried down the stairs. Just as he pulled open the front door he heard her following him. They both raced for the barn and Geordie tried to find exactly where the fire was, finally spotting it at the back corner of the roof.

Belle was fighting to open the doors when he ran to help her. The moment they started to open it, the two of them were driven back by a wave of heavy, choking, thick smoke. When it cleared enough for them to see, they both ran inside, and Belle went straight to her animals, Abel raced in to help her, but he followed a little more slowly, staring up at the place where he had caught a glimpse of flame.

Opening the rear door of the barn, Bella got a bucket of water from the well just outside the barn and handed it up to Geordie, who had found a ladder, then ran to get another one. As he tossed the water on what flame he could see, he realized what would allow her to save her barn with only a good patch on the roof. The roof leaked, so the hay stored in the loft had not actually caught fire.

He turned to tell her and saw that he had an odd bucket brigade. Robbie and Will both helped to pass water to him and yet stay off their injured legs. "Ye have wet hay up here, Belle, and it isnae catching fire well at all. The fire either dies out or sputters as it tries to catch hold."

"Then we best smother it well, as a sputtering fire still has the potential to become a dangerous one." She turned to look at their ragged bucket brigade and gasped as six young men came running up to them from Bennet's land.

"Did someone ring the fire bell?" she asked.

"I pulled it a few times, Belle, when Rafe brought us here," Abel said. "I'll take the goats out."

"Thank you. Put them in the outdoor pen. I will get the donkey and a couple of horses."

Belle hurried up the ladder to help Geordie as the helpers brought by the bell made a stronger, more efficient bucket brigade. It did not take long to soak down all hint of fire. She looked at the soaked hay and sighed. That was going to cost her. So was the rebuilding of that corner of the barn roof. A moment later Geordie was by her side.

"That willnae take long to fix," he assured her, and several of the men gathered around murmured their agreement.

"Hell, MacEnroy, that should be an easy fix for a man who helped build a stockade."

Geordie spun around to stare at the man standing behind him. "James! Did ye just get here? Oh, do ye need our help now?"

"Just arrived, and am actually going back soon. My mind has turned to staying in Maine." He took Geordie by the arm and turned him toward his horse. "There has been a bit of a complication. Remember the lady on the train?"

"Aye." Geordie had a bad feeling about what was coming.

"I heard from her a few days ago. Nice letter except for the sad news that her mother had passed. A little gossip then a thank-you for giving her my address. I wrote back with condolences and reaffirmed that it was fine for her to have my address. Signed off with the words that she should get in touch if there was anything she needed. Maybe should have left that off," James muttered.

"Why? Nice thing to say. Proper."

"Oh, I know. My mother worked hard to teach us what was proper and courteous and all that. Just wish she'd taught us what the hell to do if someone took us up on it."

"What has happened?"

"She is dead now, too, might have been dying when she wrote to me. Probably just checking to see if she had the right address. It seems someone hunted her down for that chest of coins. Killed her mother and then tried to beat the truth out of her. Her neighbor came and shot him. She had her injuries tended to, but it wasn't enough. The beating was too harsh. She asked if we could look after Morgan, save her from the harsh life of an orphanage."

"Oh, hell. And ye cannae take her in?"

"I could. Even my folks were willing. But Morgan wants you, old friend. She was very clear on that."

"Why me?"

"Who knows how a child thinks? Could be that accent of yours or that you talked with her or that you helped save her mother from those men on the train. And, it seems, you remind her of her papa."

Geordie sighed and dragged his hands through his hair. "Damn. Weel, where is she?"

"Over near the carriage, talking to that boy."

"Abel?" Geordie looked harder and then nodded. "Yup, that's Abel. Who's the mon?"

"He is the one who is handling the estate, fulfilling the last wishes of the woman."

"So, he kens about wills and all of that?"

"He does. He says he needs to talk with you anyway. So, you'll have a chance to find out what he knows."

"Better get it over with." Geordie took a moment to thank the boys who had come from Bennet's to help, then started to walk toward the carriage, only to have Belle run up beside him and take his hand in hers.

Abel was showing Morgan a frog when James, Geordie, and Belle reached them. The wobbly smile the girl gave Geordie broke his heart. He curled his arm around Belle's waist to steady himself. James introduced Morgan to everyone and Belle took a moment to quietly tell Abel to put the frog back into the little pond he stood near. Clutching her doll, Morgan told Belle what had happened and why she was there.

Morgan frowned at Abel, who was talking earnestly to

the frog, and then looked back at Belle. "Does he think the frog understands him?"

"I don't know." She spotted Thor trotting towards Abel. "Abel! Drop the frog. Thor is coming."

Abel turned to look back, which made the frog in his hands easily visible to the dog. Thor woofed and started to run. Abel tried to run away, glanced back at how close Thor was getting, tossed the frog into the pond, and dropped to his knees. The dog leapt over him and landed in the deeper water with a splash of murky water that soaked Abel. Abel looked at Belle as Thor splashed around, and he shrugged.

"Do you think he got the frog?" asked Abel, then grinned at Morgan as she started to laugh.

James and Geordie caught up with the dog and checked its mouth for any sign of a frog. They told the children that it appeared the frog had escaped. Belle rolled her eyes, took each child by the hand, and started to lead them up to the house. Mr. Hobbs hurried up from the carriage to tell them what they needed to know.

"Come with us to the house, Mr. Hobbs."

"I'll see to your carriage," James offered and hopped into the driver's seat.

"Come with me, Mr. Hobbs," said Belle as she took him by the arm. "We'll go up to the house, have a bite to eat, and see what needs to be done. Geordie will bring Morgan up. So, you are a lawyer and deal with wills and all that, are you?"

By the time they entered the house, Belle was determined to get her aunt to talk to the gentleman. He could be the answer they had been looking for.

After Geordie came inside he found himself nudged to the far side of the kitchen and Morgan came to stand next to him. When Auntie showed up and began to set the table, Belle came to join them. She quietly asked Morgan what had happened, and the little girl told her. She also told Auntie why her mother had sent her to Geordie.

"Ah, hell," Geordie muttered and edged over to James as Belle took Morgan's hand.

"Darling, I am so very sorry. Of course you can stay here. You will have to learn how to get along with frog boy though," Belle said.

"Ah, so that is why Abel is such a mess. Thor tried to get a frog?"

"Yes, Auntie. Thor saw the frog Abel was holding and thought it was playtime." She saw Mr. Hobbs at the back of the crowd in the kitchen and nudged Geordie. "Bring him forward. He said he has things to say that you need to know."

Geordie slipped through the group and grasped Mr. Hobbs by the arm, urging him forward. "Mr. Hobbs has a few things he needs to say concerning Morgan. Sorry to put ye on the spot, Mr Hobbs."

"No trouble. Got me through the crowd."

Everyone sat down and Auntie poured coffee, plus juice for the two children. She then began to bring in the platters of food. Mr. Hobbs slowly laid out all his information as he ate and put the papers on the table in case anyone wished to read the dry legal words about what he had just said.

"I don't need a house," said Morgan. "I would rather have my mother and Nana back."

Belle felt tears sting her eyes and fought them back. "I know, darling, and I wish that was something we could do, but we can't. This is your mother's way of being sure you are well taken care of when she can't do it anymore. Sometimes it is all a parent can do. My father left me this house, and although I love it, I would also much rather have him. So would Abel." Belle saw her brother vigorously nod.

"I would really like my father to come back so we could catch frogs together," said Abel.

"Aye, that would be a fine thing," said Geordie. "My brother Iain did things like that with me and my brothers sometimes."

"Well, he probably was not all that much older than you," said Belle.

"Even a year older seems a lot to a younger brother. And when there are six of us and half are older than you are, it makes even more clear that you are younger."

"But older brothers can do more for you," said Abel.

"If they feel like it."

"Well, I think that all pretty much covers the joys of having a brother, don't you, Mr. Hobbs?" Auntie said sweetly and smiled at Mr. Hobbs, causing the poor man to blush. "I will admit to an interest in the work you do. In truth, I am having a bit of trouble over a will, or rather, over how my brother is using what a will says."

Belle rolled her eyes and looked at Geordie. "I believe I heard the sound of patients gasping from hunger."

"Or lack of morning coffee. You get the coffee and I'll get the food."

"Will do," said Geordie as he followed Belle into the kitchen.

Belle and Geordie started to walk by the table, pausing only to add a few things to the trays they were carrying. Then Morgan tugged on Belle's shirt. "Are you taking food to Robbie?"

"We are. How did you guess that?"

"It was not that difficult, and I also heard him laughing with someone else just down that hall." She pointed down the one that led to the infirmary. "Can I come with you so I can say hello to Robbie?"

"Of course you can," said Belle.

As they walked into the infirmary, Belle and Geordie were greeted with a few loud complaints. "Whine, whine, whine. Food is here now and it is not that late. Still only a few hours after sunrise." She handed each young man their coffee and placed a plate of food on the table by each bed.

Belle tugged Morgan over to the side of Robbie's bed. "We have Morgan staying with us now. I fear that tale of men hunting a certain chest finally brought the men to their door, but Morgan escaped. Your brother Geordie was named guardian."

"I am sorry for ye, Morgan. Your mither was a lovely woman. The world is made less by her loss." Robbie reached out and gently rubbed his hand over her hair. "Geordie isnae such a bad choice." He smiled when the little girl actually laughed a little.

"No, I rather like him."

"Good. Maybe ye will get to see where I live soon." He glanced at Belle, who studiously ignored him.

"I am sure it is nice." Morgan glanced at Belle. "I like the ocean too, though."

After Robbie and Morgan talked for a bit and then she met and talked with Will, Belle took her back to where the others still sat at the table nibbling on what food was left. Then she grabbed Geordie's hand and tugged him off to the back porch. She sat on the steps and he cautiously sat down beside her.

"So, you now have a child."

"It seems that I do."

"One who does not know where she is going to live."

"I thought she would live with us," he said quietly as he took her hand in his.

"All right, so you have decided I will be there with you—but, Geordie, where is *there*?"

"Ah, well, I have not made up my mind on that."

When she growled he tugged her into his arms and kissed her. "I ken it. I need to make up my mind. But got one answer already."

"What?"

"That ye will be *there* with me."

"I did not actually say that, just commented on your assumption."

"Weel, I certainly dinnae want to be *there* unless ye are, even when I figure out where *there* will be." He pulled her into his arms. "I love ye, lass. I want ye to be where I am. It is just that the choice to make is a demmed hard one."

She rested her head on his shoulder. "I know. I also love you," she confessed and grinned when his hug grew tighter for a bit and he kissed her neck, "but, just like you, cannot decide which part of the country to live in. Your hills sound lovely, as does your large family, but I also love the oceanside and my large family. But then I get to pondering silly things like how it is always the woman who follows the husband." She glanced towards Bennet's home. "I could do with new neighbors though."

He chuckled. "Aye, ye could, but I cannae say all of ours are much better, and there is that lingering friction about what side you were on in the war. I think we should just allow that decision to ride for a while."

"But you were going home with Robbie when he is ready to travel."

"I am, and ye are coming with us, to meet my family and have a good look around. Breathe in the air, meet the neighbors, all that sort of thing. Then come back here and see if ye can give up this to go stay with me there, or I can decide if I want to give up the hills to live here."

"Okay. A deal. I will go and see your hills and you will come back here after being well reminded of them, so we can both make a better decision."

He kissed her again and then, hand in hand, they went back into the house. "Ye do realize that all we have decided means we should get married, dinnae ye?"

"Maybe," she said and skipped off into the kitchen.

After a moment of stunned surprise, Geordie growled and hurried after her.

Geordie having caught her in the kitchen and dragged her up the stairs, it was much later in the day before Belle got a chance to sit with her aunt. The woman had spent a lot of time talking to Mr. Hobbs. Belle was curious about what she had found out. Judging by the happy tune her aunt was humming as she mended some of Abel's clothes, Belle suspected, and hoped, her aunt had received some good news.

Sitting down on the porch swing next to her aunt, Belle nudged the woman with her elbow. "Did you and Mr. Hobbs have a good talk?"

"Harold did answer a lot of questions for me."

"Harold, is it?"

"Hush. Yes, it is Harold."

"But was there good news in those answers?"

"Good possibilities."

"Did he need to see all the papers we found?"

"He asked, and I handed them right over."

A little annoyed at how her aunt was answering the questions so curtly, with absolutely no embellishment or even hopeful talk of possibilities, Belle wanted to scream.

A narrow-eyed look at her aunt's face told her the woman knew it, too.

Then Belle noticed a faint blush on her aunt's cheeks. Was there a hint of romance in the air? she thought. Then she thought about the men who had attempted to court her aunt after her husband died. Harold was nothing like any of them. Harold was a bit overweight, with thinning hair, and might even go bald in the near future, quiet, somewhat studious, and just a bit shy.

Then she thought on it a bit more and realized her aunt had never shown much interest in those men. Belle could recall how insulted they had been by her disinterest. She would never have called any of them studious and certainly not shy. In truth, Belle's late uncle, Mary's husband, had been the complete opposite of those men as well.

"Huh."

"Huh, what?" asked Mary.

"Nothing. I was just waiting to see if you found out anything useful in all the talk you shared with Harold."

"The only thing that might be useful is if he finds anything in all those papers I had."

"No hint that he thought he might?"

"Not really, because he said he really needs to see the papers, as they are what judges go by when it all ends in court. I so want it to end in court." Then Mary turned to stare at Belle. "So, what have you and Geordie decided, now that you are parents?"

"We aren't. We are like an uncle and aunt."

"I doubt that was what that poor woman was trying to find for her girl. She wanted a family for young Morgan. I suspect the child spoke of Geordie and even Robbie a lot after they got to Boston. Morgan's mother decided after hearing about his family and all, and seeing how he watched over his brother, that he would be a perfect parent for her child if ever needed."

"Well, we have her and we will keep her. Now we just have to decide where." She eyed her aunt closely, but the woman just calmly kept sewing. "What? No opinion on that?"

"I have opinions, but you know I keep them to myself when it is a life decision."

"A what?"

"A life decision, like Where will I live? Should I marry him? Should I have a baby? Should I buy a house or rent one? Questions like that."

"I am sure I have heard you give opinions on things like that," Belle said.

"I may have, but I do try not to. I will say I tend to have strong opinions"—she ignored Belle's snort of badly choked-back laughter—"but I try very hard to stick to that rule about not pushing my opinion on any decision other people are making for their lives. I learned what a bad idea that is, and what bad consequences come from it. After all, I told my brother not to marry that wife of his and look what has happened."

"Oh! Oh, dear. Is that why you say she heartily dislikes you?"

"It is and she does. But you will let me know what you decide, right?"

"Of course I will. Exactly where is Mr. Hobbs? I haven't seen him around since we all ate together."

"I told you, I gave him the papers and he is studying them. I can only hope he finds what he needs to plan a strategy. What is that look for?"

"What look?"

"A surprised look. You don't think the man can come up with a strategy?"

"He may be perfect for it, but I just can't think of legal business and strategy together."

"Truth is, neither can I, but Harold assures me all good

lawyers have one before they face a judge." She put aside the pants she had been patching for Abel and stood up. "I am going to bake some biscuits and sweets."

As her aunt walked off, Belle hoped she had enough of the ingredients her aunt needed, because the woman used up a lot when she got the baking urge. She then went to look for Geordie.

Chapter Seventeen

Belle held Abel's and Morgan's hands as Geordie went to buy them tickets. She watched as James took their horses to the stock car. Her stomach was tied into knots as she failed to push aside the nerves twisting her up inside. She looked at Robbie, who sat so calmly on a bench she wanted to slap him. He had nothing to worry about as he was going home to show his family how much he had improved. She was going to meet Geordie's family, and then take him away from them when she left.

She felt a small, soft hand pat hers and looked down at Morgan. "Am I holding your hand too tight?"

"No," Morgan answered. "I was just trying to calm you down."

"I am fine. But I haven't traveled on a train before."

Belle wondered if she should pretend she did not notice the way Morgan looked at her. Since Morgan did not actually roll her eyes at her, she decided she could pretend that look was not equal to her doing so. The child was very good at sensing people's moods. She was also very skilled at letting one know how she felt about things. Not always a welcome gift in a child.

"Here comes James," said Abel. "Where's Geordie?" he asked as James stopped in front of them.

"Trying to strike a bargain on the tickets."

"Why? They have a list that tells you what everything costs."

"They do indeed, Abel, but the man is a Scot and I think they always feel compelled to try to deal." James grinned at her. "Something you might wish to become accustomed to."

"I am accustomed. My aunt does it too. She claims it is the Yankee in her."

James frowned in thought. "We had a few hard-nosed ones in our troop and they did the same. I can't be bothered. I either think the price is reasonable and pay it, or it isn't and I walk away. And here is our bargainer."

"And here is Robbie," said Geordie as his brother joined them. "Where have you been?"

"Getting us something to eat on the train."

Before Geordie could try to see what he got, the call came to board the train. They hurried onto the train to find enough seats so they could sit together. Geordie and Belle sat with the two children while Robbie and James sat across the aisle from them. Robbie gave each of the children a sweet and Belle read to them. Before long Morgan was sprawled against Geordie, sound asleep, and Belle had Abel sprawled on her legs. She looked at Morgan, then at her peacefully sleeping little brother, before she finally looked right at Geordie.

"I think this is going to be a long journey," she said, and he laughed as he put his arm around her shoulders.

"It is a bit long but much quicker than riding all the way there or going by wagon. On the last leg, we will rent a wagon and ride it up into the hills."

As Belle looked around at the other passengers, a question stuck in her mind. They were heading to Geordie's home, to his family. Did that mean he wanted her to stay there with him, or was he just bringing her for a visit?

They really should have cleared such things up before they left.

Now was not a good time to have such a talk, not in a car full of people and two small children close by. She had come because Morgan had seemed rather determined that they would all go together. Abel had demanded that he come, although she was not sure if it was to make sure he stayed with her or because he wanted to see where Robbie lived. The more she thought on it, the more she realized even her aunt had been of a like mind, helping her to pack and rushing her out the door.

"Was Mr. Hobbs headed back to Boston?" she asked Geordie as she began to wonder why her aunt had so heartily assisted in what was beginning to look like a conspiracy.

"I dinnae ken. Forgot to ask him, but I would think so."

"Why? He has no job back there at the moment."

"He doesnae? He must. Lawyers always have work."

"He said his only job right now was to make sure Morgan was settled. He saw to that. Auntie mentioned he was going to help her keep her house and told me he had been part of a law firm, and Morgan was his first job now that he was on his own. That carriage he loves so much was given to him when the firm shut down."

"So you are worried about him staying there alone with your aunt?"

"No, just wondering if it was why she shoved me out the door."

He chuckled. "She didnae shove ye out the door, just stopped ye from dawdling."

"I was not dawdling, I was merely making certain we had everything we needed for this trip."

When he just mumbled a sound of agreement, she glared at him, only to find him asleep. Belle shook her head, then settled herself more comfortably in her seat and closed her eyes.

It was growing dark by the time the train stopped. They all got off so that Geordie and James could get tickets for the next leg of the trip. Belle did not like standing there in what seemed like a huge crowd to her. And the air itself felt dirty. Hanging on tightly to Morgan and Abel, she waited tensely for the men to return. When they finally did, she breathed a big sigh of relief and followed Geordie back onto the train. It was not until they were seated and the train started on its way that she realized she had seen nothing of the town they had stopped in. She hoped she could regain enough courage to look around more the next time they stopped.

Sleepy and struggling to remain steady on her feet, Belle let Geordie lead her off the train. Three days on trains had wrung her out. They all went to a rooming house and soon had the children tucked in bed in the room she and Geordie would share. Knowing she needed to eat, she went to get a meal with James, Robbie, and Geordie after they had securely locked the children in the room and paid a housemaid to keep a watch on them. It was the last thing she could recall until she felt herself set down in the back of a wagon. She knew she ought to ask what was going on, but she fell asleep again. The thought of how she should learn more about why she was in a wagon when she had been on a train brought her back to wakefulness quickly. She was abruptly awake and alarmed.

Even as she sat up so fast her head spun, Belle saw Morgan and Abel staring at her with openmouthed surprise. She pressed her hand to her forehead until the dizziness faded, then looked at Geordie, who was sitting on the seat next to Robbie while James drove. "Did I finish my dinner?" she asked.

Geordie laughed as did the other two men, and that annoyed her. "Aye, ye did. Ye didnae fall facedown into your food. I am nay quite sure what happened. Took us a while to guess that ye had gone to sleep. It was the not waking up that worried us."

"You didn't wake up when he brought you into the bedroom, either. You just rolled over and went to sleep, or back to sleep," said Abel and then he giggled. "If I hadn't been able to see you breathing I would have thought you had died."

He then hopped out of the wagon when James stopped in front of a stable. She let Geordie help her down and found her legs still a little wobbly. She really needed to find out why she had gone out like that, as it appeared to have taken a lot out of her.

"It was frightening, funny, and inexplicable all at once. One man on the train was a doctor and he said it was either a very deep exhaustion or you were having trouble with what was coming out of the smokestacks. That is why we have been riding in a wagon, which we have been driving to the next stop but we'll now try again."

Morgan nodded. "He felt that, since you couldn't leave the train yet, you should be kept away from the windows and taken a distance away from the train whenever it was stopped. Geordie was happy when we reached that last town and he could rent a wagon."

"Maybe you aren't one who can ride a train," said Abel.

"But I have to be able."

"Why?"

"Because Geordie and I need to go back and forth from his house to my house, from the hills to the shore."

"And we will," said Geordie. He helped her onto the

train and started looking for seats. "Either by train or by wagon or by horse. I did notice, Belle, that if ye are at the clear end of the train and there is a goodly amount of circulating air, ye are fine. I will admit that when I was headed east on the train I started to feel as though a piece of rock was caught in my throat."

"Lozenges," said a woman and held out a small wrapped thing for him to take. "I take them a lot when on one of these contraptions. Next time you get that feeling, try one. Be sure to save the wrapper so you know what to buy if you want more."

"Thank you, ma'am." He frowned a little when the woman scurried across the aisle to sit next to Belle, then he quickly bit back a smile when Abel sat on Belle's lap with his arms crossed over his chest.

The woman looked at Abel and smiled. "Good lad. Protecting her, are you? But, not to worry, I am a nurse."

"Belle is a nurse, too. She says I can't say *doctoring* about what she does because it will hurt the feelings of the ones who get the piece of paper."

"Hush, Abel. Can I do something for you, ma'am?"

Her eyes widened when the woman leaned very close and whispered, "Are you with child?"

"I do not believe so," she replied equally softly, shaking her head a little.

"Just wondering. Extreme exhaustion can be a sign."

"Thank you. I will keep that in mind."

The woman hurried back to her seat and Belle could see no sign that anyone else had overheard their whispered conversation. Geordie was about to get in the seat when Morgan tugged on the sleeve of her dress. Belle turned to face the girl and worried over how pale the child was.

"What is wrong, Morgan?"

"Are you feeling better now?"

"I am. It was just all that smoke from the train, but that

is something I can somewhat protect myself from." She brushed a few strands of hair off the girl's face. "Now we should get ourselves settled. Geordie might be getting tired of waiting for his seat."

"And the train is soon to pull out, and I would appreciate being able to be seated for that," Geordie said.

He slid along the back of the seat in front of them until he reached the window seat. Abel sat next to him and Morgan sat next to Belle. Morgan slipped her arm around Belle's and kept a hold on her until she fell asleep. What had happened to her mother had obviously scared the child, Belle thought. She would have to take more care with herself. She had thought violence would be what the child was worried about, but it appeared it was any hint of weakness or illness in the woman who took care of her that frightened the child.

It was somewhat dark, and that, along with the regular rhythm of the train, soon put her to sleep. Belle had tried to fight it but then wondered why she bothered. If nothing else, it would make the trip go quickly.

Geordie looked down the row at Belle, who was asleep again. It did not look like the last sleep she had taken, which had definitely appeared wrong, looking more like she had passed out or, at times, was even slipping into a coma. He wondered what Belle and the woman who said she was a nurse had whispered about.

He knew one thing that could make a woman go to sleep fast and hard. He had caught Emily and Abbie in that state several times. Once Emily had been out cold on the floor, with her nephew and baby curled up with her, and he was sure she had not been fully aware that they were there. There was certainly a chance he had gotten Belle pregnant, but the shake of her head when the woman had whispered to her left him with doubts. He gave up worrying about it. When she knew she would let him know. Looking around and seeing how many people had gone to sleep, including Robbie and James, he decided he might as well join them. At the next stop, they would switch to traveling by wagon. They were close enough to his home to drive a wagon there, and he wanted Belle to get a good view of his home and the land around it.

Geordie closed his eyes, and it surprised him to see the beach in front of her house. Maybe, in his heart, he had already made his choice. It was not one his family would be happy with, and he was sad about that. Yet the thought of sitting on the front porch and listening to the music of the waves did make him happy. There was the storm season to consider, but her home was at a distance from the water. And he liked her family. Plus now, with the many trains starting to cross the country, coming home for a visit or having his family come visit him was not such a great concern. He decided that no matter where Belle wanted to stay, he could be content.

As he stepped down from the train, Geordie squinted against the sun. It was going to be a hot day and he was glad to be off the train. He just hoped Belle did not mind riding in a wagon. With James, he went to rent one. Once James started negotiating the price, he went to get their horses off the train.

While James and he hitched up the horses and spread blankets on the wagon bed, Robbie went and got them what few supplies they would need.

Robbie came to pack the supplies in the wagon and then went to collect Belle and the children. Abel leapt up into the wagon, then helped Morgan get up into it. Geordie went to lift Belle up into the wagon and she immediately set to dividing up the blankets and camp pillows Robbie had found, after giving each one a careful sniff. By the time James got into the driver's seat, she and the kids were settled comfortably and a spot awaited Robbie for when he decided he had used his leg enough for now. Robbie and Geordie mounted their horses, tied James's to the back of the wagon and started toward home.

Belle watched the countryside go by as the wagon rolled along the road. There were occasional glimpses of wildlife, such as a deer leaping through trees after being startled from its feeding, or a hawk swooping down and then rising with its prey in its beak. She had the feeling there were a lot more watching them from the woods. There was a wilder feel, more untamed, to the woods they wound through than she was accustomed to.

She liked to look at the wild landscape, but was not sure she could live in it. Belle did not like a crowd of people around every corner, but the emptiness here bothered her. It was like an itch under the skin. The town was a nice distance away, which suited her, but there were no small villages either.

When the people living here needed something they could not grow, mill, or make, they had to travel a long way to get it. A long way through the empty, dark woods. Belle could not see herself dragging her little wagon off for several miles through the dark woods and then heading calmly back. She used to get nervous when she did it at home, where it was much more civilized. There was a lot she needed to learn about this area before she made any decisions.

They turned onto a road that was wider, better tended, and with less impenetrable forest surrounding it. In the distance she could see beautifully green, rolling fields neatly fenced in and dotted with a lot of what she assumed were sheep. Next they started past a house tucked off to the side, surrounded by rocks and gardens. There were a lot of children and two women sitting in big wooden chairs set beneath a large, healthy shade tree.

Robbie and Geordie yelled out greetings to the women. The redhead leapt to her feet and grabbed hold of two boys who had started running toward their wagon, and did it with a speed and skill that deeply impressed Belle. The woman then brought the boys closer to the wagon, and the other woman, largely pregnant, levered herself out of her chair and carefully drew nearer.

"Feeling all right, Abbie?" asked Geordie. "Think I need to smack Matthew around for ye?"

"That might be an idea," she said and laughed. "He is up at the house. Tell him to come and get me if he plans to stay up there for a while. Me, Red, and the children."

"So he will need a wagon. Got it." He pointed at his companions in the back of the wagon. "This is Mehitabel Ampleford, Abel Ampleford, and Morgan Haggert. Brought them from the oceanside to see the fort."

After Belle exchanged greetings with the women, James started off toward the main house. They rode up a small rise, and at the top she could see the family home they'd called "the fort." It was a fitting name. The walls were tall, the wooden posts tightly packed and sharply pointed at the top. The gates, which stood wide open, appeared huge and she had to wonder how easily they could be closed, especially if the men were not at hand. Iain was evidently a man deeply driven to keep his family safe, and had learned two vital lessons: Hold fast to your land, and protect your family.

"That is truly impressive, especially considering how young many of you were when you built this," said Belle.

"Weel, we were raised to do for ourselves. Learned carpentry and learned the value of finding a book about it. My fither always said ye can find most everything in a book. People who ken how to do something often want to share their knowledge."

"And Iain wanted it."

He laughed. "Aye, I fear we had fallen into the habit of obeying him like we would our da. That annoyed us about ourselves, not him. After a few drinks, once in a while we would all decide he wasnae our da and the next time he told us what to do, we would say nay. Unfortunately, the next thing he wanted us to do was to give Mrs. O'Neal and her kids a place of their own inside the stockade."

"And you couldn't say nay."

He shook his head. "She was so happy, and she cried. Most unfair. Plus, she said she would make us cake as a thank-ye." He grinned when both James and Belle laughed. He looked at Robbie. "Are ye ready?"

Robbie nodded. "Nervous. Afraid the leg willnae cooperate."

Belle patted him on the back. "It will. Just make sure you don't keep standing and moving about if that leg lets you know it is tired."

"Understood."

"I will try to stay close, if you want."

He nodded. "Might give me some added confidence."

James halted the wagon in front of the door and helped Robbie get down. Belle got out of the back of the wagon and Geordie helped her collect their bags. As she started to put some down on the ground because Geordie's arms were full, two young boys came bounding out of the house yelling the brothers' names. Three older children came around the corner and waved at them. A tall man with red hair strode over and clapped Geordie on the back.

Just as she was being introduced to Iain, a pretty young woman with blond hair hurried over and then began a long series of introductions. Iain turned to offer Robbie a hand, only to stare as Robbie stepped over to the pile of bags and picked up his own, revealing his improved movement and his stronger hand.

"Ye didnae mention this in that tiny letter ye wrote," Iain said to Geordie.

"He was still newly hurt from his fall, and we could only hope that fixing the bones correctly would help."

As the rest of his brothers wandered out, Geordie introduced them to Belle, Abel, and Morgan. He continued to introduce them to the rest of his family as they made their way into the house. By the time they got inside and seated at the kitchen table, Mrs. O'Neal was setting out food and had a pot of coffee brewing. Belle was also deep in admiration of Nuala, Emily's little girl, and the baby. Geordie broke up the lovefest and started to take Belle up the stairs, Mrs, O'Neal telling him what room he could have.

"She only told you one room," Belle said and blushed.

"Weel, dinnae correct her. One room is all we need."

Setting her bag on the bed, she said, "I really want some of that coffee I could smell brewing."

"All right. And I want some of the food. And, I suspect the mob wants to ask ye a few things."

Belle bit her lip and then sighed. "If I get the coffee first, I guess I can manage answering some questions." She crouched down and ran her hand over the carpet at the side of the bed. "This is beautiful. Does someone in town make them?"

"Robbie made it. Remember, I told ye, he used to weave things. Think I even mentioned that he had done the carpets in the house."

"You did. I remember now, but I never pictured this kind of work. I hope his hand gains the nimbleness and strength needed to get back to weaving. It is art, really. If he lived in Boston he could make some decent money with this skill."

"Dinnae tell him that now. He might feel compelled to

push himself too hard. It isnae just the weaving ability he needs to get reacquainted with, it is the art of it," he said as he took her by the arm and started to take her back downstairs. "He hasnae got any grand dreams of becoming a fancy, rich mon, but he isnae averse to making a fine income. That was why we did so many tours of cider mills, even though he was in that chair that he hated for some of them."

"At least he had the sense to use it when he needed it."

When they walked back into the kitchen it was a lot more crowded than it had been. Matthew had collected his wife, Red, and all the children. Reid had arrived and he and Robbie were deep in discussion about the cider mill works Robbie had seen and the mixes he had tasted and heard about. When Belle returned to her seat near Emily, Geordie sat down and abruptly found himself the focus of his whole family.

"What?" he asked as he poured himself some coffee.

"How was the ocean?" asked Nigel.

"Beautiful. We stayed at Belle's house, which is up a hill but on the ocean. Just have to get down the hill."

"Walk down some stairs," said Robbie, "which is where I stumbled and broke my already broken leg. Abel"—he nodded toward the boy—"called it my bad leg."

"But Belle fixed it," the boy said.

"Well, we are not sure of that yet, Abel."

"What did you do?" asked Abbie.

"Just put the bones together as they should have been put together the first time. We have discovered that massaging his leg and hand appears to help with the muscles and nerves."

Abbie frowned and slowly nodded. "I can see how it might. What do you use?"

"A lotion my father made up. Nothing special, except it does help ease any cramp or pain the patient may suffer from. Robbie is the one who noticed that when it was massaged into his leg or hand, it also aided in the mobility of both."

"So, how often do you put on the lotion?"

"Twice a day on his leg and whenever he wants some on his hand. The hand appears to be more of a problem because the muscles and nerves were damaged. From what I could feel beneath the skin, the bones in his hand have healed correctly, no thanks to the men who hurt him. But the bruised muscles and nerves need more help."

"So massage. Well, there are three of us who can work on that regularly."

Belle wondered which three the woman meant, but decided not to ask.

Conversation was constant and often there were several going on at the same time. Belle found it interesting yet oddly tiring. When Geordie quietly took her by the hand and tried to slip out of the kitchen, she thought he was insane to think he could sneak away from this crowd. Noah stood in the hall and grinned as if he thought the same. It surprised her when Geordie bolted for the stairs.

"Get a good night's rest, lad. We'll get to the ceremony tomorrow," said Mrs. O'Neal.

"Running willnae save ye, brother. Didnae help me or Matthew at all. Ow! Dinnae pinch, Emily."

"Bastards," Geordie muttered as he ducked into their room and dropped onto the bed.

Belle watched him for a moment, then asked, "What was that all about?"

"Mrs. O'Neal." He sat up and took his boots off. "Ye ken I said we sort of accepted Iain as our da?" Belle nodded. "Weel, Mrs. O'Neal has become the other parent. I ken it is an odd thing."

"No, not when you think on how young you all were. But that really doesn't tell me what was meant by all of that."

"I'll show ye where the washroom is." He took her by the hand and led her down the hall. "We can talk when we get back to the room."

They each took their turn washing up and using the facilities. Then he led her back to their room. She opened her bag and put away the clothes she had brought with her, then went to sit on the bed. When he sprawled next to her, she turned to look at him.

"Ready to explain?"

"Ye said ye love me, aye?"

She leaned over and gave him a kiss. "Aye," she said and smiled.

He wrapped his arms around her and pulled her down, giving her a kiss that left her breathless. "Then ye would-nae have any objection to marrying me?" He kissed her throat.

"Now? We have not really decided where we will live."

"I have been leaning toward us returning to the ocean after a nice visit."

"It is pretty here."

"Oh, aye. But I cannae sit on the hillside and listen to the waves kiss the shore. I cannae take a deep breath and smell that ocean air. I cannae go rowing. I was just getting good." He turned his head to hide his grin over the questionable look she gave him.

"But your family . . ."

"Love them, every single one, the ones who are blood family and all the rest. But it is nay such a chore to come for a visit, is it, and I can contribute to them so they can come to us now and again. And, if we change our mind, we can always come back and set up house."

She settled down in his arms and laid her head on his chest. "All right then. I could not really decide. As I said, it is pretty here. But I did worry about where you go when you need a lot of supplies, and the forest we drove through was so thick and dark. I don't know about the wildlife here, so didn't know how dangerous it might be."

"I will be honest—a lot more dangerous than any wood ye would ride through at home. Though that moose I saw when I was there didnae look all that peaceful."

"No, moose can be difficult. Unpredictable. You don't get them here?"

"Never seen one. Bucks, but no moose. What we have are cougars, wolves, snakes." He smiled at her when he felt her twitch at that.

"Poisonous?"

"Aye.

"I think we have cougars, or mountain lions as they are sometimes called, but they rarely come down out of the hills. Animals seem to have the sense to stay away from people and their places. But here there is not much divide between settled and open land. The wildlife at home are mostly racoons, skunks, woodchucks, and the like. We have some rattlers in the mountains. Oh, and wild turkeys walking about in packs, or is that flocks?"

"Flocks."

She idly undid his shirt and slid her hand over his chest. "So you wish to marry me?"

"I do. Rather thought ye would be agreeable, since ye said ye loved me and were discussing with me where ye might like to settle."

"Ah, yes, I was doing that." She slid her hand down to his pants and undid them.

He kissed her and gently undid the buttons on her gown. By the time he ended the kiss they were both mildly feverish in their need to be skin to skin. Geordie pulled her over until she was sprawled on top of him. About to say something concerning the marriage he knew they would soon be pulled into, all thought of warning her went right out of his mind when she began to kiss her way down to his stomach. That small, soft hand of hers curled around his erection and she began to stroke him. Her long, silken hair caressed his thighs as she kissed him there and he jerked in reaction, his whole body tensing. She pulled away a little, watching him through the tangled fall of her hair around her flushed face.

"No?" she whispered.

"That wasnae rejection, love—just surprise." He threaded his fingers in her hair and very gently urged her to continue.

Geordie was beginning to think he had completely misjudged his ability to endure the pleasure she was giving him when she took him into the warm heat of her mouth. He clenched his teeth in an attempt to keep as quiet as possible. It was not long before he decided he was going to waken the whole house or end this too soon, and not as he wanted to. Catching her beneath her arms, he pulled her up his body. To his relief she took care of settling herself on his body, sliding them together in the slow, careful way that he needed her to. He reached up to caress her breasts as she rode him before pulling her down to kiss her as his release rolled through his body. Geordie then swallowed her cry as her own pleasure peaked, her body tightening around him in a way that nearly brought him to release again. Then he held her close, stroking her back to soothe her as she slumped on top of him.

He knew he was falling asleep when he finally told her, "Ye ken how ye asked what all those fools meant as we came up here?"

She slid over to curl up next to him. "You mean all that yelling?" She felt him nod. "Yes, so what were they on about?"

"Be prepared," he mumbled as his eyes closed. "The wedding will be tomorrow."

Belle sat up to stare at him, and clenched her fists when

she saw that he was already fast asleep. "Coward," she scolded him as she curled back into his side, closed her eyes, and joined him in sleep.

Mehitabel snuggled next to Geordie and he slid his arm around her, holding her closer. She was just sliding into sleep when she abruptly snapped awake again. She was sleeping with Geordie, in his family's home, and they were not married. What had she been thinking last night?

Belle was just swinging her legs over the side of the bed to get up and move when she realized that she had no idea where to move to. She yanked on her undergarments and frowned as she struggled to recall last night. After all, she had been daft enough to just accept that they were sharing a room, so she was not confident she would correctly recall where the washroom was, or what he had said.

Belle was still sitting there when the door opened and Mrs. O'Neal walked in with Emily. Right behind them was Matthew, who set a table up next to the bed. He grinned and winked at both of them, then walked out as Mrs. O'Neal set down the tray she carried.

"Eat your breakfast," said Emily. "We'll be back after we break our fast and bring your gown, Belle."

They left before Belle could say anything. She looked at Geordie. Then, unable to think of what she wanted to say, she drank some of her coffee in a desperate attempt to clear the fog her mind was trapped in. *Go simple and be direct first*, she told herself. "Where's the washroom?"

"Go out the door, head left. White door with a wooden sign hanging on it. If it says *unoccupied*, turn it over to say *occupied* and go in. Slide the bolt inside to secure it. Towels and all, already in there." He lifted the lid of a dish. "Oh, heaven. Mrs. O'Neal brought us bacon."

Shaking her head, Belle left him to enjoy his bacon and

hoped he left her a few pieces. She grabbed a robe and her little bag of necessities, then left. Following his directions, she found the washroom and it was unoccupied. As she darted inside, she turned the sign to *occupied*, and also secured the door. She had never seen such things as a sign and a bolt to secure a door in a bathroom. Then she remembered how many people were in the house and decided both were needed.

As she washed up, she tried to decide if she was afraid or excited. She was going to be married soon and realized that she had never really planned to be, even when she had decided she was in love with Geordie. She would have preferred a little warning, some preparation time. She would also like to be closer to her family so that she could have Auntie with her.

After washing up and cleaning her teeth, Belle hurried back to the bedroom. She was pleased she met no one in the hall as she made her short dash back to the bedroom. Ducking into the room, she shut the door behind her and saw Geordie sitting on the bed grinning at her.

"Ye ran back, didnae ye?"

"Of course I did. I am in my underclothes. Your Mrs. O'Neal and brother walking in caught me by surprise but don't plan to let that happen again. I see you got dressed."

"I did." He hopped off the bed and pointed at the tray with a couple of covered dishes on it. "I left ye some bacon." He stopped next to her and gave her a quick, hard kiss. "Now I am going to wash up."

He was annoyingly cheerful, she decided, and smiled sweetly as she asked, "Are they bringing your gown, too?"

She squealed in shock when he picked her up, walked over to the bed, and dropped her on it. Belle sat up just in time to see him shut the door behind him. She was about to indulge in a long litany of curses when the door opened and Emily stepped in, Mrs. O'Neal right behind her.

Emily held up a gown and spread it out on the bed. Then she and Mrs. O'Neal turned to face her, and Belle wondered why she had the urge to run—far, and fast. Which was silly, she decided. She wanted to marry Geordie and she liked the two women. Yet, she could not shake the feeling she was being pushed into something that might go badly.

"She has that look, Emily," said Mrs. O'Neal.

"I can see that. I remember it. You know, Belle, you are allowed to say no. We would never push you to the altar. We just know it is where you want to be, and we want to be the ones to get you there."

"All right." She shook away her unease and smiled at them. "Then let us get started."

Chapter Eighteen

Geordie tugged at his suit coat and glared at his brothers. "Ye ken, I never had a chance to propose to her."

"Dinnae worry on that. Ye would have bungled it anyway," said Matthew.

"Ye cannae be sure of that. I might have proven verra eloquent." Geordie did not think his brothers should laugh so hard and loud at that. "Rude bastards," he muttered.

"So where are ye going to live?" asked Lachlan.

"We will start by returning to her home," said Geordie, and he could see that his brothers were not too pleased. "I gave it a lot of thought and I want to be near the ocean. She has a fine home and it has an interesting history. I know that I can come back here if it turns out to be no more than a whim." They all murmured agreement with that. "I just like it there. Like the ocean. Like that her house is above and set back from the ocean. And remind me that I need to show ye all my drawings of a shower bath. She has one on her back porch. I like what I have met of her family. I even like her pets—Thor, Odin, and the cat, Loki."

"Aye. Ye need to go back and see if it is a good fit," said Iain. "I was hoping everyone would stay around here, but suspected some of ye would find something ye liked more.

And she seems to be a good lass. Took in Morgan without a complaint, I am betting."

"Och, aye. I was a little bruised by that as she was actually sent to me, yet she has taken to Belle. And Abel, too."

"Aye. Um, why does she call him frog boy?"

"Belle called him that," Geordie said and told them the story. He grinned as they all laughed. "He is a good lad. Smart, too, I think."

"Aye, one of those ye will have to keep a keen eye on." Iain stood up and stretched. "Best we wander down to the kitchen or wherever Mrs. O wants us to be. And dinnae worry, I will be wanting those drawings of the shower bath."

As they all left the room, Geordie talked to Iain about the shower bath. As he had suspected, all his brothers were interested. When they reached the downstairs hall he saw Morgan standing in front of Abel, her hands on her hips, one hand gripping her wooden doll tightly.

"Something wrong, Morgan?" he asked as he moved to stand next to her.

"I was just trying to explain something to this *boy*. He is being thick-headed." She raised her doll and glared at Abel. "I was just going to fix that."

"Och, nay, lass. Ye cannae hit him with your doll. Annoying as he may be, that could cause an injury ye will feel bad about later." He almost laughed because the look she gave him told him she did not think she would regret it. "It is wood, after all."

Iain bent to look closely at the doll. "Huh, it is oak. Must have taken a lot to make it."

"My papa did it before he went to heaven."

"And a verra good job he did, but, dearling, ye hit the boy with that and ye could do him some real harm. Ye dinnae really want to do that, do ye?"

As Morgan glared at the boy and considered that, Abel said, "Nope. You don't."

"Why don't I?"

"Because I am Mehitabel's brother. Her only brother, so I'm important to her."

From what Geordie could see, Abel was in danger of being whacked just for the arrogant statement. Then he noticed Belle standing in the kitchen doorway. She was smiling and shaking her head, then assumed a stern expression.

"Mrs. O'Neal is making sweets for the wedding and there might be some spoons to lick for well-behaved children."

Both children turned toward her. Then Morgan nudged Abel aside and marched off to the kitchen. Abel watched her with narrowed eyes, then glanced at his sister.

"That wasn't very well-behaved," he told his sister as he hurried into the kitchen.

Geordie looked at her and grinned. "Are ye still certain they will get along?"

"Yes. Well, as long as he doesn't throw a frog at her, and she doesn't crack his head open with her doll. Go into the sitting room for a while. We are trying to make a nice luncheon for everyone."

He watched her go into the kitchen. She was looking very fine. The gown fit her nicely, hugging every curve on her slender body, and the ivory color brought out a slight copper tone to her skin. Her long black hair was pulled back from her face and braided to stay there. Then he wondered who "everyone" was and hurried into the sitting room.

Belle looked at all the food they had made and, after taking off her apron, rubbed at her lower back. It was a feast. She had to wonder just who was coming to this wedding.

"You look a bit frightened," Emily said as she handed Belle a cup of coffee.

"Just how many people are coming? And why?"

"Most of our neighbors, the Powells and their families, and several people from the tiny collection of shops we call a town. I am not all that sure they care why, because for them the why is Mrs. O'Neal's cooking. I don't recall anyone even asking which brother was getting married." She grinned when Belle laughed. "It is a gathering. The ones that can get away are always ready to come to one of those."

"It is pretty much like that where I live."

"Small towns."

"I fear so."

"We'll take some coffee into the men." Emily got a tray and Belle moved to help.

By the time they got into the sitting room, the men were deep into conversation about the shower bath. After handing out the coffee, Belle sat next to Emily. When she glanced at the woman, Emily just grinned and shook her head.

"Do you think they will try to make one?" asked Belle.

"Oh, yes. It is a new and fancy thing. They will not be able to resist."

"Inside or outside?"

Emily listened to the men for a few minutes, then sighed. "It is sounding as though they want to try to get one inside, which means a lot of hammering and cursing."

"Oh, I'm sorry."

"Not to worry. It does sound like something nice if they can get it together. I just wish they could try to build something quietly."

Belle was still laughing when Mrs. O'Neal brought over a tall, thin man with a wild mop of graying brown hair. He wore a white collar and a black suit. It was difficult not to worry too much about what he thought of this business. It had been arranged and announced with no warning and no meeting or conversation with the pastor. She knew their pastor at home would have found some way to make his disapproval plain to see.

After a surprisingly polite talk, the man went over to the brothers. "Did he marry Emily and Iain?" she asked Mrs. O'Neal.

"He did. Matthew and Abbie, too. He moved out here many years ago. He was somewhat too worldly for many people in the town he came from. They love him around here. Does all the weddings, all the christenings and all the burials. I go to his church when I can."

"He does do a nice sermon," Emily said.

Two men entered the room. They were dressed nicely if a bit roughly, and each had a wife. Belle easily recognized that the women were of Native heritage. They each had a child and one of the wives was soon to bear another.

After she was introduced to the Powells, things began to move fast. People began to arrive and Belle began to feel nervous. Geordie, on the other hand, was enjoying the teasing and congratulations he was getting. Then Iain's lawyer and his wife came over to say hello. After only a short talk, Belle had information about a few lawyers that dealt in wills and offered them a place to stay if ever they wished to wander back East. By the time they went to talk to someone else she realized she may have also found a way to do something with the house in Boston that Morgan had inherited, a way that could build her a nice account for the future, something that would be of far more use to her than a house.

Then Mrs. O'Neal pulled her out of the room. Emily grabbed her friend Red and disappeared into the fancier sitting room. Several of Red's army of children went with them as did her large redheaded husband. As Mrs. O'Neal pulled her up the stairs, Belle caught a glimpse of Geordie surrounded by a bunch of men all fascinated by his talk of the shower bath.

"Time to give you some finishing touches."

Belle frowned at Mrs. O'Neal. "Like what?"

"Something that sparkles, some flowers, and something blue."

"I have a few things that sparkle. Not sure why I brought them, but it has become a habit to keep them with me." She pulled a small case out of the drawer she was using in the bureau.

Setting it on the bed, she opened it and found the things her mother had left to her. There was a necklace of shells and stones all nicely polished, with a set of earrings to match. Mrs. O'Neal oohed and aahed over a wide, etched silver bracelet, then quickly put it on Belle's wrist, making Belle think she would have to do her best to find one for the woman. She sat on the bed as Mrs. O'Neal placed a small wreath of flowers on her hair. Then Belle stood up to carefully don her necklace and earrings. She took a look at herself in the mirror and blushed, for she felt she looked beautiful and believed that to be very vain.

"Child, you do look pretty. For just a little while I worried about the necklace of stones and shells, but, no, it sits on the ivory dress perfectly."

"They were what my mother left me when she died. She never much liked jewelry, but these things she clung to."

"And that makes them even more perfect. One should always wear some family heirloom if one can. Emily wore a locket of her sister's. I cannot recall what Abbie wore, but it will come to me. Well, ready to get married?"

"You like doing this, don't you?"

"I do. I really do, and when you walked in with Geordie and those two babies, I knew I would get to do it again. He had that look."

"What look?"

"That *this one is mine* look. Iain had it, as did Matthew. And both of them came with children, too. Beginning to wonder if that should be my sign."

"Ah, well, that fool war left a lot of children needing someone. A lot of women, too."

"It did indeed. Enough sad talk for a wedding day. Ready?"

"Ready."

Geordie tried to stand still, to not reveal the attack of nerves he was suffering from. He knew Belle would not humiliate him with any public desertion or refusal, but now the fact that he had not formally proposed troubled him. Women expected one, not just agreeing with someone else's plan for them. Then he saw Belle walk in through the door and caught his breath. He had seen her many guises, but he did not think he had ever seen her in her full beauty. He slowly walked over to her.

"Belle," he said as he took her hands in his. "Ye look stunning. I ken Mrs. O'Neal pushed this, as she is prone to. Are ye sure?"

She stretched up on her tiptoes and gave him a light kiss. "Yes, I am sure. And when we get back home, remind me that I want to try to find Mrs. O'Neal something like my bracelet."

"No more of that, you two," said the pastor as he took them by the arms and led them to the spot where he would perform the marriage. "Let us get on with making it all proper and legal."

"The rings," Belle whispered to Geordie. "We do not have the rings."

"Oh, aye. Taken care of."

She started to wonder about that, but then set all her

attention on the pastor and his words. Strangely, she calmed with each vow they had to repeat. It made her more certain that she was doing the right thing. Then Abel, dressed up neatly, stepped up with the rings resting on a fancy little pillow. Belle found herself shaking a little as Geordie slid hers on her finger.

When she slid a wide gold band on his finger, she suddenly thought of her father's ring at home, and decided she would see if he would allow a switch. Then Geordie kissed her, and despite some of the hoots from the small crowd, she did not shy away from his response.

Wrapping his arm around Belle, he led her to the dining room where all the food was laid out. Mrs. O'Neal had done them proud yet again. As expected, the table was swarmed and he allowed Belle to pull away to make sure Abel and Morgan got some things they wanted and were seated in the kitchen with the other children. He found himself with the Powells.

"She should be back soon," he told the women. "She was just getting Abel and Morgan settled in with all the other children and grabbing some food before it disappears."

"A big possibility. The people round here do love it when you have a gathering. And they ain't coming just to look at your pretty faces."

Belle was headed back to the room where everyone was gathered, when two women approached her. It took her a moment but then she recalled they were the Powell brothers' wives. She had a feeling she knew what they wished to discuss. So she led them to seats so they could all sit as they talked and, in this corner of the room, be relatively private. Just as she was about to say something, one of the women leaned forward and ran her finger over Belle's necklace.

"This has some age to it."

"It does. It belonged to my mother's mother." She turned the bracelet on her wrist. "So did this."

The other woman smoothed her fingers over the animal carved into the silver. "What is this animal?"

"A seal."

For a while they talked about the making of jewelry, how those of mixed races survived where they had each lived. By the time the women left with their husbands, Belle felt there was a lot more holding those marriages together than the need for a home and some kind of acceptance. It was an impression strengthened when the brothers came to gather up their wives and take their families home.

Seeing how the house was clearing out, Geordie started to move Belle out of the room and up to their bedroom. She watched as the crowd started to thin out, people pausing and offering them congratulations and good wishes. They were all very nice, even though she had seen that many of them had noticed she, as well as the Powell women, shared Native heritage. She was tired out though, not used to hours spent with a boisterous crowd of people she had only just met. By the time Geordie stepped close enough to grasp her hand, pull her to her feet and lead her up the stairs, she really gave no thought to why the men all clapped him on the back as if he was some conquering hero.

As they entered the bedroom and he led her to their bed, she began to understand what all the back slapping, and laughter, and whispered jokes were about. When he pushed her down onto the bed and sprawled on top of her, she punched him in the arm.

"Ow! What did I do?"

"Laughed at those dumb man-jokes."

"What dumb man-jokes?" he asked as he undid the front of her gown.

"The ones they told you as you brought me upstairs."

"That is just the silly way men celebrate such occasions," he answered as he slowly removed her stockings, then her petticoats. "And do ye mean to tell me that women dinnae make any jokes about it? I dinnae believe that."

"Well, try. Unwed women have little to no knowledge or understanding about it all, so how could they make jokes? She would also be considered a fallen woman or something like that if she did reveal the knowledge with a joke. My father told me all about it, so I could have told a few, but I am not sure it is something to joke about."

"Your father told ye everything about it? Really? Why would he do that?"

"Because he thought it was a silly rule to keep women ignorant about such an important part of life. He also thought it silly for a man to send his daughter out into the world ignorant of what men are capable of doing, or of how she might keep the man she chooses happy enough not to be tempted by some buxom dance-hall girl."

He tugged her gown off and tossed it to the floor. "Well, why dinnae ye show me what he taught ye and I can verify it or nay."

"Sneaky man."

He kissed her and stood up to shed his clothes. Belle told herself not to look at him too much or he would preen, thinking she was ogling him. Then she saw the slow smile grow on his face and knew she *was* ogling him. Annoyed with herself as much as she was with him, she reached out and grabbed his erection, then tugged him down on the bed. While he lay there clutching himself and acting like she had done him serious injury, she stood up and slowly pulled off her chemise. She laughed when he lunged at her and wrestled her under him.

Playfulness quickly disappeared as he stroked her

body. Belle fought to keep her need tamped down so they could go slowly and savor each other, but soon knew she would not be successful. This man belonged to her now, had taken vows with her, and that knowledge added a ferocity to her need for him that both thrilled and frightened her.

Belle found herself pinned beneath him as he kissed his way down her body. She burrowed her fingers into his hair as he kissed her breasts, licking and nipping gently until she was squirming beneath him. He reached her belly. There was barely enough time to catch her breath when he nipped the inside of her thighs so that he could push them apart and nestle himself in between them and leisurely feast upon her. She could barely smother her cry as her release tore through her, and then he was there, driving into her and finding his own.

They lay side by side, panting. After a few moments, Geordie patted her backside. "I think married life could kill us."

She laughed and slapped his thigh. "If you finish that with some comment on how we will at least pass with smiles on our faces, I will do you a serious injury."

Geordie laughed and pulled her into his arms.

Iain was walking quietly past Geordie's door with Robbie and Lachlan and he smiled faintly as he heard the laughter behind the closed doors. "He will be leaving with her."

"Och, aye. He will," said Robbie. "He did love being near the ocean. The quiet rhythm of it in the night is hard to resist. And it is beautiful. So is Belle, and that house she inherited is in her blood. The whole area is. And, aside from her family, I think she is close to the land in a way we might not fully understand. Rather like us and Scotland."

"Or like us and being part of a clan."

"I suspect so. Ye said ye kenned we might nay all stay around."

"I did, but I had hoped."

"To make your own clan?" drawled Lachlan and earned himself a swat on the arm. "But there can be visits whenever we wish. And, truth is, I will be one of the first to trot out there and see what there is. Sounds like she has a fine place and works hard to keep it up and flourishing. I'd also like to take a gander at the ocean when it isnae tossing around the ship I am on. I got to thinking I might even like to try digging clams, although not sure I would want to eat any," he added as they went down the stairs.

"I would like to ken who ate the first one and was he just joking when he told everyone they were all right to eat. Was it just a joke on all his neighbors?"

"And I just hope her great-grandfather achieved what he wanted to with that complicated will."

"Two things worked in his favor even then, I think. The heir was a female and he was a white man with a long history in the area. The Powell sisters had a nice long chat with, um, Mehitabel? And what the devil is that name?"

"Bible. One of the wives got a little book that lists names and what they mean, to help mamas choose something magnificent to name their children. Hope there was something learned that the Powells can use as I ken the brothers are worried about what could happen to their wives and kids if they die and havenae tied the title to their land without every chain possible."

"Good plan," said Robbie. "They dinnae have the advantage of an old, weel-kenned name and people round here wouldnae bow to it as they are doing back East. And that lawyer ye hired, Iain, had a long chat with Mehitabel. Think he was verra impressed by what her grandfather had done to protect his family. By the time they face the problem of no male heir, there will probably be even less chance of anyone trying to negate that will."

"I smell bacon cooking," said Lachlan, and hurried down the stairs.

Belle looked at Geordie and tried not to sigh as she watched him dress. It was a little hard to believe he was hers now. Since she had gotten a lot of good advice from Iain's lawyer, she could even set aside any worry about someone trying to steal her family's land because she had married and the man was a stranger just off the boat.

"Get dressed, Belle." He gave her a light slap on the backside, which was well protected by the blanket she was under.

"Do you know how annoying a rise-and-shine person can be to those of us who do not rise or shine in the morning? Why are you in such a hurry?"

"I can smell bacon."

"Ah, of course." She slid out of bed and went to find something to wear as well as tidy up her clothes from yesterday. "Cannot miss a chance at bacon." She began to pick up her wedding clothes. "I guess I will have to learn how to cook it properly now."

"Ye dinnae ken how to cook bacon? I am sure I had some at your house."

"You probably did, but Auntie would have been responsible for it. That is why you didn't get it every day."

"I dinnae ken what to do about this. May have to re-think the wedding," he said as he started out the door, shutting it after him just before the shoe hit it.

* * *

"Already fighting with the wife?" asked Iain as Geordie hurried into the kitchen.

"Not really. Just told me she doesnae ken how to cook bacon." He started laughing when he saw the shock on his brother's face.

"Is that why ye came home?" Iain asked.

"Nay." He laughed and shook his head. "Seems her aunt fixes it when she stays for breakfast."

"Seems a sensible solution," said Mrs. O'Neal.

"Maybe, but it would help if she learned how and nay just for my pampered belly. She rents rooms during the summer season, with meals included." He filled his plate and took a seat, keeping an empty one by his side.

"That is a lot of work for a lass on her own."

"It is—the gardening, the caring of the grounds and house, the orchard and fruit bushes and a cranky neighbor who wants a large piece of her land for himself. But she appears to have a small army of cousins. There are also people who feel beholden to her father, who was a doctor. They might help out."

"That is good. So the town helps look after her."

"It appears so. So, Geordie, ye are leaving the West, aye?" Iain asked.

"Aye. I am. I want to. Never really felt settled into this area. With the family, aye, but nay this place."

"Ye think the East is more like home?"

"Weel, she will be there for a start, aye? But I do think it is a place my soul will settle to."

"Just dinnae settle in a way that makes ye just a new chapter in the book of the ocean's history. It's a long and bloody one. We will come to visit ye though, so ye best have enough room to house us."

"There is plenty of room. Just try to avoid the storm season."

"And when is that?"

"In the late summer. August and into September, although the occasional storm can happen whenever the mood takes it."

"They are bad storms?" asked Mrs. O'Neal.

"They can be. It is usually the high water and high winds that cause the most trouble."

"They talk about it as if it is a fifth season," said Robbie.

"Well, you just wait for one to come along and you will see why," said Belle as she entered the kitchen and sat next to Geordie.

They talked more about where he was moving to and Belle reissued her open invite to come and stay when they wanted to. Belle noticed Mrs. O'Neal's children kept watching their mother and she suspected they would eventually see the family come for a visit. The Powells had also spoken of coming to visit, and she hoped they did.

Chapter Nineteen

Despite the sadness of leaving such a nice group of people, the leave-taking was relatively painless at the end of three weeks. The brothers all went out to look at a place where they could make a swimming hole and then spent a lot of the evening looking over Geordie's information and drawings of the shower bath. Belle visited with the women, gaining recipes and some patterns for sewing, knitting, and crocheting.

Robbie's decision to leave went harder. His partners in the cider business were saddened, yet cheered by the thought of Robbie gaining them some new recipes. They all spoke of coming to visit now that there was the convenience of trains. Robbie's family saw the ocean as part of his healing and they embarrassed Belle with their thanks.

Robbie followed Belle up the stairs, stopping outside her bedroom door, and she asked, "Are you very sure about this, Robbie?"

"Aye. Oh, I feel sad, but not about moving to the ocean. That might change when I try to find a place to live and a job to do. Although my hand has improved so much, I can actually do some weaving." He grinned and wriggled his fingers. "I am taking my loom back with me to keep working. If I can get back to what I used to do, I might be able to make a living as a weaver."

"I hope so, Robbie. I saw some of your work and it was lovely." She grinned. "And if you feel a need for your own house, it appears we may have one to be rid of soon."

"Get some sleep. Geordie will be wanting to head out early."

Belle was tucked up in bed and just about to close her eyes when Geordie came in. As she enjoyed watching him undress, she tried to listen carefully to what Geordie had to say. As he spoke about Robbie, she had the feeling he did not know about his brother being able to do his weaving again.

"He won't have to try, Geordie, he can already do it."

"He has tried?"

"He has, and he proudly wiggled his fingers at me and said he can do it. Well enough that he is taking his loom back to the coast."

Geordie got into bed and flopped back onto his pillow. "He actually thinks he can get back to what he used to do?"

"Yup. He said he just needs to find a place to live and a job. That was when he mentioned his weaving."

"That would be wonderful." He frowned. "Of course, I need to figure out how to make a living, too."

"Well, you could take up digging clams." She giggled when he rolled onto her and started tickling her. "Never mind then. Never mind."

She stopped laughing when he kissed her. "I saw the furniture you made, Geordie. You have a skill to make a living with. But don't think you can cut down my trees for it."

"I dinnae think getting the wood will be hard. Now, we are married, and I think since we have the luxury of a bed this night, we should take advantage of it."

She put her arms around his neck. "You do have the best ideas."

In the morning, leaving proved a little harder than it had the night before. Iain and a couple of his brothers filled a cart with some things to send back to the beach. Belle welcomed them all to come and visit. They even loaded up some yarn for Robbie to use and some wood they had collected for Geordie.

The brothers followed them to the train and helped load everything onto the rail car for shipment to Boston. Belle hoped the arrangements worked well. The trains were still too new to packages and passengers for her to trust them. Robbie obviously had some doubts as well, as he had wrapped his loom in such a way he could take it on the train with him, with Geordie and Belle helping.

As Belle slid into the seat next to Morgan, she bumped into the doll. It hurt, and she looked at Morgan. "That doll weighs a lot, love. What have you stuffed it with?"

"Gold coins," Morgan said in a whisper.

Belle just stared at her, then said, "Just be careful with it and we'll talk about it at home."

When Morgan nodded, Belle sat back and tried very hard not to sweat with worry all the way home.

Chapter Twenty

By the time they got off the train in Boston, Belle was exhausted and feeling a bit sick after two weeks of travel. They looked around for her aunt and Harold Hobbs, who had sworn they would come to collect them. Geordie finally noticed their carriage, with a wagon tied up beside it, and moved over to start filling the wagon.

"Thank you for coming. I wouldn't have troubled you except we brought a lot of stuff. Hello, Harold."

"Harold has been a gem," Mary said, as the man got down and hurried over to help Geordie, James, and Robbie fill the wagon while Belle got into the carriage and sat across from her aunt. "He contacted Iain's lawyer for little Morgan. Harold has written to him several times since then. So, how is marriage treating you?"

"Very nicely, thank you. It appears marriage is doing you some good as well," Belle said, staring at the gold band on her aunt's finger. "I just cannot see the man, nice as he is, sweeping you off your feet."

"Oh, he didn't do that. I am far past that sort of nonsense. Had the luck to find that once. This time I was lucky enough to find I had a good man even though the stars in my eyes are dim. As we looked for which papers would be helpful, I guess he rather grew on me.

"So quiet and intelligent. Soft-spoken, yet never condescending to me, even when he was trying to explain something, and I think you know how difficult that can be. But I think the moment of awakening came when he carefully listed every person, alive or to be born, that Bennet would have to be rid of to get even a small piece of your land.

"Yet, I think what really shut Bennet up was that Harold pointed out everything in that will that allows us to help Bennet keep his own farm solvent and healthy, which I think was a load of what makes the grass grow green, but Bennet liked the sound of it. Just hope he doesn't think on it too much." She smiled when Belle started to laugh.

"I had never thought to look at that angle of things," Belle said. "Might have stopped a few of the confrontations."

"I doubt it would have helped. Bennet is a man who will only heed what another man says. I also think the old fool enjoyed those fights, up until Will got shot."

"Really? I thought he was getting very serious about them. He did start bringing his gun."

"Good point. Started to believe his grievances were real, I guess."

The door to the carriage opened and Geordie lifted Abel in and then Morgan. "We got the baggage loaded. These two want to ride inside with you ladies. Get yourselves tucked in safely and we will head out."

While her aunt chatted with Abel, Belle quietly touched Morgan's doll and asked, "How did your father get this money, Morgan?"

"It was from some men who tried to kill him in the war.

He got them instead. When he looked through their things, because he told me soldiers always try to take what might help them, he found the chest. He figured they had stolen it from someone or robbed some shipment and now it could be a nice inheritance for me and Mama. I put as much as I could into my doll when the men came and killed my mother and Nana because my father had wanted us to have it."

Belle decided that was all she really needed to know. It was sad Morgan's father had not realized that there had obviously been a larger group who had known about the coins, ones who could bring trouble to the family he had thought to help. She would help Morgan find a safe hiding place for it.

"Where is the ocean, Geordie?" asked Morgan.

"Just keep a watch out on your right and ye will see it soon." He set a basket of food on the seat, then stepped back and shut the door.

"Auntie, I was hoping you would bring Thor. I have missed him," said Abel, "although Mrs. O'Neal had pups and the Powells had herd dogs for their sheep."

"That was good of them. They let you play with them?"

"It was nice. They said I might as well play with the herd dogs, because their wives do and they spoil them. That started an argument, so I went and played with the dogs. Could not understand most of what the adults were saying anyway."

Belle leaned toward her aunt and said, "I suspect the Powells were speaking a lot of Welsh and their wives were using a lot of Native words. It was actually very fascinating to listen to, even if it was confusing."

Mary laughed and reached out to nudge Abel. "Thor will be pleased to see you, Abel. I do believe the fool dog has been pining for you. I really couldn't bring him because it wouldn't leave enough room for all of you and your baggage."

Abel nodded and then grinned. "He is a bit of a big dog. Loki and Odin are all right, aren't they?"

"They are fine. Loki does sulk and Odin has only begun to sleep with Harold and me. He sleeps down at the end of the bed and, fortunately, chose Harold to get up and take him out for air early in the morning. I kept waiting for you to ask for them to be sent to you."

"They never would have mixed with the herd dogs, or the few cats not left to go feral. And Loki would have been left out a lot of the time, I fear. The men treat cats much like they treat the dogs. A select few are cared for and watched over by the wives. Some of the outdoor cats have been lost to the coyotes and wolves. If we had stayed longer I would have collected a few."

"Ah. Probably for the best that you didn't take them on. Loki is feeling very protective now that she has kittens to raise."

"What makes you say that? And why are you calling him a *she*?"

"I believe it was when she had the kittens that I started doing that."

Belle stared at her aunt. "But . . . but . . . she never went into heat. And we looked her over carefully."

"I know. Young Will was most surprised. Sadly, he said he doubted she would have any more, as it was a very difficult birth. Not something one expects with a cat. But she had four of them, and they are lovely."

"You kept them?"

"Felt it was best to let them grow a bit and to let you see them first."

"Thank you. I know you have never been very fond of kittens."

"The ones I knew tended to be very destructive. It appears Loki is a very strict mother."

"Oh, dear. Wait, how did she get out? She rarely goes outside, and when she does it is mostly to linger on the porch."

"We never did figure that out. I feared we had lost her, but then she sauntered back in." Mary looked out the window as the carriage turned to go up the hillside and head up to Belle's house. "And it looks as if all your pets await you, along with my two nephews who have come to visit."

"Aunt Sarah sent her boys, Joseph and Malachi, to come stay with you?"

"Why wouldn't she? I know how to care for boys."

"No, no, you misunderstand. You live very close to town. She remembers the town as being dangerous. And, well, hateful."

"It has grown since she was a child. But, the biggest push was that she and her man are taking a small trip and she didn't want her boys left alone. I do think she was pleased I was staying at your house for a time."

The carriage came to a stop and Harold gallantly helped Mary down from it. Then he did the same for Belle and Morgan. Belle was smothered by the welcome of her dogs, even as she greeted the boys. Then she stepped into the house, took one look at Loki sitting proudly with her kittens, and knew she would be keeping them all.

Belle had barely shut the door behind her when there was a knock at it. She opened the door to find the sheriff with a tight grip on Charlie Bennet's arm. "Can I help you, Sheriff?"

"I believe I can help you with this fool. Sorry it has taken me so long. I heard your fire bell the night your barn caught fire, but it took a while for me and some of my men to get to your house. That actually proved helpful. I caught this fool redhanded. He had come back to pick up what was left of the torch he had tossed into your hay loft. That was going a step too far. He has a choice now. Charged and jailed, or fix your barn and replace your hay. There will be signs of him doing that within a week or it is back to jail. And he will do it, won't you, Charlie?" He gave Bennet a shake until the man grunted an agreement. "Will that satisfy you?"

"Yes, Sheriff, I believe it will."

"Now I just have to find something that will calm down Will's father about his son being shot in the leg by this fool. Come along, Charlie."

After thanking the sheriff again, Bella went into her house and turned to face her aunt, grinning at her. "I think the sheriff finally got fed up with being dragged away from his meals so often."

Belle laughed and then looked around for Loki and her kittens. She sat on the floor and was soon surrounded by kittens. She only worried about telling Geordie she was keeping them all for a moment, until he sat down beside her on the floor and joined her in playing with the kittens.

"Do ye plan to keep them or sell them? Or just give them away?"

"Since these are the only kittens she has ever had, I plan to keep them," Belle said.

"Ye kept her locked up?"

"Not really, she has always stuck very close to home. She just never had any kittens."

Her cousins Joseph and Malachi joined them, then Morgan wandered over. Abel came to look at the kittens, but then went back to stay with the dogs. Belle sat on the sofa, and one of the kittens crawled up. It curled up on her lap, and as she patted it, she fought to stay awake and failed.

"Cousin Belle has gone to sleep," said Joseph. "Long trip?"

"Long enough, but she slept on the train, too," Geordie said and frowned down at the kitten in Belle's lap. "Can you move the kitten for me and I will tote her up to bed."

Geordie got her tucked into her bed, even removing most of her clothing. Then he studied her. All his instincts told him she was probably with child, but he had no idea how to get her to face the possibility. Giving her a kiss on the forehead, he left the room, his mind crowded with plans for ways to get Belle to recognize her condition.

When he got back downstairs he did not see Mary, so sat down next to Harold.

"Has Mary gone to bed for the night?"

"I think her plan was to relieve herself but I believe she changed her mind and went to bed." He sighed. "I am just going to have to tell her."

"Tell her what?"

"That she was caught on the change, as I believe they say. She is with child. I have no idea how she is going to take this."

"Well, how are ye taking it?"

"Oh, I am thrilled. I have only one child. A son who lives with his wife and children in Boston. He has already congratulated me on getting a new wife." He smiled. "And getting one who owns land near the ocean." He laughed along with Geordie.

"A lawyer, is he?"

"Oh, yes, and he deals in property law. He has started speaking against those men who use sneaky ways to steal people's property. Has even taken some cases to win the land back. He does good work."

"A boy to be proud of. Well, you and I have an interesting time ahead. I need to make Belle realize she is with child, too."

Harold started to laugh and Geordie quickly joined in. One had to laugh, he decided. They were definitely in for an interesting time ahead.

Chapter Twenty-One

Summer, 1869

Lightly bouncing her son in her arms, Belle held the letter Geordie had given her. His family was coming. In fact, it appeared most of them were on their way. She was just about to say something to Geordie when her son suddenly lunged toward the floor, reaching for Loki. She was scrambling to get a better grip on him when Geordie took hold of him.

"Oh, thank you. He wanted to pat Loki. Don't think that would have gone well."

"Nope. He is a bit rough."

"There is a mob coming."

Geordie laughed. "It seems so. That's all right, is it?"

"Of course. I will have to tell Auntie. Mrs. O'Neal is coming and so are the Powells. She will be delighted. In her letters, Mrs. O'Neal often asked about Mary's twins," Belle said. "And enjoy our son, because I have a lot of work to do. Hope the twins are napping."

"Harold is still shocked that they have twins."

"He is pleased one is a girl though. That breaks through the shock now and then."

"He better start saying the name right or Auntie is going to bop him."

Geordie frowned. "Nothing wrong with Abby."

"Her name is Abrielle, his son's name is Aydan. Well, I have to get moving. It sounds like they could be here within a week."

A week later her cousins rode up to announce Geordie's family were arriving. It seemed only moments before two wagons rolled up. Children poured out of the first, and a moment later adults poured out of the second. Belle was shocked at how quickly the women ran to pick up the babies. Mrs. O'Neal was fascinated by Mary and her twins; the Powell wives huddled around her boy, cooing over his thick black hair and dark brown eyes.

It was loud and enjoyable, but after a small feast and the guests had been shown where they would sleep, Belle collapsed on the settee. The older single men were shown to her infirmary where Mrs. O'Neal had spent so much time, earlier, fascinated and intrigued by everything in it. If the woman had not started yawning and then agreed that she needed to rest, Belle suspected she would still be in there explaining things to her.

Mary sat down next to Belle while Harold and Geordie sat on the sofa across from them. "It will be a busy few days ahead," Belle said.

"But enjoyable," said Mary. "It is always a little crazed when a family comes to visit. We had just about enough room. It will also calm down when they get to the water."

"Mrs. O'Neal seemed fascinated with your twins."

"Fascinated that I even had them." Mary laughed. "I told her she could not be more surprised than I am. Well, I am headed for bed."